DEATH&TEXAS

Also by Clive Sinclair

Novels

Bibliosexuality

Blood Libels

Cosmetic Effects

Augustus Rex

Meet the Wife

Stories

Hearts of Gold

Bedbugs

For Good or Evil: Collected Stories

The Lady with the Laptop

Travel

Diaspora Blues

Clive Sinclair's True Tales of the Wild West

Essays

A Soap Opera From Hell

Biography

The Brothers Singer

DEATH & TEXAS

Clive Sinclair

HALBAN
LONDON

First published in Great Britain by
Halban Publishers Ltd.
22 Golden Square
London W1F 9JW
2014

www.halbanpublishers.com

A CIP catalogue record for this book is available from the British Library.

ISBN 978-1-905559-63-3

Typeset by Spectra Titles, Norfolk
Printed in Great Britain by
Berforts Information Press, Stevenage

Acknowledgements

Thanks are due to Philip Davis, editor of *The Reader*, wherein "Storyville", "The Venus Mosaic", and "A Bad End" first appeared; Nora Gold, editor of JewishFiction.net, wherein a section of "Death & Texas" first appeared; Matthew Asprey Gear, co-editor of *Contrappasso*, wherein "Billy the Yid", and "STR82ANL" first appeared; and David Albahari, guest editor of *Descant*, wherein an earlier version of "Prisoners of the Sun" first appeared. The author should also like to acknowledge the encouragement of early readers: Yosl & Audrey Bergner; Pamela & Jonathan Lubell; Judy Stewart.

Contents

For Seth & Kate Sinclair
&
Haidee Becker

On the knees of your soul?
Might as well be useful. Scrub the floor.

Saul Bellow, *Herzog*

STORYVILLE

IN THE END the boy became so febrile that Adele snatched him from the arms of Mama Congo and rushed him to the surgery herself. She was surprised to learn that Dr Tacrolimus had been replaced by someone called Astrov. Even more disconcerting was the news that Dr Tacrolimus – who had always gleamed like an immortal – had been poisoned by an invertebrate from the Gulf.

The first thing she noticed about his replacement was that his hair was not oiled, his jacket not pressed, and his shoes not shined (no excuse for that in a city full of shoe-shiners). He looked vulnerable and fallible. Not the sort of characteristics you seek in a doctor. Nonetheless he asked about the boy's symptoms in a confident manner. Adele could not place the accent, but guessed that he was raised some ways east of the Mississippi.

"You were right to bring the child, but wrong not to bring him sooner," he said. "Your son has influenza, and is very ill. But I shall not permit him to die."

For several days the patient seemed to be toying with the idea of doing just that. But Dr Astrov was as good as his word. He did not let the boy die.

The boy's parents wanted to demonstrate their gratitude, so they invited the doctor to their home for dinner. They lived on Esplanade Avenue in the Vieux Carré, in a petit palais painted a pretty pink. The front door was framed by white pilasters. Dr Astrov rubbed one of the columns, then licked his finger, half-expecting it to taste of icing sugar. He pulled the bell, and seconds later was admitted by Mama Congo. Above his head was a chandelier ablaze with light. Artfully placed mirrors multiplied the individual candles beyond human reckoning.

Mama Congo led the doctor up a staircase that rose like the whorls on a spire shell. His host and hostess awaited him at its summit, as if they were the rulers of a minor principality. Both were formally dressed, in contrast to their guest. They led him to a dining room, the like of which he had not seen since he left Russia. Three places were laid at the far end of a polished wooden table.

Over the meal Mr Beaufait congratulated the doctor on his professional skills.

"Do you come from a long line of doctors," asked Adele, "was your father a doctor, and his father before him?"

"No," replied Astrov, "my father was a store-keeper, whose only talent was an ability to out-fox his creditors."

"So what inspired you to take up medicine?" she asked.

Mr Beaufait apologised for his wife's curiosity, but Dr Astrov said an apology wasn't called for.

"It happened in Moscow, where I was educated," he continued. "At school I made friends with a little girl, whose father was a money-bags. Compared to her I was a country bumpkin. Imagine. Until I went to her twelfth birthday party I had never seen a water closet before. I made its acquaintance after my fifth glass of lemonade. There was a chain hanging above the toilet bowl. I didn't know what it was for, but I pulled it anyway. At once a torrent cascaded into the bowl. Thinking that the flow would never cease I leapt out of that room as though pursued by a tidal wave. Unfortunately my pants were still around my ankles. But that is not the story. The real story concerns the balloon I was given at the end of the party. It was filled with helium, and accompanied me home like a bird on a leash. When I finally let it go in my bedroom it flew straight to the ceiling. The next day I saw that it had descended a few inches. It descended a few more the day after that. And so on, until it was nothing but a wrinkled sack of rubber on the floor. I attempted to administer the kiss of life. To no avail. That balloon was my first patient, and it died. In my despair I declared war on gravity, and have been fighting it ever since. I know it is a lost cause, but that is no excuse to shirk the battles, many of which can be won."

Mr Beaufait filled the doctor's wine glass.

"Gravity's my enemy too," he said, "a fall from a horse can be a worrisome thing, and has oftentimes proven fatal."

That night Adele had an discomforting dream. She dreamed that her husband threw a saddle over her bare back and rode her to victory in the Kentucky Derby. When she mentioned it to the winning jockey over breakfast he tapped his hard-boiled egg, and blamed an excess of soft-shell crabs. At the time of her marriage Adele had been a virgin, and would have been happy to remain that way. But Mr Beaufait was no novice, and had introduced her to such pleasure that her very insides had churned and curdled, and turned to the creamiest butter.

After the unwelcome dream, however, she noticed that her husband really did look like a rider mounting a horse when he swung his left leg over her naked belly. For the first time since their wedding night she felt she needed more than expertise. Not wishing to disappoint her husband (or make him suspicious), she rehearsed the motions and the cries that had previously been spontaneous. Before long even she couldn't tell the difference.

The boy grew a year or two older. His parents remained in robust health. Dr Astrov became a figure once removed. Adele heard rumours of unwise liaisons with married women, but there were no scandals.

When the boy was four she began to detect hints that it was time he had a sibling. Although the idea was by no means unreasonable she identified with the mares at the stud farm that was her husband's pride and joy. Nor could she resist the suspicion that he had chosen her because of her pedigree, and the likelihood that she would be a good breeder. With a shock she realized how simple it would be to replace her. After the wedding she had moved into her husband's house, and as yet had left no mark upon it, save for a portrait that hung beside his in the bedroom. It wasn't a bad likeness, but it was utterly conventional. The artist, a local man, made his living from beautifying the Beaufaits and their peers.

The house had been built four generations previously by the maternal grandfather of Edgar Degas, the French impressionist, and acquired by the Beaufaits a generation or so later. This was not accidental. Her husband's family and that of the French painter were partners in a cotton brokerage, albeit junior partners. When the senior partners moved to a larger property on Royal Street, it was natural that the Beaufaits should take over the smaller. Visiting New Orleans in the 1870s Degas sketched both families at work in the Cotton Market.

One of the oils that resulted had hung for years in the dining room above the mahogany sideboard. The man at the centre of the canvas was apparently her husband's grandfather. His idea of work was to stretch his legs in a bent-wood chair and leaf through the *Daily Picayune*. Behind his back his partners were fingering the cotton spread before them on a long table. The windows were open, so it must have been a hot day, but all the brokers sported jackets and bowlers, or even toppers. A second painting by the same artist could be seen in the library. It was a particular favourite of her husband's, since it showed highly-strung thoroughbreds and their silkshirted riders at the Paris races. The two mounts in the foreground had their backs to the viewer. Never before had Adele seen horses look more feminine or more naked.

One day, quite by chance, she discovered that Degas liked to draw women even more than horses. Looking for a particular book on the library shelves she found a portfolio fastened with a purple ribbon. It contained a collection of erotic sketches executed by the Frenchman. Who were these women, thought Adele? What were their stories? Did they experience shame at being naked, as Eve had done when she became conscious of her state? Or did they open themselves slowly but freely to the artist's penetrating gaze? How would she have responded? She stroked the pinks, browns, and earthy reds with which Degas had conveyed the mass of their flesh and hair, and felt in her finger-tips an inkling of the planet's molten core.

At the beginning of 1912 Mr Beaufait ceased to use contraceptives when they coupled. One morning in mid-April Adele arose from the bed and vomited. A fortnight later Dr Astrov confirmed the pregnancy. Since her first visit he had made the surgery his own. Gone were Dr Tacrolimus's framed diplomas, and photographs of his more famous patients; in their place were maps of the delta, and luxurious paintings of local trees, executed it seemed by the arboreal equivalent of Audubon. The maps, however, had a childish quality, as though they had been coloured in by a juvenile hand. The hand, it turned out, belonged to Dr Astrov.

"Those maps are very picturesque," said Mrs Beaufait, "but I am at a loss to know what they signify?"

She was rewarded with an answer as dense as ebony.

"What is man when compared to a tree?" exclaimed the doctor, after several minutes. "Nothing but a puny dwarf!" he said, answering himself. "A tree stands despite all possibilities to fall. A man falls at every opportunity. A tree lives for hundreds – even thousands – of years. A man is here today, and gone with the wind tomorrow. The best efforts of his doctor notwithstanding. A tree creates, a man destroys. My maps are evidence for the prosecution. The first shows Louisiana as it was fifty years ago. Because the state was mainly virgin forest I have painted it various shades of green. See how green turns to emerald around the coast, and along the banks of the Mississippi, where the trees grew most abundantly. You'd think that Louisiana was some wild man of the woods, with those shaggy locks and thick beard. But you would be wrong, for the state's history is more like Samson's."

The doctor looked at his patient. "Is this too much for you? Shall I stop?"

In truth it was a little too much for Adele, who needed to sit down. But she was enchanted by Dr Astrov's passion, and the way it animated his body. She shook her head.

"The second map jumps twenty-five years," the doctor

continued. Three-quarters of the green has vanished. It gets worse. The third shows how things are today. Most of the trees have been felled, so only a few splashes of green were needed to represent the survivors. It goes without saying that the majority of the animals and birds that were sustained by the forests have disappeared too. We are assured that all this butchery has been done in the name of progress. If that were true, I would probably consider the sacrifice worthwhile. But I ask you, Mrs Beaufait, are the poor any better off? Are they more comfortably housed? Do their clothes appear to be cut from finer cloth? Are they less superstitious? Are they more healthy? I can assure you, Mrs Beaufait, that they are not. And all this has been done with no thought for the future. You may not reap the whirlwind, but your children will, or your children's children. The negroes believe that when the last bald cypress has been cleared from the coast, New Orleans will be defenceless, and ripe for destruction by Sango, the bringer of storms. Few take such prophesies seriously. I number myself among that minority."

Adele could not help herself. She yawned loudly.

"Forgive me, Mrs Beaufait," said Dr Astrov promptly, "I can see that I am boring you."

"Not boring," she replied, "scaring."

****

Mama Congo would have been surprised to hear Dr Astrov evoke one of the spirits in which she put her trust. Ever since the boy's flirtation with death she had regarded him with caution. In her opinion he was a dangerous charlatan. She knew who had really saved the boy. It was her Mambo, who had interceded with Ogou Balanjo on his behalf. When she heard that Mrs Beaufait was pregnant for a second time, she insisted that her mistress take herself and her unborn one to receive a blessing that would ensure the safety of both.

And so Mama Congo led Adele – as Virgil had led Dante – deep into the unseen world that existed parallel to her own. They walked a block or so from Esplanade Avenue, to a crossroads where a negro boy was waiting in a cart.

"This here is the apple of my eye," said Mama Congo, "my last-born, my Benjamin. When he sing in church the angels tap their toes in heaven."

Adele was astonished. It had never occurred to her that Mama Congo had a life outside the house, let alone a large family. How many other sons and daughters were there? And what of their father? Adele knew it was none of her business. But she could not resist asking how Mama Congo was able to reconcile a belief in Christ, with a continuing adherence to the ancient ways of Africa.

"A body can't have too many gods watching out for her," was all she said.

Blankets had been laid over bales of cotton in the back of the cart to make passable seats. When they were settled the boy heaved the horse's head away from the foul-smelling trough from which it had been drinking, and flicked the reins lightly over its back, raising both dust and flies.

They left the city, passed through a small wood, and followed a track that skirted fields full of the crop upon which the Beaufaits' fortune was founded. The knee-high plants were green-going-brown. Each supported a galaxy of swollen pods, some of which had prematurely popped to reveal the white froth within. Bins to receive the harvest were already in place. On the other side of the field Adele could see wretched dwellings with sagging roofs, and broken fences.

Mama Congo's boy directed the horse between two fields, and slowly the cart approached the shacks. Old negroes sat outside, their faces turned to the sun, like pot-plants long starved of light. Some smoked pipes. Their eyes were shut. Nor did they open them as Adele passed. The horse skirted a filthy cafe, which stank of burning chicken feathers, and then entered a dense stand of pines, at whose heart stood an isolated cabin. The resinous air was full of bird-song, probably coming from some sort of warbler. *Churry-churry-churry-churry*, it went, *churry-churry-churry-churry*.

"This is the Humfort," said Mama Congo, "our church."

The Mambo was waiting within. The light was dim but Adele could see that she was arrayed splendidly. A rainbow-coloured turban was wrapped around her hair. Long earrings made of shell hung from her lobes. Her coffee-coloured neck and shoulders were bare. Her dress was a patchwork of imperial purple, red, and gold. Statuettes of Jesus and the saints stood on the mantelpiece. A cockerel with a scarlet comb ran about the dirt floor. Mama Congo whispered a few words to the Mambo.

Having established what was required of her, the priestess gathered up a copper bowl, and walked around Adele, spilling cornmeal as she went, until a distinct pattern was visible on the floor. That done she picked up some dried gourds and shook them until they rattled. Then she danced. As the rhythm became more insidious Mama Congo stepped forward, as if summoned to the dance by a denizen of the spirit world.

The Mambo began to chant, in a language entirely unfamiliar to Adele. What was the meaning of *Ayizam, Beni Dawo, Kwala Yege?* Or *Kaki Oka ki anba?* She would have asked Mama Congo to translate, but the woman was flat on her back, apparently being pleasured by her invisible dance partner.

Mama Congo's performance was certainly disturbing, but all in all Adele was more worried about the chicken. Or rather she was worrying about how she would react if it were suddenly beheaded in her presence. As it turned out all the Mambo did was offer a short prayer on her behalf to her possessed house-maid, or rather to the spirit that was possessing her. Subsequently named by Mama Congo as *Ayza*.

Outside the bird-song had been replaced by the sound of fife and drum. Three negroes emerged from a deeper part of the wood. They were wearing crumpled suits and sweatstained hats, and were moving together in a kind of soft-shoe shuffle. The drummers were leaning over their instruments, while the wind-man was slowly charming himself to sleep. Lower and lower he sank, until he was curled upon the ground, shrill notes still emerging from his twitching body.

"I feel like I'm spying upon ghosts at play," whispered Adele.

"They's the opposite of ghosts," replied Mama Congo, "they's zombies. Ghosts are spirits with no bodies. These men have bodies, but their spirits have done gone away. The music has transported them all the way back to Dahomey."

Suddenly Adele became convinced that someone was watching her. She turned around and found herself staring into the eyes of Dr Astrov.

"What are you doing here?" she demanded.

"Unfortunately some patients do not feel at ease in my surgery," he replied, "so I call upon them at home."

There was a pause, filled only by the hypnotic beat of the

drum and fife. What could Adele say? She could hardly tell Dr Astrov the truth. *Boom-boom-boom*, went the drum.

"I was so captivated by your enthusiasm for our native trees," she said, "that I asked my maid to show me some."

"She made an eccentric choice," he said, "but even these can teach us something."

So saying he handed Adele his stethoscope, and instructed her to place its bell against the trunk of the nearest pine. Adele listened and immediately squealed with horrified delight; something was moving within the tree.

"It's the sound of sap rising," he said, "the army of life on the march."

Mama Congo kept her distance, knowing that the spirits who hid in these trees would not take kindly to eavesdroppers.

"These specimens are but saplings compared to the Goliaths and Methuselahs that live on in unvisited backwaters," concluded Dr Astrov, "if you are really interested I should be happy to guide you to them."

The following evening Mr & Mrs Beaufait (a handsome couple) promenaded arm-in-arm along Chartres Street, and then across Jackson Square to watch the full moon rise above the Mississippi. Adele recalled that there was a story attached to the apartments that lined its east and west flanks. They were financed by a certain Micaela Almonester de Pontalba, a beauty of Spanish descent, who had presented her gorgeous red hair to the Emperor Napoleon, and afterwards painted her investment brick-red in memory of that squandered glory. Adele loved her husband, but secretly lamented the fact that he was not the sort to excite or even appreciate such romantic gestures. In life as in bed he was a man dedicated to good practice.

"Let's not go back just yet," said Adele.

Illuminated by the moon they wandered down to the river and entered the French Market. Gas lamps created corridors of light in which fish fresh from the Gulf was being sold, as well as oranges straight from the tree. Beyond all the silver and gold they happened upon a stall displaying a selection of flutes and penny whistles, some very like the one the alleged zombie had been playing.

Without forethought Adele raised a replica to her mouth. She blew hard, but produced only a silent jet of air. The stallholder ran his fingers through his long black hair, and approached his new customer.

"Flutes are like people," he explained, "you pick one up and straightaway you know you are made for each other, that you will make music together. But others won't play for you, no matter how hard you try. What do you think? Is this one Mr Right?"

Adele blew again, with the same negative result.

"Let me give you some help," the salesman said. Taking the flute from Adele he assumed a position behind her, and held the instrument to her lips, which parted to receive it.

"If it isn't comfortable there's no hope," he said, rolling the flute around on her lower lip, and forcing the fleshy part out a little. "You tell me when it feels right," he said.

It may have felt right to Adele, but it didn't to Mr Beaufait, who was just about to intervene when his wife caused the flute to emit a long plaintive note, like the mating call of an extinct bird. He had no choice thereafter but buy the thing for her, though he hated it, and felt like he was bringing a Trojan horse into the house.

****

Toward the end of April Mr Beaufait and some cronies took the train to Louisville in order to watch the Kentucky Derby. While he was away his wife volunteered to receive a natural history lesson from Dr Astrov.

Born and raised in New Orleans, Adele had never before seen anything like the bayou. For a start its main ingredient appeared more like hot chocolate than water. Secondly it didn't look like it belonged to the twentieth century. In fact Adele felt that she had been transported back to the beginnings of life on earth, and would not have been a bit surprised if a dinosaur had arisen from the back-water's primordial depths. Or she had heard God's voice booming through the canopy of leaves.

The trees that bore them emerged from the water like the columns of a temple, creating the impression that this was indeed a sacred place. Adele already knew (thanks to the doctor's running commentary) that those growing nearer the banks were bald cypresses, while those that colonised the deeper parts were water tupelo. Both species had swollen or even buttressed bases, tapering to long clear boles, that emphasised their classical appearance. Some of the water tupelo were still in flower, and the buzzing of bees augmented the chirruping of cicadas, the plash of the paddle, and the sibilance of the doctor's lowered consonants.

He was facing the direction of travel, so that he could better describe the wonders of the wild arboretum as they manifested themselves; and she was facing him, so that she would miss none of it. Although the sunlight was diffused, and fell upon them in shades of yellow and green, the air was stagnant and humid, causing every pore in their bodies to overflow. Another consequence, of which she had an acute awareness, was the way her summer dress clung to her body, as if deliberately designed to emphasise her ripeness.

Fortunately it seemed that the doctor only had eyes for the trees.

"There is a pumpkin ash, and there a redbay," he said, "and there among the shrubs are dahoon, bayberry, and poison-sumac . . . "

And then he broke off and knocked her to the bottom of the boat, as if he had indeed noticed, and mistaken her ripeness for readiness. The canoe rocked from side to side, but did not tip either out. Nor did Adele scream. She was certainly surprised by the doctor's action, but equally surprised that the shock of it was not entirely an unpleasant one. She could not, in all honesty, call what was about to happen "rape".

She closed her eyes and anticipated the weight of his hand upon her breast, the desperate hunger of his lips on hers.

But instead of kissing her the doctor spoke (albeit in a whisper): "Forgive my transgression against your person, Mrs Beaufait, but your life was in immediate danger and I had to act without delay."

She opened her eyes and saw, hanging from the branch of a tree, a snake the length of an average basketball player. The entrance to its maw was wide open, revealing the deadly fangs and eponymous whiteness of a cottonmouth.

"You are indeed a miracle worker, Dr Astrov," said Adele, "first you snatch my son from the jaws of death, and now me. My husband will never be able to thank you enough."

Slowly the boat drifted away from the reach of the snake, and they resumed their journey.

"Et in Arcadia ego," said the doctor, by way of conclusion.

But we cannot be Adam and Eve, thought Adele, because I am already spoken for. She didn't see the word coming, any more than she had seen the snake. It ambushed her, jumped straight into her mind. "Unfortunately". She tried to cast it out, but it wouldn't budge, kept insisting that it was le mot juste.

Eventually the trees began to thin, until they found themselves in open water. The curious aroma of floral perfume and fermenting vegetation was replaced by the vinegary odour of raw wood and sawdust. The land had been laid to waste, temples become ruins, their columns nothing more than stumps protruding from the surface.

"East of Eden," said the doctor, "the end of paradise. Loggers claim that the trees will regenerate, but here there is nothing. Only coarse grass and scrub."

"Turn the boat around," said Adele.

Their parting dialogue went like this.

She: "Today was a revelation. Are there others in store?"

He: "There is one for sure."

****

On the very day of the Kentucky Derby (always the first Saturday in May), Dr Astrov called upon Adele.

"Come," he said.

Obediently she left the boy in the care of Mama Congo, who clearly did not approve of the adventure.

"Where are we going?" she asked.

"For a little walk," replied the doctor.

They marched one block north on Esplanade, then turned left on Bourbon, turning north again after ten blocks.

"You are carrying your professional bag," she remarked,

"from which I deduce that we are on our way to see a patient."

"Several," replied the doctor. He sniffed the air.

"Here is life!" he exclaimed. "Can you not smell it?"

She inhaled a sample, recognizing magnolia, tobacco, horse dung, rye, and below that the musky odour that lingered in the marital bed after sex. By the time they crossed Rampart Street she didn't need the smell or all the sailors on shore leave to tell her where they were heading.

"Dr Astrov," she exclaimed, "I believe we are on our way to a house of ill-repute!"

"Precisely," he replied, "I have an agreement with Minnie White to examine her girls on the first Saturday of every month. We can turn around if you find the idea offensive."

Rather to her surprise she didn't.

She was even more astonished by the grandeur of Minnie White's establishment on Basin Street, whose entrance hall boasted a phalanx of jardinières, and a mirror the size of Versailles. There was even a pianist. Equally astounding (to her) was the constant procession of prominent citizens. Well aware that many of Mr Beaufait's peers patronised the prostitutes, or even maintained mistresses in Storyville, Dr Astrov had carefully chosen a day when there was no danger of an unscheduled encounter with an errant husband. What he hadn't accounted for was the photographer.

***

"See how far I have come from that water closet in Moscow," said Dr Astrov, as he took possession of his temporary surgery; a public washroom on the ground floor that would have suited the Tsarina herself.

The girls lined up to see him in order to have their privates checked, some coming straight from work. Adele had been expecting to feel superior to these fallen women, but found herself respectful of their arcane knowledge. She quickly judged that they deserved their privacy, and informed the doctor that she would await him in the lobby. The piano player acknowledged her presence, then continued with his unusual syncopations. Copulation, it seemed, was a round-the-clock business.

While the doctor continued to practise his trade among the gilded faucets and the marble nymphs, the photographer lugged his 10 x 8 plate camera from room to room in search of willing sitters. This was no easy task, since he came from the same mould as Toulouse-Lautrec. For all Adele knew they were cousins, or even brothers. He certainly dressed in a Frenchified manner, and had an accent to match.

She first became aware of it when he unexpectedly approached her.

"A debutante, I presume?" he gasped.

Adele wrinkled her nose. His breath smelled of mint, his clothes of lavender and moth-balls.

"My name is Bellocq. As you see I am a photographer. Probably you require pictures to make your presence known. Also your charms, if you wish, which I can show to their best advantage."

The presumptuous dwarf had mistaken her for a prostitute. Her initial response was insult and outrage, but on second thoughts recognised that his assumption had been wholly reasonable. What else could a woman be in such a place? Finally she felt rather excited, even flattered.

"A portrait of my face will suffice for now," she said.

"Bon, bon," he said. "Do you have your own room?"

"Not yet," she replied.

"No matter, no matter," he muttered, "there are several that are vacant this morning."

He found one that contained a large wooden bed (which must once have supported more puritanical folk), and a divan (raised at one end). There was some sort of pelt on the floor. In rapid succession Bellocq steadied his tripod, fetched his spotlight from where he had last used it, posed Adele, focused the camera, loaded a plate, and pressed the rubber bulb that released the shutter. Re-emerging from beneath the velvet drape he said, "C'est tout." Though he obviously wished it were otherwise.

"Normally I pay the girls to take off their clothes, and they pay me to take the photographs," he explained. "Since the amounts are equal no money actually changes hands. But as you have not taken off your clothes, the equilibrium is disturbed, if you see what I mean."

Adele did, or thought she did.

"How much do l owe you?" she asked, snapping open her purse.

"You are too hasty, mademoiselle," he replied. "I am seeking to increase your fortune, not diminish it. You body is your business, and you have an excellent one. Why not advertise the fact? You need have no fear of standing naked before me. Monsieur Bellocq knows the meaning of chivalry."

The once and future Mrs Beaufait recognised that her bluff had been called; if she was to sustain her pretence of being a prostitute she had no choice. Was she royalty? No. Was her modesty more precious than that of Miss White's other employees? No. Was her flesh fashioned from finer materials? No.

"You have a deal, Mr Bellocq," she said.

Rising from the divan she noticed a coal-black mask hanging from the wall above the bed.

"I shall take off everything else," she said, "but I shall wear that."

Bellocq raised no objections.

Adele calmly removed the cameo that was fastened at her throat, then undid all the buttons on her blouse including those on the cuffs. She unbuckled her belt, loosened her skirt, and let it drop to the floor. Bellocq, pretending indifference, meanwhile prepared his camera, and positioned the spotlight. Adele unrolled her stockings and kicked off her shoes. At length nothing remained but her knickers. Go on, she ordered herself, for once in your life do something daring! In such a way she divested herself of everything save her rings; those she retained so that anyone who looked at the photograph in years to come would know that she was a married woman not a prostitute.

Did she feel shame? Not a shred. On the contrary she was shameless, felt herself responding like a coquette to Mr Bellocq's candid stare. Little did he guess that he was the first man ever to look upon her naked body in its entirety, not excepting her husband. Mr Beaufait had witnessed it all, of course, but only a bit at a time. What would he say if he could see her now? The idea of transgression and retribution both thrilled and frightened her. She slipped on the mask, which covered her eyes and mouth, and immediately felt less vulnerable, as though body and identity were now separate items.

"Are you familiar with the Goya portrait called *Maja Desnuda*, by any chance?" inquired Mr Bellocq.

"Naturally," replied Adele, reclining upon the divan like the Spanish noblewoman.

"Excellent," cried the photographer, "but not perfect. Your skin is very white, making it too easy for the viewer's eye to slide the length of your body without stopping. Whereas we would prefer his gaze to linger on your breasts. The mask offers a buffer at one end. Perhaps you should replace your stockings and shoes to do the same at the other."

Adele was conscious of the sway of her bosom as she bent to replace her stockings, and sensed that Mr Bellocq was no less aware. The knowledge only encouraged her to emphasise the motion. Newly shod she leaned back on the divan, rested her torso on her left elbow, and laughed.

Pat on cue the door opened and Dr Astrov walked in, as Adele had half-hoped he would. Like some vagrant bluebottle his gaze alighted upon the patch of hair that marked the delta of her private Mississippi. She recalled the maps in his surgery, and became convinced that this perverse voyeur was dreaming only of trees.

"A penny for your thoughts, Dr Astrov," she said merrily, as she removed the mask.

"Mrs Beaufait," he exclaimed, "have you taken leave of your senses?"

"Isn't that the point of Storyville?" she replied.

Sans mask, sans everything, she arose and stood upon her high heels. The doctor noted that her breasts, much enlarged by pregnancy, remained perpendicular, and showed no sign of ptosis. As a matter of fact they were stupendous. Her recklessness, and her courage moved him; as did lust for what they made visible.

Bellocq invited him to view her likeness on the ground-glass screen at the rear of the camera, where it hung upside down like a bat, then exposed a final plate. That done the unlikely Cupid made his exit. Lacking a bow his camera had proved equally effective in discharging the arrows of desire (one of which was now firmly lodged in Dr Astrov's breast).

They were in a bordello, in a room dominated by a massive double bed. She was already naked. And she desired the doctor. Of that there was no doubt. So what was to stop them? Only the fact that she was worrying about Mr Beaufait and the boy. How could she betray them both like this? Fortunately Adele was also a woman of some skill in the art of sophistry. She rapidly conceived a way of proceeding without causing damage. She would simply play her role to its logical conclusion.

"If you want my body," she said, "you'll have to pay for it."

She reasoned that if he did it would cease to be hers for the duration of the hire, and therefore she would have no responsibility for its actions.

"How much?" asked the doctor.

"The going rate," she replied.

So he handed her twenty dollars and they retired to the bed. Even so she still experienced some guilt when Dr Astrov entered her. And when he finished she wondered if it had all been worth it. The experience had undeniably been pleasurable, but so it was with her husband. In truth the two men were disappointingly similar.

She began counting slowly to fifty. By the time she reached forty-five she expected the doctor to be asleep. At ten, as anticipated, he withdrew his penis, but at fifteen he surprised her by attaching a finger to that mysterious knob at the head of the delta. She had often wondered after its purpose. On bad days she even feared that it might be an inoperable tumour. But if this was the way it was going to kill her, then dying might not be such a bad experience after all. She never reached forty, let alone fifty. Her last conscious thought was that she was losing control over her body. Of their own accord her arms rose above her head. Her back arched and fell with increasing momentum.

To the doctor it looked as if she were some earth-bound creature trying to recapture the art of flying. Her eyes rolled in her head, her mouth opened, she began to babble, and then to scream, actually to scream. One moment she was ecstatic, the next terrified, terrified that her body would no longer be able to contain all the passions within. And when the pressure finally proved too great she felt as though she had been transformed into a gigantic cotton pod that had split asunder and spilled all of its contents over the white sheets.

"Oh my God, Michael," she gasped, "what have you done to me?"

Adele dozed and awoke with a start, convinced that a price had been extracted for her unbridled freedom, that her skin was now as black as the mask. Of course it remained spotless.

"How do you feel?" asked her partner in crime.

"Like I've just won the Kentucky Derby," she replied.

But how did he feel? He had fallen in love on several occasions before and dreaded repetition of earlier performances, when he would frequent the woman's house, annoy her husband, abandon his duties, and loath himself a little more with every passing day. This time he would behave with more dignity and honour. He would make a grand gesture, yes, he would renounce his past, and offer to start a new life with Adele in this land of new lives.

****

All the way back from Kentucky Mr Beaufait wondered how he would tell his wife that he had lost his shirt on Sonada. He need not have worried. When he returned home he discovered that she was gone, and that New Orleans was short of one doctor.

"He done bewitched her," explained Mama Congo. "We met him in the woods one day, and he tell us that he's there to heal the sick. But that was a big untruth. He only done bribed a Boker to perform some lefthanded voodoo."

Mama Congo assured him that her Mambo had the power to break the doctor's evil spell. But Mr Beaufait preferred to enlist the services of a private investigator. The trail was still warm and the detective quickly traced the doctor and his mistress to a plantation house just shy of the border with Mississippi.

It was a two-day ride from New Orleans. On the second afternoon Mr Beaufait left the road and entered a dense grove of live oaks and crape myrtles. Ahead he could see the establishment where his fugitive wife was living feloniously as Mrs Astrov. Sunlight cascaded over the roof and the jalousied galleries, making it look more like a blessed place than a house of sin. The white columns and walls must have dazzled his eyes, otherwise he would have surely seen the two riders before they saw him. The pair were already trotting away through the trees when he realized who they were.

"Come back, Adele," he cried, "the boy misses you."

But she gave no sign of having heard him. He spurred his horse, but it was tired and uncooperative. In a fury he unholstered his Colt Navy Model revolver, and aimed at Dr Astrov's back. He was a good shot, but it was a moving target, and besides he was agitated. The bullets did not even come close.

He waited for two nights and a day for them to return, but the scandalous couple were never seen in those parts again.

In fact eight months elapsed before the private investigator picked up their scent again. A woman, matching Adele Beaufait's description, had given birth to a baby girl in a Baton Rouge hospital. There was even an address.

Mr Beaufait surprised his wife breast-feeding. It was, of course, the first time he had set eyes upon his daughter.

"Does she have a name?" he asked.

"Of course," she replied.

Mr Beaufait's fond assumption that his wife was alone was conclusively disproved when Dr Astrov emerged from the shadows waving a revolver at the intruder.

"Go!" he demanded.

"Not without my wife and child," came the bold reply.

Dr Astrov did not waste any more words. He fired four shots in the direction of his rival. All were well wide of the mark. Nevertheless, Adele screamed, and the startled baby cried until it was red in the face.

"I accept your challenge," said Mr Beaufait, "and will await you outside."

"You mustn't go," said Adele, as soon as her husband had left the room.

"All my life I have used stories as a form of protection," replied Dr Astrov. "They enabled me to turn my enemies and my fears into objects of ridicule. Then I felt safe again, because a figure of fun could not also be a cause of fear. But now there is no escaping the facts, which are awaiting me on the other side of the door. What will happen, will happen. I am a doctor, Adele; more than anyone I know that none of us can remain in Storyville for ever."

"I'll be your shield," pleaded Adele, "my husband will not fire if there's any danger to me or the baby. He may have his faults, but he is a gentleman."

Dr Astrov smiled and walked to the door. He looked back but once before he went out.

"Don't worry about me," he said, "I'm not the only Fabergé egg in the room."

When Adele thought about those words in later years she puzzled over their true meaning, eventually ascribing their obscurity to her lover's Russian origins.

****

Although duelling was illegal in Louisiana Mr Beaufait was never charged with any crime, possibly because his brother was the district attorney.

Visiting her husband in his cell on the day of his release Adele hugged him and said: "You should have done that long ago."

It was a phrase he was to hear again in the bedroom, when she directed his hand to a place he thought only whores allowed access.

Mr Beaufait did not attend the Kentucky Derby in 1913, for obvious reasons, nor again in 1914. But in 1915 he took his wife and two children to Louisville. Remembering her dream of long ago Adele placed a small fortune on a filly called Regret. Her husband scoffed at her choice, informing her haughtily that no filly had ever won a Kentucky Derby. But she had the last laugh. Regret led from start to finish, easily beating Pebbles and Sharpshooter into second and third place.

Over dinner on the train taking them back to New Orleans

Mr Beaufait informed his family that he had decided to move his money from cotton to timber.

"It will be a new beginning," he said.

They bedded down in their cribs, while the locomotive rolled on through the southlands, spitting fire from its smokestack. Had Adele awoken and looked toward the heavens she would have seen only darkness, for that night the moon and stars were hidden by gathering clouds.

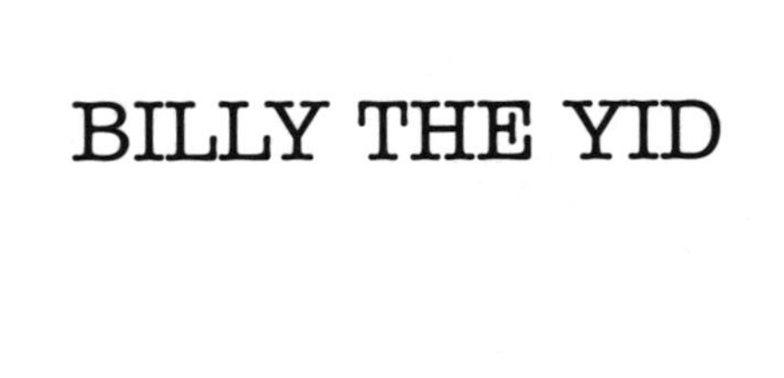

BILLY THE YID

IF YOU'VE HEARD of me at all, it's on account of a novel I wrote in the 1980s called *Rabbi Goldfinch's Folly*. Should you be unfamiliar with even that, suffice it to say that the Rabbi's folly consisted of trying to rape a German au pair at the barmitzvah of one of his congregants. His excuse was that the boy's mother had lied to him, leaving him with the false impression that the girl was Swiss. This assault in turn leads to a series of pogroms which bring havoc and mayhem to places such as Hendon, where I happened to grow up.

The rabbi of the synagogue to which my parents belonged chose to take the book personally, and – to their mortification – delivered a sermon in which I was denounced as a new Josephus, a latter-day betrayer of Zion. Others – in the congregation – called me a self-hating Jew, a circumcised antisemite. One anonymous correspondent even cursed me: "May all the tortures and indignities you visit upon your characters be visited upon your own body, you bastard. May you be spared nothing." I tossed the note in the dustbin, but to no avail, I still recall every word of it. The BBC, however, made a documentary about me, and the book sold well. It is out of print now, but still taught at various universities, both here and abroad. I do not think about it often, in fact I barely give it a second thought.

So it is a surprise to see "Rabbi Goldfinch's Folly" in the subject line of one of my unopened emails. The sender, Evelyn Turteltaube, is a mature student, studying English and American Literature at the University of Bonn. Apparently *Rabbi Goldfinch's Folly* was one of the works discussed during the course of a term-long seminar entitled, "The Book & the Holocaust", and was (in the opinion of my correspondent) the best of the lot.

"Discussion of your novel was quite amusing," I read. "When Dr S asked us if we liked the novel there was a long silence. After some coaxing a fresh-faced and innocent-looking male student (young, of course, I was the only older person, apart from the lecturer) commented as follows: 'Yes, I liked the novel, but I didn't like the author's sick fantasies.' Dr S: 'What do you mean by sick *fantasies*?' Student (blushing): no answer. Dr S: 'Are you, by any chance, referring to the scenes involving the narrator's Israeli mistress?' Student (blushing even more): 'Yes.' Dr S: 'What about the rest of you? What did you think?' Female student (hard-working and tight-lipped): 'I think those scenes are really tasteless, utterly sick and disgusting.' Dr S (slightly taken aback by now): 'Perhaps I should have warned you, but such behaviour is the norm in modern Anglophone literature.' Male student (an intellectual type, who as the course neared its end rather surprisingly made a pass at me): 'That does not alter the fact that the scenes are embarrassing at best, repulsive at worst.' Me: 'You are all so prudish. Did you not think it in the least amusing when the Israeli woman astonished the narrator by slipping a finger into his pants and . . . well, you all know what she did with it?' 'I did.' This from a Bulgarian student (female with – I don't know how to put it – an erotic flair – can you say it like that?), who continued: 'It's exactly like real life, natural.' This comment led to everyone looking astonished, but me it emboldened. Before the author himself I am too ashamed to repeat my interpretation, but in the class I am not shy. It was greeted with hoots – or is it 'howls'? – of derision. There are eighteen students in the seminar, of whom a handful (I regret to say) call it the Boo-hoo class (and giggle every time at their silly joke). Perhaps they are not typical, but I have noticed gradual shifts in attitude in Germany over the years. More and more voices are heard proclaiming 'enough is enough' (about the Holocaust), while the young say, 'Why blame us? It wasn't our fault.' A new so-called healthy form of patriotism is being propogated, encouraging my fellow-countrymen to be proud to be German again. I have also observed a growing (and quite extreme) hatred of Israel on the left. All this makes me sick."

At which point Evelyn Turteltaube must have paused, taken stock, and decided to make the switch from polemical to personal, to get a little flirty: "I think I'd better stop writing now; after all you are a complete stranger and probably not in the least interested in my ramblings. Also, I'm getting into this strange, tired, slightly unreal late-night mood. I know I probably shouldn't send this email anyway, but I'm feeling slightly adventurous now (or rather bored, my boy-friend is away at a conference, and my imagination is beginning to wander where it shouldn't). Tomorrow I shall certainly be mortally embarrassed by what I have written, but by then it will be too late."

My wife is in her studio upstairs. Illuminated by a shaft of light she looks like she's fencing with her easel. A famous actor is balanced on a stool opposite her. She diverts her attention from the canvas to stare at me.

"Well," she says, "is the house burning down, or what?"

"Nothing like that," I say, "but I've just received this extraordinary email . . ."

"From the Nobel Committee in Stockholm?" she says.

"No," I say, "from a student in Bonn."

"I think he – or more like a she, judging from your excitement – can wait until dinner, don't you?" But I have to tell someone about it immediately.

How long since I telephoned Vivian Ben Duchifat in Caesarea? Ten years, or more. But I still remember her number by heart. Why not? I used it often enough when she was auditioning for the role of the outrageous Israeli mistress in *Rabbi Goldfinch's Folly.*

"My God," says Vivian, when she hears my voice, "it's the murderer himself. Do you intend to ask forgiveness for killing me off so horribly in your nasty little book?"

"Dead right," I say.

"Idiot," she says. "I forgave you for that years ago. Now tell me just why you've decided to reenter my life at this late stage?"

I read her extracts from the email. Her laugh is a sound straight out of the past.

"Did we really do half the things you wrote about," she says, "or was it just wishful thinking on your part? To tell you the truth, Izzy, I don't remember any more."

I do. I took notes. What else is a writer to do with experience, however ecstatic?

In the kitchen my wife is uncorking a bottle of Sicilian red. We have it with a plate of Trofie al Pesto Genovese. This is a placatory gesture. My wife knows how much I adore this dish. The plates are white, the cutlery silver, and there are wine glasses not tumblers. And she has exchanged her paint-spattered dungarees for a purple dress.

"You should know better than to interrupt me when I'm at work," she says. "What was it you wanted to tell me?"

"It doesn't matter now," I say, "the moment has passed."

As does the moment of reconciliation.

"What?" says my wife. "Are you sulking? Could it be that you are a little bit jealous that I've been commissioned by the National Portrait Gallery to paint X, while you are forced by a reluctant publisher to write on spec? How galling it must be for you."

"Bollocks," I say, "the very opposite is true."

Believe me, I mean every word. Years ago my pinch-faced Latin master predicted that I would be hung. No idle threat, when the most famous alumnus of the secondary-modern across the road was James Hanratty, the last man to be executed in England. It follows that if my wife's portrait of X is a masterpiece, as I hope it will be, she may well be asked who she'd like to paint next, and she will of course say, "My husband". And when the portrait is done I will unveil it with the words: "Mr Hunter spoke the truth. I have been hung."

"Why are you in such a foul mood," I say when we are in our double bed, "isn't the portrait going well?"

"Fuck off," she says.

"Well, it seemed a good likeness to me," I say, "from what little I saw."

"How long have we been married?" she says.

"A long time," I say.

"And still you do not know that a good likeness is not the same as a good painting," she says. "They are not synonymous."

"But the painting cannot be anonymous either," I say, "surely it must bear some resemblance to the original."

"Let me put it in terms you might understand," says my wife. "When we make love you begin by kissing my face and uttering all manner of false endearments. But they're soon forgotten as desire mounts. And if it turns out to be a good fuck so's my face. In both the studio and the bed appearance is only a starting point."

****

My wife's taunt about my career was insulting, but fully justified. None of my subsequent books has become anywhere near as notorious – or famous – as *Rabbi Goldfinch's Folly*. Most have been well reviewed, but the sales of all fall into that dismal category called "Disappointing". These days I have only minimal contact with my publisher, my credo being: "If you have to ask your publisher a question, you don't want to know the answer".

Every six months, however, my agent takes me to lunch at his favourite restaurant, Bocca di Lupo, to demonstrate his abiding interest in my progress. We order. Plates are presented. My agent twirls blonde curls of spaghettini, to which the flesh of tomatoes and lobsters has adhered, around his fork and says (before filling his mouth): "Astonish me."

So I start to tell him about Morris Bernstein.

"Who the fuck is Morris Bernstein?" he says. "Your accountant? Why should I be interested in your fucking accountant?"

"Bernstein's a character in a book called *Extras*," I say. "It will consist of maybe fifteen mini-biographies of people who are – at present – only walk-ons in the biopics of the immortals. It is my intention to give them above the title-billing for once. Six or seven are already done. At present I'm working on Bernstein, whose only claim to fame is that Billy the Kid shot him dead. We know the date of his death, but not of his birth. Most likely he was born in London on February 11 1856, to Fanny and Julius Bernstein. He's next heard of in Santa Fe, New Mexico, where he finds work in a department store owned by co-religionists – did I mention he was Jewish? – the Spiegelberg Bros. He's all of seventeen. Coincidentally, Billy the Kid, only twelve, and yet to kill his first man, is also living in Santa Fe. Did their paths cross there? At least one of the Kid's biographers maintains that Bernstein served Billy in his employers' store."

My agent gives such a grimace that one of the waiters rushes to our table, for fear that a dish he served contains poison.

"Why are you doing this to yourself?" says my agent. "Why are you wasting your time on a book that has only one message: minor characters, minor author?"

"Let me finish," I say, refilling my agent's glass. "I won't tax you with the minutiae of the Lincoln County War, except to mention that one of its victims was Billy the Kid's employer, a rancher he was being paid to protect. It was after John Tunstall's murder that Billy went gun-crazy. Why? I suspect that Tunstall (English-educated and only twenty-six) was more than Billy's boss. I think the Kid was his catamite."

"I smell money there," says my agent, "though you need to be more dogmatic on the catamite thing. I don't suppose Bernstein was also a feigele?"

"I don't know," I say, "but I have seen it claimed that he wrote poetry."

"A queer love triangle," says my agent, "that might be really something."

"Are you ready for the climax?" I say.

My agent pours himself another glass of Barolo. "Fire away," he says.

"On August 5 1878 Billy the Kid and his gang – known as Regulators – decided to round-up Tunstall's herd, which had scattered after his death. Because there was so much ground to cover, the Kid took a short cut across the Mescalero Indian Reservation. What happened next is still disputed. Apologists for the Kid maintain that an official working at the Indian Agency mistook the Regulators for bandits, and opened fire without warning. One of the Regulators – not Billy – returned fire with fatal consequences. The dead man was Morris Bernstein."

"So where's the story?" says my agent, pouring us both a third glass.

"According to his defenders the Kid was not within earshot – let alone gunshot – of the killing. Apache witnesses tell a different story. Percy Big Mouth (quoting his father) described how some Apaches came into the Trading Post, where Bernstein was distributing rations, and reported that rustlers were stealing their horses. Bernstein immediately picked up his rifle and said: 'I will send them back'. 'No,' he was warned, 'they outlaws. They will not listen.' 'They will mind me,' said Bernstein, mounting his horse."

"He was a fool," says my agent, "but a brave one: The Jew who stood up to Billy the Kid. Maybe that I can sell."

"He approached Billy and said,'You go back,'" I continue. "'Who says so?' replied the Kid. 'I am saying so,' said Bernstein. The Kid's reply was to unholster his pistol and shoot him dead."

"Poor boy," says my agent.

"He died for nothing," I say. "The Kid took the horses anyway. But the sacrifice made a martyr of Bernstein; by dint of blood spilled on Apache land he became a blood-brother to Cochise, Geronimo and other heroes of the resistance."

****

My version of Morris Bernstein's short life and dramatic death is published in the *Jewish Chronicle*. It elicits but a single response, from a reader who has heard that the Governor of New Mexico is considering offering the Kid a posthumous pardon. "May the ghost of Morris Bernstein haunt him if he does," he concludes.

But I am forgetting the phone call from my cousin, Tatum, a long-time resident of East Talpiot.

"Boychick," he says, "I loved your article in the *Chronicle*. Always sticking up for the little man. That's our family through and through. But right now I need someone to stick up for me. And I say to myself, Who better than my cousin Izzy?"

When my wife finally emerges from the studio (followed by X, who sneaks away like a guilt-ridden analysand) I venture to tell her about Tatum's request.

"My meshuggener cousin in Israel telephoned," I say. "It seems he's getting married for the third time and wants me to be his best man. I don't think I can refuse him."

"But I can," says my wife. "I've done my duty by him. I attended his first two weddings. Enough is enough. When is the third?"

"In a fortnight," I say.

"That settles it," says she. "I can't just break off in the middle of painting X's portrait. You go without me."

****

And I do. My cousin lives in a house on Rehov Klausner, opposite the erstwhile residence of SY Agnon, still the only Israeli writer to have won the Nobel Prize. Our fathers were brothers, and because there was but three months between us, we were raised as if we were too. Now we are the only living witnesses to the manifold ingratitudes and misdemeanours of our childhood. This keeps us close, even though we have little else in common. We attended the same grammar school, but thereafter our paths diverged; I went on to the University of St Albans, while Tatum became an untutored autodidact. As a result he's always seeking to find gaps in my knowledge, or to show off his own.

We are sitting on a terrace at the end of his garden. The dense foliage of loquat trees shades us, each leaf an emerald toupee with a precise centre-parting. There is no wind, the air is pure, and the Judean wilderness is visible before us, like a herd of sleeping camels.

"Did you know that Agnon took his nom de plume from the word 'agunah', the term for a woman who cannot remarry because her husband has denied her a divorce?" says Tatum. "He obviously saw himself in a similar bind; estranged from God, but by no means free of him. It certainly helps explain why he was so attracted to the subject of failed marriages. Pity he's not across the road any more. What stories I could have fed him! But it was one of his that I recalled, just as I was in the process of shruging off the second Mrs Nesher. The one about the divorcing couple who realize that they have made the biggest mistake of their lives. Was I about to do the same, I thought, as the rabbi began to coax from me the words that cannot be taken back? Instead of them I tasted on my tongue another of Agnon's delicious phrases, 'Flesh such as yours will not soon be forgotten'. But then I recollected the vindictive soul that dwelt within that temple, and couldn't follow the rabbi's promptings quick enough. Thank God I did, otherwise I would never have met her successor."

"And when will I have that pleasure?" I say.

"Probably not till we're under the chuppah," he says.

The view from beneath the chuppah – which has been raised al fresco on the edge of the Armon Hanatziv Promenade – is of the solar system in miniature. At its centre the Dome of the Rock scatters light as if it were a scion of the sun. It illuminates the mountains of Zion and Olives, and the three valleys called Tyroppean, Hinnom and Kidron, that surround the Old City. And it gilds the couple standing before me, about to become man and wife.

The rabbi is small but has lungs as huge as zeppelins. His voice shakes the hills, and can probably be heard in Damascus and Cairo, as well as in Jerusalem. I bear witness as Tatum takes his vows, stamps on the wine glass, and kisses the latest Mrs Nesher. Only then am I introduced to her.

"Yonina," says Tatum, "meet my cousin, Izzy Adler, the famous writer. He's been married to the same woman for twenty-five years and counting, which makes him something of an anachronism, if not an outright freak."

"On the contrary," says Yonina, looking at the woman who has linked her arm to mine, "I think he is a man of sound judgement. You are very welcome, Mrs Adler."

"A reasonable assumption," says my companion, "but an incorrect one. My name is Vivian Ben Duchifat, and we are just good friends."

"Thanks for letting me bring her," I say to Tatum, as we make our way to the bar.

"She's kept her looks well, I'll give her that," he says.

But Tatum has no interest in discussing my date. All he wants to do is talk about his wife.

"I think she's the one, Izzy, I really do," he says. "Between you and me, we've already decided to start a family. But do I want to raise my children in this hard place, that's the question? To be honest with you, Izzy, a lot of what you write goes straight over my head. But your article on Morris Bernstein got me right here, right in the heart. It made me cry, Izzy, made me cry for my unborn children. When I first came to this land, I was one among a generation of Morris Bernsteins. We were not saints, God forbid, but we cared, Izzy, we cared for one another, and – here's the rub – for others as well. All that has changed now. In the settlements, but elsewhere too, we are raising our sons to take what is not theirs without pity or remorse. God help us, Izzy, but we are raising a generation of Billy the Yids."

Our glasses are filled with champagne. Again and again. I win the prize for providing the wittiest caption to a photograph of Tatum at an earlier marriage. It is my first literary award in many a year, and I milk the moment. My acceptance speech is longer than the one I made in my official capacity as best man. A bassist, a guitarist, and a fiddler eventually take the stage and play Western Swing like they were raised in Texas. At some point Tatum – having found a shoulder-length purple wig – seizes the microphone from the singer and invites the assembled company to smell his armpits. The singer reclaims the microphone, and croons soothing ballads, until the guests slowly begin to waltz up the hill and homewards.

****

Since the Armon Hanatziv Promenade is but a fifteen-minute stroll from Rehov Klausner, I had accompanied the groom to the ceremony on foot. But now it's after midnight, and Tatum has no more need of a best man.

"Look," I say to Vivian, when we are standing beside her Toyota, "Tatum and his new bride have a suite booked at the King David. Apart from me his house is empty. Why not spend the night, and drive back to Caesarea in the morning?"

"Can't be done," she says, opening the door, "the dog is expecting me. I'm late already." She places the key in the ignition, and her hands on the wheel. "Well," she says, "what are you going to do?"

It would not be very gentlemanly to allow her to travel alone at this ungodly hour, but it would be even less gentlemanly to get in the car with her. For a few moments I stand on the brink, vaguely aware that I am being called upon to make a moral decision.

"Nu?" she says.

"What the hell?", I think, and choose the greater of the evils.

Descending the hill, Vivian unexpectedly takes the Harel cut-off at speed.

"Are you trying to kill us?" I say.

"Don't be such an old woman," she says. "The car's running on empty, and – if my memory serves me well – there's an old Paz station just around the corner."

Her headlamps pick out a beat-up old hatchback in its otherwise deserted forecourt. On the automobile's hood is an open parcel of food; some pitta, hummus, and what looks like babaghanouzh. Around it are a pack of six young yeshiva students. They circle the food, like wolves around a kill, each darting towards it in order to snatch a share, then jumping back, and eating while still in motion. All are wearing the same uniform; flat black hat, and long gaberdine coat. But not all wear them in the same way: some balance their hats on the back of the head, a few on the crown. One tilts it forward, so that his eyes are hidden. Half have their gaberdines buttoned tight, the remainder leave them hanging open. Five of the youths have dark sidelocks, which swing like plaits as they move. The sixth has blond hair and straight peyot, which are flattened against his cheeks like a flapper's bobs.

I work the pump, and pay in the kiosk. As I return to the Toyota, I can see that the ravenous boys have turned their appetites from the victuals to Vivian. The majority are staring at her through the car's windows. The sixth – the blond one – is reclining on its hood, his face pressed hard against the windshield. I shove aside the boy who's blocking my access to the passenger door, and grab the one on the hood.

"You go back," I say.

He raises his head, and turns towards me. His pupils are dilated, his lips flecked with saliva and food. He is clearly high on something other than testosterone, and could well be as dangerous as he looks.

"Who says so?" he snarls (his voice slurred, but clearly American-accented).

"I am saying so," I shout.

At which point Vivian, having had enough, fires the engine, and activates the wipers and the washers, instantly achieving what words did not.

"So my cousin was right," I say, as we resume our journey, "this place really is swarming with Billy the Yids."

"If you want my opinion," she says, "that sounds a touch antisemitic."

****

Even before Vivian reaches her front door the dog is yelping for her. When she opens it the creature leaps straight into her arms.

"Did you miss me, Muzzy?" she says, kissing its tiny brown snout.

Muzzy is short for Mazel – luck – and is some sort of hairless chihuahua. Mazel avoids me like the plague, and when I reach out to pet it, the thing growls with evil intent.

"Okay," says Vivian, when she has seen to her dog's needs, "where do you want to sleep tonight. In the guest bedroom, or upstairs?"

"Upstairs, I guess," say I.

So we ascend in a line; Vivian, the dog, and me.

"I don't have a toothbrush," I say.

"You can use mine," she says.

When I come out of the bathroom Vivian is putting on her pyjamas.

"How do you want to play this?" she says. "Do you want to sleep like spoons? Or do you want to fuck?"

"May as well be hung for a sheep as a lamb," I say.

"Just so long as you aren't going to be stricken by guilt afterwards," she says.

"My mishegoss is fear not guilt," I say.

So Vivian takes off the pyjamas she has just put on, and climbs into bed naked. I follow her example. As does the chihuahua. She lies on her back and lights up a cigarette. Leaving her to smoke I work my way along her body.

"My goodness," she gasps, "you're the most bristly man who's ever been down there."

I toil to the brink of lockjaw, but can't make her come.

"Don't take it personally," she says, "but I don't come as easily as I once did. To tell the truth, none of my lovers can make me come better than I can myself. Be warned, Mr Big Ears, if I ever read what I've just said in a story of yours I'll have your guts for garters."

When I awaken it is light. I sit up, not entirely certain where I am. My confusion is multiplied by the fact that my sleeping companion seems to have the face of a minor demon, with reddish skin, pointed ears, and a long snout. When I try to push the horrid vision aside, it barks and bites my hand.

"By the by," says Vivian, sitting up in bed, "I liked the way you handled yourself with those yeshiva bochers last night. I'd always had you down as – how shall I put it? – a cautious man. But I was wrong. You surprised me – and I may add – turned me on. If you had behaved differently, of course, you'd be waking up downstairs right about now, with not even a dog for company."

So saying she scoops up the disconcerted chihuahua and clutches it to her bosom.

"Tell me," she continues, "have you heard any more from that German student, the one I must thank for last night's debaucheries."

"Lots," I say. "Although she has a live-in boyfriend she admits to wondering what it would be like to have an affair with a Jew. She also wonders whether I've had sex with a German in reality."

"Sounds like an invitation to me," says Vivian. "Have you replied to it yet?"

"No," I say.

"Okay," says Vivian, "let's have some fun and do it together. What sort of person do you think she is?"

"Insecure," I say, "intelligent, highly-sexed, though I think she has some issues with her body."

"Write that you had a dream," says Vivian. "And in this dream you were in an unfamiliar German city . . ."

"And in this city there was a house," I say, "and in this house there was a room. And in this room there was a table laid for a tea-party. But there was only one person present, whose face I could not see."

"What happened next is not clear, you must write," she says. "In one version you and the unknown guest sat at the table all night deep in conversation. But in another the two of you were in a bed-chamber, your bodies entwined in an amorous embrace. Do not forget to use the word 'bed-chamber'. It has the necessary dream-like quality, which you need to avoid actual committment at this early stage."

Even before I leave Caesarea I receive the following reply from Evelyn Turteltaube: "I am reading *Rabbi Goldfinch's Folly* for the third time. I am reading it in bed. I am naked of course, and can feel your words crawling all over my body. Nor do they stop there. They respect no laws of privacy. I can feel a particularly long adverb crawl up my back passage. It seems our dreams are very much alike. It will be my pleasure to ensure that yours come true."

"The question is," says Vivian, "just how much reality can you handle?"

****

"Confess," says Tatum, on my last morning in Jerusalem, "did you get to fuck Vivian Ben Duchifat on my wedding night?"

We are drinking mint tea in the garden, beside a pomegranate tree. A yellow-vented bulbul alights upon a branch to which a large but damaged pomegranate is attached. The bird swivels acrobatically until it is hanging upsidedown, its chromium rump fully exposed, and its beak precisely aligned to the fruit's gaping wound. Then with extreme delicacy, as if its beak were tweezers and the pomegranate's seeds the rarest of rubies, the bird extracts its breakfast. I identify with that pomegranate as Tatum tries – with less finesse – to drag the secret from me. Eventually I nod with feigned reluctance.

"You dog!" says Tatum. "You dirty dog!"

I sip my tea, as if he were talking of someone else.

"And today?" he says. "Should anyone inquire. Will you be here or there?" he says.

"Officially, here," I say, "but not in reality."

****

My flight is due to leave Ben Gurion at 5.00 am. Vivian has booked a taxi for 2.30. It is ten-thirty and we are in bed, having drunk two bottles of wine.

"I really am very good at this," she says, lighting another cigarette, "I missed my vocation. I should have been a call girl."

We doze a little, but at 1.15 I arise to take a shower.

"There's really no need," she says. "I leave no trace. Your wife won't be able to smell me on you."

Why take the chance? When I have finished she is half asleep.

"You know where the light switch is?" she says as I take my leave.

I decide to descend in darkness, so as not to waken her fully. At a certain point – maybe five steps from the ground – the stairs make a ninety degree turn to the right. Take it too early and you're in big trouble, as the staircase has no bannister. Take it too late and you're in equally big trouble. So I use my leading foot to feel for each step, before committing the rest of me. This works fine, until the next step isn't there, and I find myself tumbling through thin air. I drop for five feet or more, and hit the marble floor; first my legs, then my back, then my head. Bang, bang, whack, like the sound a spoon makes when it hits a soft-boiled egg.

Considering the knock it received my head is surprisingly pain-free. I manage to sit up, then stand up, without keeling over. I touch my head. It is wet. There's obviously a lot of bleeding going on. I enter the downstairs bathroom, and switch on the light. I look in the mirror and see something out of a horror movie. Rivulets of blood are pouring down my face. A large piece of skin – or even skull, for all I know – is sticking up. I look like I've been scalped. There is blood all over my jacket and my shirt. And the floor. And the sink. The place looks like a crime scene. I try to staunch the flow with a hand-towel, but it is quickly soaked through. Standing at the bottom of the stairs, I call Vivian's name. But only the cursed dog responds. Like some dwarfish ghoul it starts to lap up my blood.

So I ascend the stairs with my bloody turban. In the en suite I grab another towel and press it to my wound.

"I think hospital is a better bet than the airport right now," I say.

"Don't be such a drama queen," says Vivian, alert to my plight at last. "In my experience head wounds always look much worse than they really are."

What does she mean, "in my experience"? She's not a fucking doctor. But – who knows? – maybe she's right. Anyway, she stops the bleeding, then tops off her handiwork with a band-aid. The one concession she makes is to walk me to the taxi, her familiar (my blood-brother) snapping at my heels.

But in the airport the wound reopens, and pumps out enough gore to make a saint turn green. I present myself at the first-aid station clutching my bag with one hand, and my skull-cap of blood with the other. The first thing the medic on duty does is declare me unfit to fly. The second is to summon an ambulance. Finally he wraps a bandage around my crown and chin. The remainder he winds around my throat, tightly enough to bring to mind my Latin master's prophecy. In the ambulance I am strapped to a stretcher in the back, but I won't lie down. I have no idea where I'm going. Looking out of the windows at the rear of the ambulance I can see that its red lights are flashing. Talk about crime and punishment. In the Holy Land, it seems, you only have to stray an inch from the marital bed, and before you know it you're on the road to the emergency room.

Once there I sit and wait with the halt, the lame, and my fears. How many times have I said (without really meaning it), "I need my head examined"? Well, tonight it seems that I really do. Doctors scrutinize it inside and out: eight stitches are required to patch up my scalp, and a CT-scan to ensure that no similar damage has occured within. At 6.00 am –

shortly after I'm informed that I won't be requiring brain surgery – I summon Tatum.

"Where the hell are you?" he says.

I can give no satisfactory answer. A nurse informs him that I'm in the Assaf Harofeh Medical Centre. He takes me from there to the airport, where I manage to get on a later flight to London.

"What the devil are you going to tell your wife?" he says.

"I'll think of something," I say, "I'm a fucking writer after all."

During the flight I explore all manner of ingenious scenarios, but in the end decide to tell my wife the truth, omitting only the character of Vivian Ben Duchifat, and switching the location from her house to Tatum's.

Anyway, with my pom-pom of cotton wool my wife cannot be anything other than sympathetic. And the whack on my head does seem to have knocked some sense into it. When Evelyn Turteltaube offers to come to London "for a mutually satisfying encounter" I counterfeit an excuse.

After the third suggestion has been turned down my correspondent begins to smell a rat: "I have been trying to suppress my uneasy feelings, but I do not think it is good for my well-being to do so any longer. Please correct me if I am wrong, but it seems to me that my enthusiasm is being met by a stone wall. How am I to know what is going on? You disclose almost nothing about yourself, which means I can only grope in the dark. Has something happened? Are you ill? Or have you simply lost interest in me as a person, now that you know I am prepared to sleep with you? I'm not just a sexual fantasy, you know, I am a real human being."

Explain to me, Evelyn Turteltaube, just why you merit special privileges? I am a writer. Everyone I meet immediately becomes a fictional character. And I – the creator – am no more real than any of them. When I married my wife, all those years ago, my parents gave us a painting as a wedding present. At first glance it looked like a conventional scene of orthodox Jews praying at the Western Wall. But closer examination revealed that each figure and every stone was constructed out of the Hebrew alphabet, as in the days of creation. If my wife were ever to paint my portrait she would do well to follow the same procedure, to fashion me out of words instead of oils. Though I know exactly what she would say were I ever to make such a recommendation.

The eight stitches are removed, and my head heals, leaving a visible scar. I say farewell to Morris Bernstein, and begin to research the life of Solomon Nunes Carvalho, who crossed the Rockies with Captain John Fremont in the 1850s (he was the expedition's daguerreotypist), and – like my wife – painted portraits of several celebrated men, among them Walkara, Chief of the Utes.

"No 'all it will require is a dozen visits to my studio' for Carvalho," I say to my wife. "He just set up his easel, asked his sitters to pose, polished off the portrait, and if they didn't like it they scalped him."

"Fuck off," says my wife.

But then she changes her mind.

"Maybe you're right," she says, "maybe I have become corrupted by the ideal of perfection, by the delusion that what I do has some kind of importance."

"Like it or not," I say, "you can't do anything else. You're stuck with painting, like I'm stuck with writing."

****

The Travel Editor of the *Jewish Chronicle* sends me an email which begins: "It's a crazy idea, but it might just work."

The idea is for me to visit one of the numerous Western Theme Parks in Germany. She thinks that an article about straight-laced Germans dressing up as Cowboys and Indians will amuse her readers.

"Pullman City, near Passau, seems a good bet," she writes. "Do say 'yes'," she concludes.

My wife has no interest in accompanying me, unlike Evelyn Turteltaube.

"Oh God," comes the response, "at last we shall meet."

"What about your boyfriend?" I inquire.

"He's fine about it," I am assured.

It is agreed that we will rendez-vous at the Koln-Bonn Flughafen, and from there take the train all the way to Passau.

"So you will get to know me and Germany at the same time," writes Evelyn Turteltaube.

When I enter the arrivals hall it is empty save for a man of brobdingnagian proportions with long black hair. He looks like the German economic miracle made flesh: shoulders, biceps, thighs, calves all built out of money-bags; ribs wrought from gold bars. Seeing me his face becomes animated, and he takes a stride in my direction.

"Mr Izzy Adler," he says, "it is Mr Izzy Adler, isn't it?"

How does he know my name? And what does he want of me? To that there can be but one answer. Evelyn Turteltaube lied. Or if she was telling the truth, and our trip was once okay with her boyfriend, he's obviously had second thoughts. It isn't hard to read his mind as he approaches with outstretched hand: he wants to kill me, to force the life out of my puny economy. And can I blame him?

Of course I can't! I have brought this punishment upon myself. Like the stoics of old I await my fate, knowing that as soon as I take the ogre's hand, he will hoist me aloft, spin me like the rotors of a helicopter, and fling me through the plate glass windows. But what choice do I have but grasp it? As it turns out, the hand is surprisingly soft. It doesn't crush mine, but it doesn't let go of it either. I sense that its owner is waiting for me to break the silence. Better that than my bones.

"Did Evelyn send you?" I ask.

"What do you mean 'send me'?" he says. "I am Evelyn."

"How can you be Evelyn?" I say. "Evelyn is a girl's name."

"Is the author of *Brideshead Revisited* a girl?" he says.

"When you said you had a boyfriend I just took it for granted . . ." I say.

"Lazy thinking," says he.

"But what has given you the idea that I'm gay?" I say.

"Another time," he says, picking up my bag. "Don't forget, this is Germany. Here the trains run on time."

There's no escaping him, no possibility of retreat. The *Jewish Chronicle* paid for my tickets, so I have an obligation to deliver. And I can hardly run home to my wife complaining that Evelyn Turteltaube turned out to be not a woman but a man. So I skulk after my unexpected companion, as he purchases tickets for the link between the airport and the Koln Hauptbahnhof, where our journey proper will commence. When the train pulls out of the station I repeat my question.

"For a start your books excite me," says Turteltaube, "so we're obviously on the same wavelength. Then, as I read more and more of them, I began to notice a pattern: most of the heterosexual encounters – I'd say about 95% of them –

are unsatisfactory if not actually humiliating. Indeed, I'd go so far as to say that the only enjoyable ones involve buggery. From that I deduced that you were – if only unconsciously – one of us: a queer. That was the theory I proposed during the discussion of *Rabbi Goldfinch's Folly*. I assumed you understood."

"Obviously an incorrect assumption," I say, "as is the one that you can draw conclusions about my life from my work."

"I might agree," says Turteltaube, "if you hadn't also written: 'It's easier to tell the truth in fiction.'"

****

There's seven hours on the train before we reach Passau, and then two more days and nights in the company of a man who looks like Conan the Barbarian and wants to have sex with me. Needless to say, the room he has reserved for us at the Hotel Residenz contains a double bed. In it I begin to worry that my bed-mate might be right about my secret desires. I try to bring to mind, as if to a court of law, all the scenes of sexual intercourse in my entire oeuvre. There are a lot. And I have to admit that it does begin to look like Turteltaube has a point. Whereupon a witness for the defence intervenes: "When did you last laugh at a description of blissful sex? Never! Because only disasters are funny. Give the man a break. He's not gay, he just thinks he's a comedian." The jury is still out, but at least I sleep a little easier.

Next morning Turteltaube does fifty press-ups, disappears into the bathroom, and leaves hairs in the shower stall that resemble strands of diabolical dental floss. "Relax," he says over breakfast, "you are still a heterosexual." They taught us Latin at school, but not German, so Conan the Barbarian assumes the role of Chingachgook, in order to ascertain the exact whereabouts of Pullman City.

The place, deep in the Bavarian hills, looks like a movie set. Outside the Marshal's office is a man wearing a tin star. What's remarkable about him is that he's only three feet high.

"Hände hoch!" he cries, waving his six-guns at us, "hände hoch!"

"It must come as something of a culture shock to hear a cowboy speaking fluent German," says Turteltaube. "But then so did half of the United States, back in the 19th century. Consider this, Mr Adler. If the English language hadn't triumphed there could well have been a second Anschluss, a trans-Atlantic alliance between a German-speaking America, and Hitler's European Empire. Of course, Philip Roth toyed with such a fantasy in *The Plot Against America*, but if you want my opinion, this is a much more dramatic scenario, and perhaps a writing opportunity for you."

"It's something to bear in mind," I say, "my agent is constantly badgering me to seek out bigger themes. That one should satisfy even him."

A crowd has gathered outside the Black Bison Saloon. More people are leaning over the balconies of the Palace Hotel. Visitors, all dressed for the occasion, line either side of Main Street. Down the middle shuffles a row of Indian dancers raising dust. Musicians beating tom-toms establish a rhythm. The dancers form a square; women on the outside, men within. Turteltaube is clearly entranced by the men, who wear waistcoats and breechcloths studded with rhinestones, and seem able to spin infinite numbers of hoops around their arms and legs. One dancer emerges from the pack and starts jumping through hoops with increasing velocity until you anticipate his disappearance into an uncounted dimension.

After the show we walk past St Joseph's Church (where, Tatum should know, weddings can be performed), and descend into a hollow where teepees stand amid the pines. One belongs to Devalon Small Legs, a Blackfoot Medicine Man, out of the Canadian Rockies. He has some advice for me: "Greatness begins within".

Turteltaube, however, is more interested in the most accomplished of the hoop dancers, who introduces himself as Jimmy Running Bird.

"Don't you feel – what? – sacrilegious," says Turteltaube, "performing your rituals in front of strangers? German strangers, at that."

"Not a bit," says Jimmy Running Bird, who still looks exhausted from his exertions. "It offers me the chance to counter old stereotypes, to show that not all Indians are dreaming of a return to the 18th century. Certainly not this one: my costume is a combination of traditional Crow designs, and disco. And I make sure to include a lot of crowd-pleasing touches in both my costume and my dancing."

"Well, you certainly pleased this member of the crowd," says Turteltaube.

Jimmy Running Bird takes immoderate gulps from a bottle of Coca-Cola. "Indian drink too much firewater last night," he says.

Devalon Small Legs is not the only Medicine Man on the block. His neighbour, a Mescalero Apache, is also one.

"Where is your home?" I say.

"In Schnepfenthal," he says, "and before that in Ruidoso, New Mexico. You know of it?"

"I have certainly heard of it, and of some of its famous visitors," I say, "like Billy the Kid."

The Apache spits into an invisible cuspidor.

"To you he may be famous," he says, "but to my people his is a name best forgotten. We continued to fear him, long after he was gunned down by Pat Garrett. In the 1920s my grandfather met people who swore that the Kid was living still. If we were naughty our parents would say, 'Quiet, or Billy the Kid will come and get you'."

It occurs to me that Palestinians living in Area C of the West Bank now say something similar to their kids: "Behave, or the Jews will eat you up."

"Were all palefaces spoken of in the same way?" I say (careful not to put words in his mouth).

"All bar one," says my informant. "There was talk of a good man the Kid shot down, the only 'broad hat' – that's what we called your people – who ever gave his life for the Apache. His name was something like Marcus Bearskin. Are you related to him?"

"Only by religion," I say.

"There is no stronger tie," says he.

Looking at Turteltaube flirting hopelessly with Jimmy Running Bird he grabs my wrist, and stares at my face with alarming intensity. He looks a bit like Jeff Chandler in *Broken Arrow*, whose Cochise was said to be so wise he could see straight into the soul of any man.

"Apache medicine – Indian medicine – is based upon the belief that all disease is caused by the breaking of taboos," he says. "You may not be sick yet, but you will be. And that man will be its cause. Quit him and his evil ways before it is too late. Otherwise you will have cause to remember the warning of Tsispah."

****

"Well," I say, as we ascend the path back to Main Street, "did you get yourself a date with Jimmy Running Bird?"

"No," says Turteltaube, "but he did give me some good advice about my hair. He said I should wear it in a pony-tail. I think he's right, don't you?"

"Absolutely," I say.

"And what pearls of wisdom did your Apache friend give you?" he says.

"He told me to avoid you like the plague," I say.

"It disappoints me to learn that a member of an oppressed people like the Apache should be a homophobe," says Turteltaube, "though the likelihood is that he wasn't a real Apache. Most of the Indians you see here are really Germans in mufti – if that is the correct word. They see themselves as 75% Indian, and only 25% German. Nonsense, of course. But their heads have been turned by the books of one man (as mine has been by yours). Have you heard of Karl May?"

"Of course," I say, "Hitler's favourite author."

"That's unfair," he says, "Einstein loved him too. Not to mention Kafka. In fact, everyone loved May and his hero, an Apache chief named Winnetou. 'Eleven Winnetous,' said one of our writers, referring to the national football team, 'and we would be world champions'. Winnetou is everything we Germans would die to be: wise beyond normal understanding, virtuous, romantic, healthy in mind and body, and at one with the natural world. Not warlike, but unconquerable if provoked beyond reason. Most of my fellow countrymen dream of being like him, even if they don't dress up as Apaches. Hitler was different. He thought Karl May's books were about him. He thought he was Winnetou. He was that vain."

In the evening we take a stroll along the Fritz-Schaffer

Promenade. To our right are Baroque churches, palaces, Italianate squares, and renaissance-style towers, to our left is the Danube, in whose imperturbable waters the ancient buildings are reflected. It is hard to conceive of any tempest ruffling that picture of tranquility.

Ahead is the spit of pasture from where we observe the gentle confluence of the famous drei Flüsse: the Danube, the Ilz and the Inn. Insecticide-minded swallows skim the surface of the waters, as if removing parasites from the backs of lordly beasts.

We follow the path around the headland and continue along the Innpromenade, where bumble bees buzz in the bells of wild flowers, and the city's modest glory is reflected with even greater serenity.

"Do not let yourself be blinded by the beauty of Passau," says Turteltaube. "It houses an evil soul."

"Like the second Mrs Nesher," I think.

Pausing beside something that resembles a milestone, but which has an inscription headed by the Hebrew injunction "Yizkor" – "Remember!" – Turteltaube says: "Had I but the strength of Samson I would pick up this rock and cast it into the river, in order to shatter this cursed city's self-image."

"What does it say?" I ask.

"The usual crap," he says, "about how the Jews of Passau were robbed of their livelihoods, and finally murdered in the lagers. Of course there is no word of apology. Why should there be? The criminals were not good Germans, but a gang of unheimlich villains called the Nazis. Have you seen *The Nasty Girl*, Mr Adler?"

"Of course," I say, "and, for God's sake, call me Izzy."

"Did you know that it was set in Passau?" he says.

"That I didn't," I say.

"Oh yes," says Turteltaube, "Anna Elizabeth Rosmus, the teenager who began an essay entitled 'My Hometown During the Third Reich', thinking to tell a story of heroic resistance, was born and educated right here. As you are aware, the story she ended up telling turned her original idea on its head. All her informants lied to her, including the big-shot bishop, who insisted that no Jews had been persecuted in his diocese because there never had been any Jews to persecute. But she persisted and found the douments that showed them up for what they were. Her essay won a national competition, but didn't go down so well locally. What the movie doesn't tell is that in the end persistent death threats drove Rosmus away from Passau, and into the welcoming arms of Washington DC. God bless America."

Turteltaube makes a big fuss over where to have dinner, but I couldn't care less, I am not on a date. We settle for a place that has gondolas painted on its walls, and order plates of pasta, together with a bottle of the house red. A man and a woman enter.

"Do you think they are twins," says Turteltaube, "or a husband and wife who wish they were?"

Both wear identical check shirts, and same-model slacks precision-pressed. Both have matching hair-styles – light brown, cut short – and wear the same gold-rimmed specs. They sit beside one another, not opposite, perhaps to avoid the impression that they are facing a mirror.

"What do you think their sex-lives are like?" says Turteltaube. "Do you think they swap genders on occasion, take turns being the man? Perhaps they have shown up here tonight for a reason, Izzy. Perhaps you could learn something from their behaviour. Or do you think you already know everything there is to know about yourself?"

"I thought we'd agreed that our misunderstanding was history?" I say.

"I am like the politicians who signed all those treaties with the Redskins," says Turteltaube. "I give my word, then I break it."

Although it is Saturday night, Passau is already deep in its beauty sleep, until a posse of hyper-kinetic police cars suddenly stirs the slothful molecules of darkness, and the city looks up in surprise. The noise also jolts Turteltaube out of his drunken reverie.

"Come," he says. "Something big has happened. The TV in our room will tell us what."

Turteltaube is right: the event is the lead story on the ten o'clock news. He listens with increasing agitation, while providing me with talking subtitles.

"It is as I said: the Nazi Beast refuses to die," he says. "Earlier today a skinhead knocked on the door of Alois Mannichi, Passau's chief of police, and rammed a knife into his chest when he answered. Thank God the blade missed his heart by a fraction. Before he went into surgery – from which he has only just emerged – Mannichi was able to inform his colleagues just what the swine had screamed as he plunged in the dagger: 'Greetings from the national resistance movement', and 'You won't be trampling on the graves of our comrades now'. What did he mean by the last? Well, a few weeks ago an unrepentant old Nazi had a funeral hereabouts, during the course of which one of his admirers opened the coffin-lid and slipped in an outlawed flag. Mannichi ordered the old bastard's exhumation, and had the stinking flag with its fucking swastika destroyed. All this explains the exceptional police activity. They are rounding up – how do you say it? – the usual suspects."

As a reporter speaks directly to camera from the crime scene, a skinhead pushes some spectators aside and screams something at her. I ask for a translation.

"He said that Mannichi is no martyr," he says. "All he is – he said – is just another wannabe Wiesenthal."

Incensed beyond words, Turteltaube begins to pace around the room. His eyes are bloodshot, the veins in his forehead are pulsing, and I wouldn't be at all surprised to see him turn green and burst out of his shirt. Instead he snatches up the wooden chair in front of the dressing table, as if he had just asked it to dance.

"How can you sit there so passively?" he says. "Can't you see it's happening all over again? First they come for the leftists. Then the Jews. And finally the queers. What this city needs is a wake-up call. It needs someone to break the glass and set off the alarm. It needs me, Izzy, it needs me."

Whereupon he raises the chair above his head, spins it around as if he were the demented wrestler I had envisioned at the airport, and prepares to toss it with all his might. Only when he pauses opposite the window that overlooks the Danube do his real intentions register. Accounting for the broken window will be hard enough. But what if the chair lands on a pedestrian? For that Turteltaube will be prosecuted, and probably me with him. How will I explain that to my wife?

Panic-stricken I leap from my chair and launch myself – arms outstretched – in his direction. The impact of my arrival coincides with the release of the chair and alters its trajectory, not by much, but by sufficient to ensure that it misses the window. Overcoming his initial amazement, Turteltaube uses his unemployed hands to address my grip around his waist. But I hang on obstinately, determined to prevent any further acts of anarchy.

By now, however, Turteltaube has something else in mind. Of a sudden he ceases to struggle, and drops straight to the ground. Unbalanced by the unanticipated withdrawal of his bulk I cannot help but do likewise. When I try to rise I find myself pinned to the floor by one of Turteltaube's mighty hams. With the other he unbuckles my Levis, then flips me over, maintaining an uncharacteristic silence all the while. I have no say in the matter of course. Being familiar with *Brokeback Mountain*, I know what it means when you hear a man spit behind your back. "One day," he says at last, "one day Izzy Adler will thank Evelyn Turteltaube for this night."

"That's all I need," I think, "another fucking prophet."

Face-down in the carpet I await my fate. Initially it comes in the form of a digital probe.

"Dear God," I whisper, "I don't ask for much, but please don't let me get an erection."

No sooner have the words been uttered than Turteltaube withdraws his finger as though my prostate had given him an electric shock.

"I want you to promise me one thing," he says. "When you go back to England make an appointment to see your General Practitioner – you call him that, I think – and have him examine your prostate. I have felt a lot of them, Mr Adler, but never one like yours. I can only fear the worst."

Turtletaube is not a great sleeping partner. On our first night together I spent half of it fretting that I was a closet queer. On our second I'm rendered sleepless by the fear that I may have prostate cancer. What is worse, I wonder: to actually have prostate cancer, or to have been anally raped by a crazed philosemite? I recollect the words of Tsispah, as he said I would. Was the prostate cancer – if such it be – provoked by my willingness to consort, to commit adultery with a German? But what if the oaf beside me was not the cause of the disease, but its detector, and possibly my saviour? How to explain that one in a moral universe?

"You must hate me," says Turteltaube, no less insomniac, "and how can I blame you? From your point of view I must seem like a typical German, with the soul of a Nazi, and prejudices to match. But how different it looks to me."

I can hear that he is weeping. As if that were not enough condensation from his tears begins to form in my exposed ear.

"Even as a boy I knew that I was different," he continues. "At the time there was a magazine called *Bravo*, which provided a Q & A service for confused – even suicidal – teenagers. I asked how it was that I, alone among my contemporaries, was unable to masturbate. What was I doing wrong? Or was I a freak? My letter was not published, but I received an answer in the mail. If one set of transgressive images did not do the trick, it suggested, perhaps I should try another. I found the remedy in a flea market: a book filled with images of wonder rabbis. Of course I did not purchase it with self-abuse in mind, but it was beneath the compassionate gaze of the original Hassid that I first learned to masturbate properly. This was a man who understood my displacement – is there such a word? – and my confusion. And when I learned that the Nazis had murdered both Jews and homosexuals alike, I comprehended the true nature of the bond that I had felt: I understood that we were brothers. You certainly will never want to see me again. But please – I beg of you – do not think badly of me."

****

Whatever I think of Turteltaube I take his advice, and pay a prompt visit to my GP, who is so alarmed by what he feels the he refers me to the urologists as a matter of urgency. The results of a blood test merely magnify his concerns.

Dr Streptopelia's consulting rooms resemble a Gentleman's Club more than a medical establishment. All its waiting room lacks is a stag's head over the mantlepiece. Upstairs are private chambers, in which men are on hand to practise the Englishman's vice. Pretty soon my back passage has more passing traffic than the Euston Underpass. When the rectal ultrasound proves inconclusive Dr Streptopelia recommends a PCA3 test. This involves me assuming the foetal position – in a knickerless state – while Dr Streptopelia locks the door to his consulting rooms, and concludes what Turteltaube started. With a finger encased in surgical rubber, he massages my prostate until – willy-nilly – a drop of semen is produced. The drop is then examined for a particular gene. If it's absent I'm in the clear. It's present in spades. I am marched to the theatre in the basement of Dr Streptopelia's enterprise for a biopsy.

Some people are rumoured to run hampsters up their anuses for the perverse pleasure of it, this is more like accommodating a bad-tempered crab. Not that I would mind, if the news were good. But it isn't.

"How mad do I have to be to suspect that a God in whom I do not believe is out to get me?" I say to my wife.

"It's worse than that," she says. "Let din v'let dayan, there is no law and there is no judge."

Of course she doesn't know what I know.

But at least there is treatment. I am prescribed radiotherapy at the Royal Marsden, plus three years of Zoladex to mop up my testosterone, plankton to prostate cancer cells. It is what they offer sex offenders in prison.

"My only prayer," I say to my wife, "is that if I am turned into a woman by the hormone therapy let me at least be a lesbian."

I make an appointment to see the consultant who dabbles in Erectile Disfunction. He has badger-brush hair and an out-of-season tan.

"Do you ever have erections?" he says.

"In my dreams," I say.

"In your dreams is good," he says.

"No, no," I say, "I meant it in the sense of 'I wish'."

"Ah," he says, "have you ever tried Viagra?"

I shake my head.

"Don't attempt to run before you can walk," he says. "Start with masturbation once or twice a week, and then if your partner is willing, you could try doing it together."

"My tragedy is that I was born with only one penis," I say to my wife, as I flog the dead horse.

I telephone my agent with the news.

"At last I have a theme worthy of me," I say.

"What would that be?" he says.

"Prostate cancer." I say.

"Fuck off," he says. "It's already a cliche, like consumption was a century ago. There's hardly a decent male writer well into his second wind who hasn't already done it to death: Philip Roth and Richard Ford, to name but two. Take a leaf from Tony Judt's book and find something less common or garden." He pauses, then signs off: "Prostate cancer. You've gotta be kidding."

A few weeks later my wife receives a letter from the National Portrait Gallery.

"Guess what," she says, waving it at me, "the Trustees are so crazy about my pathetic likeness of X – what poor judges they are – that they have voted to commission me to paint a group portrait of the original Best of Young British Novelists. Including you, mon petit Chekhov, if memory serves me well."

"Glory be," I say, "my Latin master was a prophet."

The survivors meet once for a collective photograph, after which the cooperative pose for individual studies in my wife's studio. For a few months our house becomes like a literary salon, with Mrs Adler as Madame de Stael. Eventually it is my turn. Needless to say my wife doesn't allow me to view the work in progress, but she remains in an equitable mood, so I deduce it is proceeding as well as can be expected. Most of my peers sat for five sessions or thereabouts.

On the sixth my wife says to me: "I don't know why, but yesterday I suddenly felt awful that I hadn't even congratulated your cousin, Tatum, on finding happiness at last. So I telephoned him. The phone rang and rang. Obviously he was out. But just as I was about to put down the receiver the new Mrs Nesher herself answered. What's her name?"

"Yonina," I say.

"That's right, Yonina," she says. "I explain who I am. And she says that she has such a funny story to tell me. It won't be news to you, of course. About how she mistook the woman on your arm for me. Remind me of her name."

As if she doesn't know.

"Vivian Ben Duchifat," I say.

"Now why would Tatum invite Vivian Ben Duchifat to his wedding?" she says.

"Because I asked him to," I say.

"And why would you do a thing like that?" she asks.

"Because you told me to 'fuck off' when I wanted to show you that first email from Evelyn Turteltaube about *Rabbi Goldfinch's Folly*," I think.

But I say: "For old time's sake."

"What 'old times' would those be?" says my wife.

Several months after that the finished painting is unveiled at the National Portrait Gallery. I am wearing my old school tie in the portrait, as you'll see, but to me it feels like a noose.

DEATH & TEXAS

AFTER WRITING ABOUT himself in a dozen or more books, Zaki Feldman decides it's time to pick on someone more interesting. His agent is not enthusiastic.

"Davy Crockett?" he says. "Who the devil cares about Davy Crockett nowadays? He's about as cutting edge as formica. And since when were you such an expert on him?"

But he is a good agent, and finds his client a publisher. He even negotiates a modest advance.

Feldman blows it on a trip to Texas.

Here he is in Fort Worth, at the Stockyards Station, a corral the size of a soccer pitch. He is wearing a Stetson, a pair of Levis, and scuffed cowboy boots, but he fools nobody, least of all himself. Perched on a splintery cross-beam he watches as half-a-dozen mounted vaqueros – bossed by a cowgirl – quoit a score of longhorns with lassos, walk the roped beasts until they are calm, and generally kick up a lot of dust.

At midday man and beast alike reappear on Exchange Avenue, slowly progressing north in a low-budget reenactment of a 19th-century cattle drive. Had they been doing it for real, cowboy and cow would have traversed

Texas, then progressed to the railheads of Kansas, where the panic-stricken survivors would have been herded into cattle cars, and railroaded to Chicago's grim slaughterhouses. Today's drive may be a sham, but the bloody abattoirs of yesteryear continue to grind away, of that Feldman has no doubt.

Although the sun remains close to its zenith it is pitch black in Billy Bob's, a darkness penetrated at intervals by shards of light ricocheting off the Rhinestone Cowboy's diamante saddle, revolving like a disco ball above the heads of the unholy drinkers. Resting his bottle of Lone Star on the bar, one of their number unpockets his AT&T cell phone, and contacts Kinky Friedman, sometime front man of the Texas Jewboys, and latter-day Dashiel Hammett.

The purpose of the call is to remind Friedman of their recent encounter in Queen's Square – home of Friedman's British publisher – where he had invited the caller to look him up when he was next in Texas.

"I'm in Texas now," says Feldman.

Following Friedman's directions, Feldman drives for several hours through territory that wouldn't disgrace Tuscany. Late in the afternoon he finds himself inching the rental over a cattle-guard and steering it along a cutting that leads – after a couple of water crossings – to Echo Hill Ranch, which Friedman's father – a professor of psychology at the University of Texas – had purchased in the early 1950s.

Finally the road discloses pastures and paddocks, a ranch-house, some out-buildings, a trailer. Striding across paddock and pasture comes a figure with three canine familiars. He is garbed in black from top to toe, and could pass for either a man with a price on his head, or some sort of super-religious Jew.

"Jesus Christ," says Feldman, as Kinky Friedman proffers his hand, "you were raised in the Garden of Eden."

"My misfortune," replies Friedman. "A happy childhood, I've always believed, is the worst possible preparation for life."

He plucks a used cigar from his breast pocket, lips it, and lights the working end with a match.

"Cuban?" says Feldman.

"Habana Montecristo No 2," says Friedman. "But don't go thinking that I'm soft on Castro. The way I look at it, I'm not helping his economy, I'm burning his fields."

They sit in the shade of a Mexican sycamore and chew the fat. For some reason Kinky Friedman and the Texas Jewboys never got to be a headline act like – say – Willie Nelson.

"Our tragedy was that those who appreciated our lyrics couldn't abide country music, while those who loved country music hated our lyrics," says Friedman. "I guess the world just wasn't ready for classics like 'Ride 'Em Jewboy', still the only song in the entire Country & Western canon about the Holocaust. So what did I do?"

He pulls on the cigar, and exhales a cloud.

"What I did was to reinvent myself as a writer of Mysteries (with a capital M). If I have learned anything in my life it is that nothing is as it appears to be. Turn that observation into a book and – hey presto – you have a Mystery. And why are Mysteries always money-spinners, while other genres remain box office poison? Because Mysteries offer comfort in the form of resolution, unlike in real-life, where the (lower-case) mysteries remain unresolved and – more often than not – insoluble. Mr Feldman, listen to me: like it or not, what the reading public wants are more Kinkstahs, not more Kafkas."

When the Montecristo finally goes extinct Friedman beckons his guest – now in the early stages of dehydration – into a trailer that stands apart from the house. Entering a small kitchen Friedman opens the faucet, and collects the water in a jug, to which he adds something red and a spoonful or two of granulated sugar. But instead of pouring the cocktail into two long glasses, Friedman fills several transparent containers, which Feldman recognises as bird-feeders.

Friedman explains that when his father died – about a year previously – he had inherited the title Hummingbird Man, as well as the duties that went with it. Unlike most of the things in his life these he takes very seriously. So it is with the utmost care that he secures the feeders to rusty nails that protruded from the bole of a long dead tree. The grateful hummingbirds create a little aurora borealis.

"As you can see," says Friedman, "things get a little hectic around Happy Hour. They'll all be flying down to Rio before the month is out. Don't ask me why. Maybe because they're already dressed for the Carnival. But they'll be back at Echo Hill punctually on 15 March 2004. My hope is that I'll still be around to greet 'em."

At which point it occurs to Feldman that Kinky Friedman might be wearing black, not because he is entering a Jesse James look-alike contest, but because – like Hamlet – he is still in mourning for his father.

"Do you live alone," says Friedman, "or is there a Mrs Feldman?"

"Not any more," says Feldman. "And you? Have you ever been hitched?"

"Only to the wind," says Friedman.

They stroll down to Big Foot Wallace Crick, named after

a frontier scout who went native. Flanked by stands of cedars, oaks and cottonwoods the creek pours down from the hills, and – even in mid-summer – continues to bubble ferociously over the pebbles.

"Non-Texans have likened you to Davy Crockett," says Feldman, "meaning to insult. Do you take it as such?"

"I take it as the biggest compliment," says Friedman. "Davy was one of the great heroes of my childhood. And not much has changed since then, neither in me, nor in my opinion of him. When Scott Fitzgerald declared that there were no second acts in American lives he obviously wasn't thinking of Davy Crockett, or the Kinkstah for that matter. In the winter of 1836 Davy was transformed from comic character – albeit one with a foothold in Washington – to tragic hero. In short order he fell out with his one-time mentor, President Andrew Jackson, and lost his seat in Congress. Turning on his former constituents he said: 'Since you have chosen to elect a man with a timber toe to succeed me,' – his opponent had a peg-leg – 'you may all go to hell and I will go to Texas.'

"He went, aged fifty, expecting to start life anew, not end it three months later at the Alamo. In January he wrote to his children that his prospects had never been brighter. A month after that he was in San Antonio, preceding his nemesis – General Santa Anna, dictator of Mexico, and would-be hammer of Texas – by eleven days. The remainder of his life can be measured in hours, during which he is said to have played the fiddle, danced a jig, drunk rye by the jug-full, rallied the troops, and taken a pot-shot at ol' Santa Anna himself, missing only by inches. The rest, as they say, is history. And historians, needing to earn a crust, continue to split hairs. Let 'em. It doesn't matter. All that really matters is that the Alamo – one of the most insignificant missions in the province – became something else when Davy Crockett and his fellow defenders crossed Travis's famous line in the sand, knowing that to do so meant certain death; it became the birthplace of Texas."

"You believe all that?" asks Feldman.

"Every last word," says Friedman.

Retracing his steps he lets slip a secret.

"My intention is to be the first Jewish Governor of Texas," says Friedman, "just as I was – in the unforgettable words of the Reverend Jimmy Snow – the first full-blooded Jew to appear on the Grand Ole Opry. The truth is that I'm the bastard child of two cultures, two cultures that have more in common than they know: for example, both encourage the wearing of hats, indoors and out. More importantly both revere sites where men willingly sacrificed their lives in liberty's name; for Jews it's Masada, for Texans it's the Alamo. So I am doubly committed."

He collects some green apples from the trailer, which he hand-feeds to a pair of donkeys: Gabby – after Gabby Hayes – and Roy – after Roy Rogers.

"I grant you that I've no political experience to speak of," he continues. "But so what? When you consider my predecessors you have to conclude that it can't be such a difficult job. I'll promise the electorate that – if victorious – I'll open the Governor's mansion to the general public – by turning it into a whorehouse."

"It's a pity that donkeys don't have the vote in Texas," says Feldman.

****

By the time he pulls up outside the Menger Hotel in San Antonio it is already dark. Across the way he can see the Alamo. Floodlights shine upon it from below, making it appear stark and proud against the dark sky. He feels like Heinrich Schliemann at Troy. But instead of Homer to guide him, Feldman only has the memories of movies seen in childhood. Thanks to them he knows that fewer than 300 volunteers, besieged by thousands of blood-crazed and battle-hardened Mexican troops, had held the honey-hued mission for thirteen days, thus buying time for Sam Houston to form an army of his own, an army strong enough to rout Santa Anna at San Jacinto and secure Texan independence (which lasted until the Republic was incorporated into the United States).

According to Friedman – who had it from no less an authority than the manager himself – the Menger Hotel was haunted, not by unquiet spirits from the battleground, but by the unavenged ghost of a murdered chambermaid, slain a century before by her jealous lover. Friedman hadn't actually seen her himself, but on one of his frequent stays at the hotel he had woken in the small hours to see a voluptuous gypsy shaking her zanzibars at the end of his bed. He figured she was some kind of succubus, because he spotted a guilty look on her face as she faded away.

No such luck for Feldman.

Upon leaving the hotel after breakfast he sees at once that San Antonio has the Alamo more tightly encircled than Santa Anna and his armies ever did. Even worse is the evident truth that in the searching light of an unforgiving sun the Alamo resembles nothing so much as an up-market Taco Bell. Of course it isn't tacos and enchiladas they are selling inside, but soul food: liberty, freedom, rebellion, martyrdom, victory, and other such abstractions.

More concrete items are displayed, Bowie knives among them, for use in defence of these propositions. One particularly vicious-looking blade is accompanied by a caption that boasts: "It was a Bowie knife that killed Dracula!"

In the Visitors Center Feldman observes a fellow writer sitting at a table in hopes of selling his new book. Called *The Alamo: An Illustrated History*, it contains all manner of arcana, such as the fact that the Alamo's campanulate facade – its signature feature – was not actually attached until 1850. In the opinion of Edward Everett, assistant on an earlier restoration, this innovation made the famous ruin resemble the "headboard of a bedstead". Signing a copy for Feldman its author – George Nelson – has this to say: "Of all the historic sites in America this is the one with the greatest discrepancy between what they say happened and what really happened."

And yet when Feldman enters the gardens, where golden carp swim with zen-like tranquillity in the acequia, and bluebonnets look like patches of heaven on earth, the mythic place begins to mess with his senses, not least his good sense. At the entrance to the holy of holies itself a Texas Ranger ensures (pace Kinky Friedman) that all gentlemen remove their hats. Although deconsecrated in the early 19th century, the old church is once again a shrine, a place of pilgrimage every bit as sacred as the Vatican or Graceland.

Within Feldman notes a stained glass window depicting, in its central panels, Davy Crockett swatting Mexicans. He knows it's Davy Crockett by the magic of semiotics, because the beleaguered hero is sporting his trademark coonskin cap, an item of clothing as recognisable, and as apocryphal as the deerstalker of Sherlock Holmes. In a nearby chapel, displayed as if it were a saint's holy relic, is one of Crockett's buckskin shirts colourfully embroidered. All it lacks are marks of the martyr's blood.

The thing has a strange – nearly miraculous – effect upon Feldman. It transports him back to the summer of 1956. He is in his bedroom unwrapping a parcel, given promise almost beyond bearing by the presence of American postage stamps. Three years previously his nanny had emigrated to the United States, back then more like a different dimension than a different continent. At Christmas he had become accustomed to receiving futuristic presents from her, but this was the first to have arrived out of season.

A note was attached to the penultimate layer of wrapping paper.

It read: "Dear Zaki, There were tokens issued with the ice-cream at our local parlour. Collect enough and you could exchange them for this outfit. How we suffered on your behalf, eating ice-cream for breakfast, lunch and dinner. You must be a big boy now. I hope it fits. Love, Mary."

Feldman remembers how eagerly he tore through the final sheet of paper, to reveal tan leggings, a fringed buckskin jacket, and a coonskin cap; a complete Davy Crockett costume. He put it on immediately. Previously a timid boy he suddenly felt invincible, wrapped as he was in his cloak of invulnerability. Feldman looks longingly at the shirt in the glass case, and wonders how different his life would be if it were only his to wear.

And would Crockett's fate have played out differently if he had been wearing the shirt on the morning of March 6 1836, when the defenders' bluff – victory or death – had been called and reworded – surrender or die?

Feldman tries to imagine the real Crockett's feelings as he stood in this very building, knowing full well that death was awaiting without, with full mustachios and a Mexican accent. In the end perhaps it had been a relief to step outside and meet it man to man.

At any rate that's how it happened to Fess Parker and John Wayne.

Of course if they tried that stunt today they'd more likely be hit by a Japanese import than a Mexican projectile.

So where can Feldman go to experience the Alamo in splendid isolation? Does such a place exist? For sure: it's a place where artifice is considered to be considerably more authentic than authenticity. It's a movie-set.

****

Feldman fires up the rental and motors west on Route 90 for maybe 120 miles. It was there, some seven miles north of Bracketville, that John Wayne had caused a replica to be raised, so accurate that it would pass for the real thing in movie theatres, and maybe even academies.

Feldman reaches Bracketville by sundown, sleeps over, and is the first visitor at the Alamo Village next morning, not counting a mean old viper. Apart from the snake, Feldman sees no other living thing until he enters the Cantina, and even then he feels he is intruding upon the privacy of phantoms.

All the tables are unused, bar one, which is occupied by a woman who could have doubled as the ghost of Bette Davis. She looks up at Feldman, coughs horribly, and curtains her face with bony hands. Moments later the long fingers part to allow the release of an even more terrible rattle, and then there is nothing, only a stillness that verges on the unnatural.

Steam rises from the old woman's coffee cup, and floats heavenwards like a homebound soul. Silence attends its passage, a silence that remains unbroken until the old woman coughs again, and then – having spotted Feldman – lets loose a miserly but commanding word: "Service!"

On cue a waitress emerges from the kitchen, and a Country & Western trio appear on a dais as if from nowhere. Their instruments already tuned, the musicians launch straight into a Willie Nelson medley. Ignoring the souls she has awakened, the old lady prefers to stare into her coffee cup, as if it contained the elixir of youth. Meanwhile the vocalist cautions mommas everywhere against allowing their babies to become cowboys, even though it is apparent that his own had discarded the good advice: he is sporting the full rig, including a fine pair of Colt .45s strapped around his waist.

After the set he and his backing musicians perform a short drama for the sole benefit of Feldman. *Even Stevens* involves minimal dialogue, a lot of shooting, and ends Jacobean-style with the entire cast sprawled on the dusty floor.

Feldman applauds and the three rise from the dead to take a bow. The vocalist address the visitor: "Where y'all from?"

"London," says Feldman.

"I guess that would be somewhere in East Texas," says the resurrected cowboy.

He holds out his cold cold hand.

"My name is Richard Curilla," he says. "I hope you liked our little production. Okay, it wasn't Shakespeare, but you have to admit that *Even Stevens* cuts to the chase a lot quicker than *Julius Caesar*."

Curilla continues to play the good ol' boy, until he discovers why Feldman is in his neck of the woods, whereupon he steps out of character, and straight into his own size elevens.

"I'm a real Alamo nut," he says. "I saw John Wayne's movie thirteen times when it came out in 1960. So you understand that for me working in this place is like I've died and gone to Heaven. This Cantina is where Wayne and Richard Widmark, that is Davy Crockett and Jim Bowie, got to know each other over some tequila, but more importantly it's where Wayne delivered his now famous 'Republic' speech to Lawrence Harvey's Col Travis: 'Reeepublic,' said Wayne. 'I like the sound of the word. Means people can live free, talk free . . . Some words give you a feeling. Republic is one of those words that makes me tight in the throat. Same tightness a man gets when his baby takes his first step . . .' Same tightness I get every time I repeat those sentiments."

Curilla is interrupted by a cough that reverberates like the deepest notes of an organ in a baroque cathedral.

"You know who that little lady is?" he says, pointing to the front runner for the Texas heat of Miss Tuberculosis 2003, "that's Virginia Shahan, widow of Happy Shahan, the man whose obstinacy – and vision – turned an obscure ranch into the capital of the Texas movie industry, a fact acknowledged by George W Bush, back when he was Governor. It was Happy who first gave Wayne the idea to build a permanent set right here in Texas, rather than to rustle up some plywood facade south of the border. Ironically it was a Mexican who was entrusted with the task of putting it up. Wayne was doubtful. 'What makes you think you can build the Alamo?' he said. 'What makes you think you can make pictures?' the contractor snapped right back. Wayne liked that. Construction started the following day, and filming within a few months. No one knows more than Mrs Shahan about the shenanigans that occurred behind the scenes. Pity she's so sick today."

There is really only one thing Feldman wants to know; how does a man get to be called Happy?

"This is where they all died," says Curilla, once they have crossed the four hundred yards of sand that separate the Cantina from the Alamo. "And if Crockett, Bowie, Travis et al were to rise from the dead today this battered place would look a lot more familiar to them than the original."

"That's why I'm here," says Feldman.

Standing with his back to the Alamo, he can see what can no longer be seen in San Antonio: low outbuildings, high ramparts, beyond them a nascent community, and beyond that the high plains. He didn't need to climb on the ramparts to recognise that Crockett et al must have enjoyed an unencumbered view of the besiegers, rank upon rank of them, as they marched ever closer, until the defenders could feel death's cold breath upon their faces.

"The final assault began under cover of darkness," says Curilla, "and was over ninety minutes later. When the sun rose it was upon the dead bodies of the Texians. We know that Bowie died in the infirmary, and that Travis met his end facing his killers, but controversy has always attached itself to Crockett's final moments. Word on the street in the days that followed, was that a handful of survivors had been executed by Santa Anna. Some said that one of them was Davy Crockett."

"Hold it right there," says Feldman. "Are you telling me that Davy Crockett didn't die fighting? That Hollywood has sold us a bill of goods?"

"No, sir, I am not," says Curilla. "I am merely reporting the existence of a rumour. Though honesty compels me to add that the rumour was lent some substance by the discovery of what looks like an eyewitness account, supposedly the work of Jose Enrique de la Pena, one of Santa Anna's adjutants. It was privately printed in 1955 by its discoverer – a Mexican book dealer named Jesus Sanchez Garza – the same year that Fess Parker's performance took the world by storm. Was it a coincidence? You tell me.

"In his report of the battle's aftermath De la Pena records how six or seven Texians were captured or maybe surrendered – it's not clear which, though the distinction is crucial – and that their captor – General Castrillon – pleaded with Santa Anna for their lives. Santa Anna screamed at him that it was already decreed that no quarter was to be given, and his men hacked the prisoners to death. De la Pena maintains that the prisoners all died like men, 'without complaining and without humiliating themselves before their torturers'. Of the victims only one was described. This man, wrote de la Pena, was of 'great stature, well proportioned, with regular features, in whose face there was the imprint of adversity, but in whom one also noticed a degree of resignation and nobility that did him honour'. Later he named him as, 'the naturalist David Crockett, well known in North America for his unusual adventures'. Two questions arise immediately. Is De la Pena's version accurate? Is it even genuine? Of course we'll never know what really happened, unless some new documents come to light. But in my mind there's no doubt that Davy Crockett went out like a lion."

Feldman asks his informant what he has heard about the new version of *The Alamo*, being shot even as they speak. Is it supposed to be any good? Curilla looks to the heavens, where a single buzzard is floating easily on a thermal, like a swimmer face-down in a pool.

"Over the years I've graduated from being a simple fan, to being something pretty close to an expert," he says, "and I'm perfectly aware that John Wayne wasn't Davy Crockett, that Arthur Hunnicutt wasn't Davy Crockett, and that even Fess Parker wasn't Davy Crockett. And I was pretty damn sure that Billy Bob Thornton wouldn't be Davy Crockett either. But when I was invited to the set of the new movie to see him perform a scene, it blew my socks off. He's got Davy Crockett nailed down. In my opinion he's a cert for an Oscar nomination. And he'll probably win it. I'm told that Ron Howard pulled out of the Alamo project because of a dispute with Disney over budget and rating. Howard wasn't prepared to hold back on the violence, which would have meant an R, but Disney insisted on targeting a PG audience. Howard's successor, John Lee Hancock, swears that his movie will be no less true to what really happened at the battle of the Alamo. If Billy Bob Thornton's performance is anything to go by he may just pull it off."

"It seems downright wasteful – and a tad disrespectful – not to have made the movie right here at the Alamo Village," says Feldman. "Do you know why they didn't?"

"Look around you," says Curilla. "It's one thing to spend a few days or even weeks filming in the sticks, but six months is another matter. John Wayne or John Ford were happy enough, but these new fellas figure downtown Del Rio is less appealing than downtown Austin. So they built another replica – out of plywood – over at Dripping Springs, within easy reach of Austin. Another reason, and it's only my opinion, is that you don't spend $90 million on a movie to use hand-me-downs, you don't win Oscars for applying a new lick of paint."

****

Whatever way you look at it, Del Rio – thirty miles to the west – is a border town. For starters there is the eponymous river itself, separating the United States from Mexico. But other boundaries crisscross the city too, invisible lines not represented upon any map. Del Rio is where the laid-back misery of Kinky Friedman gives way to the infernal cataclysms of Cormac McCarthy, where the wisecrack becomes the gunshot. Nor is this all, not by a long shot. Del Rio also marks the borderline between the quotidian and the uncanny. Wasn't it hereabouts that Fess Parker – making his big-screen debut – flew into man-eating ants of brobdingnagian proportion? To go beyond Del Rio is therefore to enter pays inconnu, in which the bizarre is the norm, and the enemy takes no prisoners. This is the line that Feldman crosses when he takes the road to Langtry, a road that beetles over land designed to make a visiting Martian feel homesick.

One thing alone stands between Langtry and oblivion: the memory of its only notable inhabitant, Judge Roy Bean. Invited by the Southern Pacific to bring some order to their new creation (one of many insignificant dots now connecting San Antonio to Los Angeles), the Judge packed his single volume on jurisprudence, his gavel and his Sunday best, and set himself up as the "Law West of the Pecos".

However, it was not his idiosyncratic rulings that guaranteed his everlasting fame – it is said that he once fined a corpse $40 for carrying a concealed weapon – but rather his unrequited passion for the actress Lillie Langtry. Perhaps Judge Roy Bean would have had better luck with her if his chief rival hadn't been the King of England. Spurred by her constant failure to even acknowledge his protestations of love, he painted a sign and pegged it above his front porch, thereby transforming the place into an Opera House. Okay, it wasn't the Royal Opera House, but if Miss Lillie Langtry was prepared to perform in San Antonio, why not in a town named in her honour (pernickety railroad historians maintain that Langtry was named for one of their own, an engineer who helped lay the track back in '83, but for the purposes of this story we'll give the benefit of the doubt to Judge Roy Bean, who told her that's what he had done).

Either way she was certainly the reason he named his saloon (which doubled as a courthouse) the Jersey Lilly (the misspelling preserved to this day). In 1904 – to the astonishment of all – their Judge's dream came true. Jersey Lily actually stepped off a train bound for California, and graced Langtry with her presence. Unfortunately Judge Roy Bean was not able to be at the depot to greet her, having given up the ghost four months previously.

Strangely touched by his visit to the Judge Roy Bean Visitors' Center, but hungry nonetheless, Feldman seeks out the town's only BBQ, which stands on Desolation Row between two shacks, both of which look as if they had been trashed by mutant insects. The restaurant, however, remains miraculously intact. Its proprietor, a grey-haired old pilgrim sits on a porch without, as if waiting impatiently for the day's last customer. She shouts Feldman's order to her husband, who prepares it in the kitchen. Framed on the wall is a photograph of both, standing on either side of their son, a young man in a graduation gown. Next to it is a sign, *Se habla*

Polish. Feldman decides not to let on that his mother's mother had been been a Jacobovitch from Lodz.

From the restaurant he hikes through sand hot enough to ignite his boots, until he gains a viewpoint high above the Rio Grande, from where he looks down upon cliffs of orange and burnt umber. Feldman squints long at Mexico on the other side, then turns back toward Langtry, pausing only to remove the numerous spikes and burrs of anonymous succulents, that have attached themselves to the soles and heels of his boots.

He is glad when they prick his fingers, because the discomfort stops him thinking about the blue plaque on the Cadogan Hotel in Pont Street, which commemorated the fact that the same Lillie Langtry had once lived there. But the distraction does not last long, and his thoughts fly back to the grand redbrick hotel in distant Chelsea.

Feldman tries his best to resist entering the place, but the doorman is already beckoning him through its open portals, and there is no option but proceed. The next thing he knows he is in an elevator with his wife. Then they are knocking on a door. The man who opens it looks like Rasputin. Why not? He is in the same line of work. He is a faith healer, a faith healer, a fucking faith healer. Despite his resemblance to a mad monk, he actually sounds like Peter Lorre. In a soft insinuating voice he explains that the cancer attacking Mrs Feldman's innards is only acting in self-defence. He begs her to cease trying to destroy it with chemotherapy or whatever, for it is nothing if it is not part of her. If she could learn to cherish it instead, she would surely be made whole again and healed. In the end he holds her face between his hands and breathes into her mouth.

On the way home she had vomited, and then made it clear

that she never wanted to set eyes on the man again. She never did.

Feldman looks up from his boots, and stares straight into the simmering inferno, hoping to cauterize the haemorrhage of unbidden images. How had TS Eliot put it? “Human kind cannot bear very much reality.”

Feldman doesn’t think he has sunstroke, and he certainly isn’t drunk. How could he be when he only had one Lone Star with his burger and fries? But how else to explain the horrid sight that assails him in that place? At first he assumes that the giant bugs are ants, but when he looks more carefully he knows they are unclassifiable to anyone other than a microbiologist. Because of the shimmering waves of heat he cannot be positive, but he suspects that some are transporting human beings in their pincers. Before long he becomes convinced that one of these unfortunates is Mrs Feldman herself, and begins to approach the creatures with her salvation in mind. But try as he might the task is beyond him. When he finally accepts defeat, he sits himself down upon a rock. And there, by the sluggish waters of the Rio Grande, Feldman remembers his wife. It seems an appropriate time to step away, leaving him alone with his memories in that unhomely wilderness.

****

As predicted Kinky Friedman announces his intention to run for Governor. It is February 3 2005 – the anniversary of his father’s death – and he is standing outside the Alamo. Where else? His campaign slogan? “Why The Hell Not?”

“Davy Crockett came to Texas and elected to die for it,” he says, “not because he wanted his fellow Texans to have a choice between plastic and paper in some fast food chain. But because he wanted us to have a real choice."

The implication being that if Davy Crockett were alive today he'd be putting his cross alongside Kinky Friedman's name. And why the hell not?

The following March Kinky Friedman commences an eight-week petition drive to collect the 50,000 bona fide signatures required for his name to appear on the November ballot. It is a feat no independent candidate has managed since before the Civil War. When the Kinkstah beats the jinx with signatures to spare it became apparent to all – not least to the man himself – that Kinky Friedman is now a serious candidate. It is at about this time that he receives a call from an old playmate.

Cecelia Mayo was the daughter of Professor Manuel "Manny" Mayo, quondam colleague of the equally professorial Tom Friedman. Cecelia and Kinky Friedman hadn't been childhood sweethearts exactly, but he had pulled her ponytail and made her cry on more than one staff cookout, so he had obviously liked her. But they lost touch when she fell in love with an Englishman and decided to study medicine in London rather than Austin.

It proved to be a productive move: she married the man, graduated from medical school, and established a practice in North West London. Many years later she heard that her erstwhile buddy was booked to give a reading at her local Waterstone's on Rosslyn Hill. Kinky Friedman showed up with a former beauty queen in tow, read a bit, played a few of his old songs, and had his companion give an impromptu lesson in line-dancing. After that he sat at a table and signed copies of *Armadillos and Old Lace.*

"Hello Richard," she had said, when she reached the front of the queue.

Friedman had failed to recognise her at the first attempt, but saw the inner girl as soon as she mentioned her father's name. When they parted with the usual protestations he presented her with a lucky plectrum engraved with his moniker.

"Call me the next time you are in Texas," he had said.

"I've a bone to pick with you, Kinky," she says, when that next time arrives. "Do you remember that lucky plectrum you gave me in Hampstead? It was a dud. I hadn't had it but a week when my husband of many years checked out of my life, preferring to spend the remainder of his with a cliché."

"Honey," says Friedman, "there was nothing wrong with the plectrum per se. You simply neglected to specify whether you wanted good luck or bad."

"I could do with some good luck, right now," she says, "because Manny is very sick. To tell the truth, I've come to Austin to say goodbye."

"I'm sorry to hear that," says Friedman, "you know that Tom died not so long ago."

When Cecelia's father is cremated, a week later, Friedman shows up at the service wearing a yarmulke, but he is a minyan of one.

"Hey," he says, "where's the rabbi?"

"My father wasn't Jewish," says Cecelia.

"Not Jewish," says Friedman, "but I remember him reciting the Kaddish for his wife like he took it in with his mother's milk."

"It was my mother who was the Jew," says Cecelia, "my father was merely a goy who chose the chosen people as his own."

As the casket rolls slowly into the fiery furnace, Friedman leans towards Cecelia and whispers: "At least you got here in time to say goodbye."

"More than that," she says, "as an only child I became the custodian of the family secret. My father, bless his soul, passed it on with the proper amount of drama, with panache even, quite an achievement for a man on his death-bed."

"So what was it?" says Friedman.

"A secret," said Cecelia.

But after she has hugged her father's former colleagues, numerous friends, and fewer relations, Cecelia opens up a little.

"It has to do with the Alamo," she tells Friedman. "It seems that one of my mother's ancestors fought there."

"Are you telling me that a Jew stood shoulder to shoulder with its immortal defenders?" says Friedman. "When I am Governor he'll have a statue. You have my word on that."

"I don't think so," says Cecelia. "His name was Nunes Pereira, and he fought on the other side. He was a Marrano, and Santa Anna's private physician. As such he never left the Generalissimo's sight."

"Am I to understand that he was the privileged witness of many things, up to and including the death of Davy Crockett?" says Friedman.

"My lips are sealed," says Cecelia.

On the seventh day after the funeral Manny Mayo's heir takes a small key down to the Wells Fargo Bank on Congress Avenue. A thin man in a grey suit – the vault teller – ushers her down a flight of stairs. Isolating a single key on his vast ring he carefully inserts it into the top lock of the safe deposit box, whose number matches that on his client's key. His job done he backs away, leaving Cecelia to view its contents. Now exposed are her ancestor's campaign medals, and a journal which contains – so her father had assured her – a precise description of Crockett's last moments. The words, she was told, were dynamite.

"Generations of your family have elected to keep the journal's existence a secret," her father had said. "But now the decision is yours alone."

Cecelia leaves the medals, but takes the book.

Returning to her father's house she picks up an urgent message from Kinky Friedman. He has something for her. Can she visit him at Campaign HQ? She stops off en route to the airport.

Friedman signals for her to wait while he fields some questions from the *Austin American Statesman*. When the journalist is done Friedman approaches Cecelia and slips a crumpled piece of paper into her hand. Flattening it on her palm she notes a name and a telephone number.

"Call him," says Friedman, "he's crazy about Davy Crockett, and maybe he'll be crazy about you too. I guess I owe you a husband."

"Thanks, Kinky," says Cecelia, kissing him on the cheek, "if I still had a vote in Texas it would be yours."

****

Dr Mayo considers herself a better than average GP, maybe even an excellent one. Over the years she has learned that a patient's cultural background is as important as a knowledge of the symptoms, because it is impossible to make any real sense of the latter without an understanding of the former.

English men, for example, would typically only show up

because their wives had forced them, and even then getting them to admit anything was wrong took the third degree.

Their wives were little better, with their tendency to tell no more than half the story. Only after she was dead and buried did Dr Mayo learn that a woman who had attended her surgery complaining of indigestion had also been experiencing severe pains in her left arm.

By contrast Jewish women were always at death's door.

After the passing of her father Dr Mayo became increasingly interested in her sicker patients, especially those whose initial symptoms turned out to be but the tip of a malignant iceberg.

She begins to record their facial expressions, body language, and verbal responses as the breaking waves of bad news began to shake the ship of state. She makes many hospital and home visits, notebook in hand, during the titanic struggle for survival. Nor does she shirk the sinking itself. As they go down some are the equal of Manny in their graceful submission, while others struggle with horrid clumsiness to stay afloat upon the waters of oblivion. Still others go to their maker in a condition of denial, shock even, incapable of assimilating the brute fact they are dying.

These tend to be the ones with irritating spouses, who mistake their GP for God, and keep asking unanswerable questions like: What are his chances, doctor? How long has she got, doctor? Will he suffer, doctor? Are there really no miracle cures on the horizon, doctor? Will prayer and good deeds avert the evil decree? At least she can answer that one: "If only."

As her notes accumulate she begins to consider the possibility of writing a book on the subject – to be called something like *Studied In His Death* – a book informed both by her personality and her clinical observations. At the same time, by way of a counterbalance, Dr Mayo thinks it healthy to invest a certain amount of energy in the project of life, and she remembers the paper Kinky Friedman had given to her.

****

Zaki Feldman is correcting the proofs of his new collection of stories when the telephone rings. An unfamiliar female voice – house-trained but with notes of a wilder transatlantic nativity – says his name. He admits ownership and awaits her offer of reduced utility bills, or the revelation that he is the lucky winner of a luxury holiday for two in the Florida Keys. He is wrong on both counts.

"My name is Cecelia Mayo," she says. "It seems we have a mutual acquaintance in Kinky Friedman. Either he is crazy about the pair of us, and gave me your number in hopes that we would get along like a house on fire. Or he thinks we're a couple of deadbeats who deserve each other. Shall we take the risk and find out which of the two propositions is the true one?"

"Why the hell not?" says Feldman.

They agree to meet outside Kenwood House in Hampstead.

"How will I recognise you?" says Feldman.

"Rely on me," says Mayo. "I've been doing my homework. I've even read a couple of your books. And I'm on nodding terms with your author's photo."

"Despite that you still want to meet?" says Feldman.

"Why the hell not?" says Mayo.

Feldman dresses for the date as he does for every other occasion, as if he were a cowpoke on the Texas panhandle.

Mayo, for her part, looks like a courier for the French resistance, with her black beret, her belted mac, and her pinstripe slacks. The newly formed couple have exotic juices and polenta cake in the Coach House, then walk off the calories. They ramble around the ornamental lake, over which parakeets are weaving a tapestry of green and gold, through the medieval wood, and across hill and dale until they reach the Highgate Ponds.

Mayo recognises pigeons and crows, and is impressed that Feldman can name so many of the other birds they disturb, from nuthatch to green woodpecker, but to tell the truth she isn't really interested in the Heath's flora and fauna.

What she really wants to talk about is the practice of writing. With apparent spontaneity, she invites Feldman back to her place in the Suburb for a modest supper.

They turn around and head back towards Kenwood, and from there they go – in Feldman's car – to Mayo's little bit of rustic make-believe on Wildwood Road.

Having entered her kitchen, she begins to prepare the meal.

"Is there anything I can do?" says Feldman.

"Sure," replies Mayo, wiping her hands on her apron: would Feldman be willing, as an experienced writer, to cast an expert eye over her experiments in prosody, her first attempts to turn her case notes into a coherent narrative, into a book even?

"Does it have a title yet?" Feldman says.

Mayo tells him.

"I recognise that," says Feldman. "It's from Macbeth: 'Nothing in his life became him like the leaving it; he died/ As one that had been studied in his death/ To throw away the dearest thing he ow'd,/ As 'twere a careless trifle.'"

"The pity is that not everyone attended the same academy as the Thane of Cawdor," says Mayo. "But one who certainly did was Mr Belvedere. Not his real name, needless to say. The way he faced death – better yet, outfaced death – was something else. Perhaps you'd like to start with his story? It's called 'The Chronicle of a Death Foretold'".

"It sounds the perfect appetizer," says Feldman.

Mayo sits him at the dining room table, and places a typescript of some fifteen pages before him. He begins at the beginning.

It seemed that this Mr Belvedere, a Caucasian gent in late middle-age, showed up at the surgery one day – like some character from a film noir – and declared himself DOA. But all his vital signs were normal, and he had no symptoms to speak of. Nevertheless he remained convinced that his organs were hatching a plot to kill him. He might be in the dark as to which among them would draw the short straw, but was certain that the assassin would strike soon. Week after week he came back, each time a little more insistent.

Eventually Dr Mayo gave in and ordered some blood work on the NHS, but the results revealed nothing out of the ordinary. How could she justify more expensive tests? All the evidence suggested the man was a hypochondriac, except that Dr Mayo's intuition was now telling her that he wasn't. So with her encouragement Mr Belvedere went private. Sure enough scans disclosed an inoperable tumour in the chest cavity. He had been proven right: he was a dead man walking.

His response was even more extraordinary: he faced extinction not fearfully or regretfully, but with a sense of vindication. His last little victory was to predict the day of his death, practically to the minute. What was going on? Dr Mayo noted that in shops the motto was: The Customer

Knows Best. But in surgeries and hospitals it was always the opposite: The Doctor Knows Best. Perhaps this is not always the case, she argued. Perhaps the patient's own sense of unease should be considered as a possible diagnostic tool. As well as kowtowing to the objective, argued Dr Mayo, medicine should also embrace the subjective.

While they devour their spaghetti bolognese, Dr Mayo invites her guest to be as candid as he likes concerning her efforts as a writer. Feldman's attempts to get away with a few generic compliments are deemed woefully inadequate. Nor is his advice to drop phrases like "dead man walking" deemed sufficient. So Feldman proposes reshaping the episode as if it were a detective story, a sort of corporeal Cluedo.

Dr Mayo is quite sympathetic to that notion, and wonders whether it would be better to cast herself or Mr B as the detective. Feldman says he rather likes the idea of a detective solving his own murder.

Emboldened Mayo wonders whether Feldman's agent might be interested in seeing the manuscript when completed.

"If the answer is yes," says Feldman, "will you reward me with a kiss?"

"I'll kiss you," she says, "whatever the answer."

"I was joking," he says.

"I wasn't," she says.

Their first kiss is a tentative peck, comparable to a lesser-spotted woodpecker testing the resistance of a tree.

Reassured that resistance is low they become ravenous for kisses, but are still not entirely convinced that their performance will be the equal of their appetite. Nor can they take the capability of the other entirely for granted. And so hands are sent forth on scouting missions.

Both sets of scouts having delivered favourable reports a decision is made, as if by mutual consent, to ascend to the bedroom. Once there they fall upon each other like teenagers, though unlike teenagers they do so in the dark. And in the dark they lose themselves, but find one another. And the combined years of their abstinence are fifteen.

She switches on the bedside light and retires to the bathroom, giving Feldman his first glimpse of her backside. Neither buttock, he is relieved to see, has yet developed a double chin.

Alone in the bedroom for the first time he examines its contents, in hopes of knowing its owner better. It does not take him long to determine that the room also serves as a study: the preferred furniture being a desk rather than a dressing table. Where a mirror might have been is an iMac, whose screen looks like polished obsidian, and reflects his face as if through the mists of time. On the wall above the desk are framed degrees, and a couple of antique photographs, the raw material of biography.

By the time Mayo returns from the bathroom Feldman knows this much about her: that she had taken a first degree – a BA – at the University of Texas, and had subsequently qualified as a doctor at Guys. A third certificate – no less prominently displayed – declares her to be a Master of Dada, whatever that might mean.

Both of the photographs are cartes de visite, one of which has a helpful caption: "Mr Frank Mayo as Davy Crockett". Since the photographer, who styled himself Sarony, worked out of New York, Feldman deduces that his bedmate's ancestor was an actor, possibly even famous in his day. Frank Mayo's outfit consists of a three-quarter-length buckskin coat, with a fur collar and fringes, and a hat made from the entire pelt of a raccoon, head not excepted. He is leaning against a log cabin, which sports – above its door – the antlered end of a stag.

The adjacent photograph is also a studio shot, though on this occasion the studio was in Jerusalem, and was the workplace of a certain Alexandre Gherardi. The name of the sitter, however, is not recorded. He too is in some sort of fancy dress, consisting of a fez wrapped in a painted kerchief, and a long silken djubba.

"I see you are interested in my gene pool," observes Mayo. "If you like I'll give it a little stir."

She sits herself beside Feldman in the bed.

"I'll begin with my paternal spawn," she says. "So famous was my father's great-grandfather at the time of his death in 1896 – on a train between acting engagements in Colorado and Nebraska – that it made the front page of the *New York Times*. The paper's obituarist lauded Frank Mayo as one of the handsomest men on the stage, the very picture of virile manhood; sturdy, attractive, magnetic."

She pauses, and points to the other photograph: "The equally picturesque gentleman in the Oriental costume was the descendant of Marranos who crossed to Mexico in the wake of the conquistadors. Many of them became medical men. Healing as well as Judaism, it seems, was in their DNA, as are both in mine."

Mayo goes on to tell Feldman what she has already told Kinky Friedman: that Nunes Pereira had risen to become Santa Anna's private physician, and that he had witnessed the fall of the Alamo. So sickened had he been by the carnage, she adds, that he had embarked upon a pilgrimage to Jerusalem, reconverted to Judaism, and found himself a Jewish wife. In time Pereira returned to the New World with his wife and children, though he settled in Texas rather than Mexico.

"It's not certain," says Mayo, "but the possibility exists that my maternal ancestors saw my paternal ancestor in Frank Murdoch's play, *Davy Crockett; or Be Sure You're Right, Then Go Ahead*, when he took his sell-out production to Austin in 1878. Susanna Dickinson, a rare survivor of the Alamo massacre, definitely attended a performance. Presumably she viewed great-grandpa Frank's impersonation with something like nostalgia, but Nunes – if he went – must have been stricken with guilt. Having a foot in both camps, so to speak, may explain why the new woman in your life possesses such a conflicted personality."

"Do you make house-calls?" says Feldman.

Finding her way to St Albans, she approaches his house for the first time. To her surprise – she didn't have him figured as a believer – a mezuzah is nailed to the doorpost.

"It's an empty gesture," says Feldman, "there's nothing inside it. I want the world to know that I'm a Jew, and the world to come to understand that I'm not buying what it's selling."

"In which case," says Mayo, "you're getting the worst of both worlds: pogroms in this, no entry into the next."

"Speaking of pogroms," says Feldman, "I thought we might watch the DVD of John Lee Hancock's *The Alamo.*"

Having been among the first to see the movie when it was originally released in 2004, Feldman already knows that Richard Curilla's enthusiasm for Billy Bob Thornton's performance as Davy Crockett was not misplaced.

In the course of his research, Feldman has read eye-witness accounts of the night in Washington when Crockett went to see James Hackett, a celebrated Shakespearian actor, in a comedy called the *Lion of the West*. He went because Hackett was playing an outrageous character named Nimrod Wildfire, accepted universally as Crockett in all but name.

In the movie the viewer witnesses Hackett in his dressing-room, applying make-up, rehearsing his silly lines, and trying on a turban fashioned from a skinned wildcat. Hancock could easily have made him look a fool, more ham than Hamlet. Instead his performance – what is seen of it – is afforded some respect. Making his first entrance he spots the original in the audience and says – somewhat nervously – "Good evening, Mr Crockett", at which the real Crockett rises from his seat and – bowing graciously – also says, "Good evening, Mr Crockett".

Billy Bob Thornton is so convincing at that moment that Feldman almost forgets he's no more Crockett than is Hackett. He feels like a traitor, but it will be Billy Bob Thornton rather than his beloved Fess Parker he'll be envisioning when he starts to write the biography.

What that scene also does – Feldman notes – is to establish the simultaneous existence of two Crocketts: David, the plain-talking Congressman; and Davy, half-horse, half-alligator, and total wind-bag. He likes the way Billy Bob acknowledges – with no more than a few wry grins – that his true self – his Davidic personality – is being gradually overwhelmed by that unruly alter-ego, that character he has so carelessly elected to play, that other Crockett, that Davy. And in the end, having lived the better part of his life as someone more than flesh and blood, he has to choose between betraying all those who have swallowed the stories, or dying like a larger-than-life hero. Of course he opts for the latter. And as David Crockett passes away, so Davy is embraced by immortality.

But Billy Bob Thornton's Davy Crockett doesn't die in the time-honoured way, doesn't die fighting like Fess Parker's and John Wayne's. Clearly John Lee Hancock and his historical advisors were familiar with Jose Enrique de la Pena's memoir. But they had gone further, had touched upon the possibility that Crockett's behaviour in extremis could have been misinterpreted as that of a coward. Why else would Billy Bob warn his executioners that he is a "screamer"? However, the screams, when they come, are hardly those of a coward, but rather of a man not prepared to exit this life quietly.

"Is it generally accepted that Crockett wasn't killed in the final assault?" says Mayo.

"I didn't know you were an authority on the subject," says Feldman.

"I'm anything but," says Mayo.

"But you're obviously familiar with de la Pena," says Feldman.

"Never heard of him," says Mayo. "I have other sources."

"Other sources?" says Feldman.

"I've said too much already," concludes Mayo.

Later that night, in Feldman's bed for the first time, she says: "You know, I'm also a screamer."

"But you came like a dove when we did it before," says Feldman.

"That's because I hardly knew you," says Mayo, "and wasn't ready to let you in on all my secrets."

"But you are tonight?" he says.

"It's a distinct possibility," she says.

When the possibility fails to become an actuality – Mayo offering up little more than a few high decibel coos – Feldman can't help but feel a sense of failure, and a little cheated. Despite her reassurances the feeling lasts for several weeks until – with no advance warning – Mayo releases from within her ribcage a scream that – in less salubrious neighbourhoods – might have alerted the murder squad. Feldman, for his part, takes it as a marriage proposal.

****

"Praise God with trumpet blast," sings the choir of the Liberal Jewish Synagogue, as bride and groom step from beneath the chuppah. "Praise God with harp and lyre. Praise God with timbrel and dance. Praise God with strings and pipe . . ."

A table has been set for fourteen in the banqueting rooms of Berry Bros & Rudd on St James's Street. A place of honour had been reserved for Kinky Friedman at the bride's right hand. Had not the gubernatorial candidate promised her a new husband, and had not his campaign promise come good in little more than a year? But he had declined the invitation with regret, sending in his stead an 18" high Kinky Friedman action figure. It isn't very active, to be frank, but it does speak, having a repertoire of twenty-five one-liners, including "Why the hell not?".

Once all are seated servers lower silver tureens onto the field of white, and ladle golden portions into bone china bowls. Mayo commands one end of the table, Feldman the other.

"Could it be that we are here today," says Rabbi Siskin (who has usurped the chair reserved for Kinky Friedman), "because Berry Bros & Rudd once gave house-room to – let me get the wording right – the Legation for the Ministers from the Republic of Texas to the Court of St James?"

"Indeed we are," says Mayo, slicing a herb dumpling with her spoon. "When I emigrated to England the only person I knew was my first husband. At the time I was crazy about him. But I could never warm to his family. The word 'prissy' was surely invented to describe them. My fellow students at Guy's came from the same mould; buttoned-up when sober, unbearable when drunk. Can you blame me for feeling homesick?"

"To tell the truth," says Rabbi Siskin, "my in-laws have never been comfortable with the idea of a rabbi in the family. Even a liberal rabbi. They see me as a redundant figure in the modern world. They would have much preferred it if – like you – I had treated bodies instead of souls. I'm not sure that my wife doesn't share their prejudice. No, I don't blame you for feeling homesick. Sometimes I feel homesick, even in my own home."

Mayo kisses Rabbi Siskin on the cheek.

"To cure my own malady I came to Berry Bros & Rudd," she says, "hoping to find a little bit of Texas. The place looked intimidating to a barely house-trained American, but I entered it anyway. A dapper gentleman in a pin-stripe suit approached me immediately. I asked him as politely as I knew how if he could tell me the exact location of the Texas Legation. He replied that a lot of Americans – Texans he assumed – asked the same question. Without saying another word to me he turned his back and walked away. Was I outraged? No, I was enchanted. From that moment forth Berry Bros & Rudd was for me the very model of England. A place that for all its apparent inhospitality had for three years in the 1840s opened its doors – and maybe even its heart – to a bunch of provincial Texans in frock coats. When I told the story to Zaki he declared – in his literary way – that the building was a metaphor for our union, and insisted that it be celebrated no place else."

Feldman had planned the whole thing behind Mayo's

back, presenting her with what he assumed would be a welcome fait accompli. But it turned out that he didn't know his bride-to-be as well as he thought.

"Have you gone crazy?" she said, dropping the estimate as if it were red hot. "How can we possibly afford such an extravagance? I'm sure everyone would be just as happy with a fancy supper at the local Greek."

"This is a wedding," said Feldman, "not some fucking birthday party. I don't know about you, but I'm not expecting to have another. We are both childless, we don't even have parents any more. So why not spend a little of what we do have on ourselves, on celebrating the small miracle of finding each other?"

"I'm not disputing the principle," said Mayo, "just its excessive cost. My income is finite, and you're not exactly a millionaire."

"Come on," said Feldman, "you're about to inherit a fortune from your father, and – who knows? – my new book may yet make mine."

"By the time the lawyers, the accountants and the IRS have finished with my father's estate," said Mayo, "what you call a fortune will be little more than a pittance."

"Be that as it may," said Feldman, "I have already put down a deposit."

In the end he compromised by reducing his order of the 2005 Au Bon Climat Pinot Noir, and substituting the culled bottles with a 2005 Ca' del Solo Sangiovese from Bonny Doon at half the price. He comforted himself with the thought that its dark and earthy qualities would complement the main course: buffalo ribeye steak au poivre.

Feldman raises high a glass of the former and toasts his wife, who responds by raising a glass of the latter.

"I don't know which is giving me more pleasure," says the woman seated on Feldman's left, "the sight of my old friend brimming over with happiness, or the taste of this Pinot Noir, indubitably the best I have ever drunk, from old world or new. Some crabby Marxists may say that a burger and Coke is America on a tray, but to my mind this divine spread is the real real deal. Right now, darling, I feel like fucking Pocahontas."

"Do you mean you feel like fucking Pocahontas," says Feldman, "or that you feel like fucking fucking Pocahontas?"

"Fuck off, darling," she says, "and pour me another glass."

Taking a gulp she adds: "Isn't this one of the wines the Paul Giamatti character was raving about in *Sideways*?"

"If it isn't," says Feldman, "it ought to have been."

"I just loved that movie," she says, "can you remember one with a wittier script, or better acting? And didn't it make you want to sample every fucking wine in the Santa Ynez Valley, not to mention Thomas Haden Church? Tell me you feel the same."

"About everything except Thomas Haden Church," says Feldman.

"My editor keeps asking me when you'll be writing another article for us," says the woman, who happens to be the deputy editor of *Terra Incognita*, a magazine that introduces travellers to places they don't yet know they want to visit. "I'm aware that *Sideways* isn't exactly a promo for marriage – what with Mr Haden Church having a fling on the eve of his – but if you haven't already got a honeymoon booked I'd like the pair of you to fly out to Santa Barbara c/o *T I* asap, to take – how shall I put it? – a sideways look at the Santa Inez Valley and its viniculture. Am I your fucking fairy godmother or what?"

The new modus vivendi works like this: Feldman spends the day in St Albans, at his desk if he's lucky, and the night in Hampstead Garden Suburb, a twenty-minute drive away if his luck holds. And so it is not uncommon for Mayo, returning from evening surgery, to find her house already occupied, as it is on this night. Her computer has been switched on, she notes, but her husband is striding to and fro like a turbo-charged child in want of ritalin.

"What's up?" she says.

"By God, I do so love a good coincidence," he says, "it almost makes you believe in a higher power."

"It'll take more than a coincidence to convert me," says Mayo, "after the run of doomed souls I've just seen. Parkinson's. Alzheimer's. Hodgkin's. You name it. They had it."

"Well here's another name that might just alter your mood," says Feldman. "Fess Parker. Fess Parker, the baby-boomers' Frank Mayo. Yes, yes, yes. Fess Parker, star of Walt Disney's *Davy Crockett*, is the same Fess Parker who owns Fess Parker's Wine Country Inn and Spa in Los Olivos, California, where we are going to spend the better part of our honeymoon. Surely the King of the Wild Frontier – if not God Almighty – is watching over every step we take."

****

"I'm glad to see he still has his name above the title," says Feldman, as the honeymooners catch sight of their destination on Los Olivos's Grand Avenue. Two flags fly above the resort; the Stars & Stripes, and the colours of the Lone Star state.

"Is the owner on the premises?" Feldman asks the receptionist.

"All but," she replies, "we're expecting him within the hour."

He paces around their room, which is surprisingly Frenchified.

"Good heavens," says Mayo, drying her hair after a shower, "you're as jumpy as an expectant father."

"Meeting Fess Parker's a big deal," he says. "When I was a kid my parents would take me – for a special treat – to that neon-lit outpost of America on Oxford Street, Studio 2, long-since demolished alas, but remembered fondly as the place where I first set eyes upon Fess Parker. To see him again, in the flesh, is some sort of miracle, an achievement beyond my younger self's wildest dreams. I don't want to betray the moment. I don't want to come over as a cynic. I want to dig deep and see if there's any of that old wonderment left in me."

As predicted Fess Parker's in the lobby when they go down: white-haired now, but tall, straight-backed and agile still. Feldman holds out his hand, which Fess Parker grasps. His grip is true and firm.

"Meet the wife," says Feldman, "not Mrs F mind you, but Dr Cecelia Mayo. Frank Mayo, like you the greatest Crockett of his day, was her great-great-granddaddy."

"I'm just about to have a small aperitif in the garden," says Fess Parker, "why don't the two of you join me?"

There are several tables outside, all unoccupied, until the local deity picks the choicest. In this other Eden it is hardly necessary to hang up feeders for the ruby-bibbed humming birds. They find all the sweetness they need in the blue cups of the agapanthus.

"I'm a true son of Texas," says Fess Parker, "which means that Davy Crockett was a big part of my childhood."

"As he was of mine," says Feldman, "thanks to you."

"I always felt a special affinity with the man," says Fess Parker, "our birthdays being but one day apart – August 16 in my case. There was even talk that Crockett was actually part of our family, once or twice removed. I was born in 1924. Back then horses and mules remained the principle means of transport. My world included old-timers who still hunted game for their pelts. I got to know them because my father was a county commissioner, which gave me a view of public life (though not quite on a par with Davy Crockett's Congressional experience)."

A waitress approaches, and Fess Parker whispers something in her ear.

"I've asked her to bring three glasses of our white riesling," he says, "slightly chill, and a little sweet, just the ticket for a pleasant evening such as this."

"Sounds delightful," says Mayo.

"Of course I read up on barnstormers like James Hackett and your great-great-grandpappy when I first heard I'd got the part of Crockett, but to tell the truth my career was of a very different order. They were true men of the theater; stage hands who worked their way up to become leading men. Whereas I was an accidental actor, beholden to random strokes of good fortune. The first of which occurred when Burl Ives showed up to give a concert at the University of Texas, where I was studying Russian, of all things. Ives didn't make me want to stop studying Russian, but he sure did put the idea of becoming a folk singer in my head, something that was to pay big dividends later on.

"Second was when my professor, who knew zilch about movies, found himself responsible for the visit of Adolphe Menjou, a big star at the time. Knowing that I did, he asked me to do the honours. I showed Menjou around Austin, and in the evening hosted a party for him in a frat house. He must have been grateful to me, because as he departed he asked me if I would like to work in Western films. And when I eventually decided to try my luck in Hollywood, he was as good as his word. But I soon began to feel that my skills, such as they were, lacked substance. So I signed up at the University of Southern California, where William DeMille – brother of the more successful Cecil B – taught drama. After I graduated I asked him: 'Do you think I should look for a career in the movies?' He replied: 'I have no idea.' At the time I thought this was a very mean-spirited answer. Now I know exactly what he meant.

"With or without his blessing I pitched myself as the new Gary Cooper. I got a few tiny parts, including one in a horror movie called *Them!*. Maybe you've seen it? It's a film of its time, for sure, but it's stood up pretty well. I played Alan Crotty, a ranch foreman, who is locked away in a lunatic asylum when he claims to have been attacked by giant ants. My big scene comes when, dressed in a hospital gown, I have to persuade the film's hero – Jim Arness – that the giant ants were not the fantasy of a madman. Well, Walt Disney, for one, was convinced. As a result I received a summons to meet him. For some reason I took my guitar along. Seeing it Mr Disney asked if I would care to play him something. So I picked out a folk song I'd learned from Burl Ives, which required me to mimic the lonesome sound of a train whistle. What I didn't know was that Mr Disney was crazy about trains. And that's how I got to be Davy Crockett. I quickly discovered that Mr Disney did nothing by halves. The film was shot in Technicolor, but first aired in black & white as a three-part TV series, starting on 18 December 1954. You can be pretty sure that as many raccoons as turkeys died that Christmas. The following June it reappeared as a 90-minute movie."

The waitress brings the wine. The toast is: Davy Crockett.

"That must be when I saw the film," says Feldman.

"You said it," says Fess Parker, "the impact was universal. I felt I needed to be in the witness protection program. In France they actually did change my name, but for other reasons. The chief among them being that in French 'Fess' means 'buttocks'. Instead of 'Fess' I was known there as 'Fier', which means 'proud'. But having done me proud Mr Disney didn't know what else to do with me. He turned down a role in *The Searchers* without even telling me about it. Then I read the script of *Bus Stop*, and really wanted to do it. But Marilyn Monroe would have been my co-star and Mr Disney said, 'I don't think this is for you.' That's when I came up to the Santa Ynez Valley to lick my wounds. First thing I notice is this property for sale. I'm not looking to buy, but its beauty is irresistible. Five minutes later I'm emotionally involved. An hour after that and it's mine. Now I have 600 acres under cultivation. The metamorphosis is complete; instead of making movies, I make wine. I hope you both approve of the result."

With dinner Feldman orders a bottle of Fess Parker's Frontier Red (complete with an image of the vintner as Davy Crockett on the label). Paul Giamatti would have held his nose at the very thought, but to Feldman it is as if he is quaffing the elixir of youth. In the privacy of their room he causes his wife to scream not once, not twice, but three times.

On the point of sleep he whispers: "I feel sort of weird. Do you think I could be experiencing something like happiness?"

"Why 'something like'," says Mayo, "why not the thing itself?"

"And you," says Feldman, "how do you feel on the first night of our honeymoon?"

"Mighty relieved," says Mayo, "relieved that someone else is picking up the tab for all this."

****

Westfall Ranch sits at the junction of Foxon Canyon Road and Steele Street. Feldman and Mayo note its gates, crowned with a W, en route to the Fess Parker Winery. By the time they return numerous SUVs, some pulling horse-boxes, are threading their way beneath the W and finding spaces in a yard baked as hard as Iago's heart. Without consulting his wife, Feldman – who's at the wheel – takes an unscheduled right and joins the line.

The yard is full of men in Stetsons and chaps, handsome quarter horses, and indispensable chuck wagons serving hotdogs and beans. At the far end spectators are sitting on bales of hay, which have been stacked to form temporary bleachers. Both cowboys and cowgirls are shielded from the broiling heat of the sun by red umbrellas, large enough to be observed from the moon.

Curious to see what they can see, Feldman finds a place alongside an authentic-looking cowpoke. Mayo, somewhat less interested, joins him.

"So what's happening?" she says.

"You from Texas?" says the cowpoke.

"Once upon a time," says Mayo.

"Me too," says the cowboy. "Weatherford, Texas, Cutting

Capital of the World, and where (don't you know it?) the Westfalls have a second ranch."

Leaning across Feldman they shake hands.

"Good to meet you," says Mayo.

"As to your inquiry," says the cowpoke, "it's one of those rare questions to which I know the answer, if you'll permit me."

"Please," says Mayo.

"Well," says the cowpoke, "the Westfalls – that's Russ and Janet – are in the business of selling cutting horses. And I'm in the business of buying em. And I ain't in the minority here. But I'll clam up for now, because you're about to get a demonstration of a real good cutting horse at work."

As he speaks twenty or more heifers fill the corral. Rising dust marks their passage, as if the ground were card and their hooves redhot. The herd is followed by three mounted cowboys; two flank the cows, while the third rides in deep to separate one from the rest.

"Now the rider has two and a half minutes to show off his horse's skills, not to mention his own," says the cowpoke. "And I have two and a half minutes in which to decide whether it's worth my hard-earned dollars."

Even to Mayo it's apparent that the heifer is driven by a single imperative; to reunite with the herd. Equally obvious is the duty of man and horse to block its way. The heifer dodges to the right, accelerates, stops dead in his tracks, raises dust, then skips in the opposite direction, like a desperate patient trying to out-manoeuvre the Angel of Death. For two and a half minutes the unlucky cow tries every feint it knows to escape the horse, but it just isn't flexible or smart enough.

The potential buyer tips his Stetson higher on his scalp,

as if in awe of what he's witnessed, and says to Mayo: "You won't see much better than that. Did you notice how the rider let go of the reins, put his hands down, and gave the horse its head? That showed right off that he had full confidence in his mount. As did the way he was sitting, his back nice and relaxed, bent even, in what we like to call the 'cutter's slump'. Yep, that was a horse trained to perfection in the art of reading a cow."

"Sounds like a description of my first marriage," says Mayo. "The bastard was also trained to perfection in the art of reading this old cow. He had a mistress for months, maybe even a year or more, and did I suspect a thing? Did I hell? Even when he owned up I could hardly credit my ears. I thought we were partners, but to him I was just breeding stock. And when it became apparent that I would never deliver, he decided there was only one place for me, the abattoir we call the divorce court."

"Ma'am," says the cowpoke, handing Mayo his business card, "if this gentleman, whom I take to be your second husband, doesn't treat you any kinder just give me a call, and I'll send one of my wranglers after him with a branding iron."

****

After returning to England Feldman secludes himself for a week in order to meet the deadline set by the editors at *Terra Incognita*. To celebrate the work's completion, he drives down the M1 to Hampstead Garden Suburb, with a bottle of Au Bon Climat Pinot Noir left over from the wedding party. While they are savouring the wine and eating medium-rare filet mignon from Waitrose, the cell phone chimes in Feldman's pocket.

"What the fuck, Zaki," says his fairy-godmother, "out of the goodness of my heart I send you to write a travel piece inspired by the movie *Sideways*, and you come back with a bio of Fess Parker. How many of our readers have heard of him, do you think, and of those how many do you think give a fuck about his career, which peaked – correct me if I am wrong, Zaki – in 1955? Minus 272, that's how many, absolute fucking zero. What our readers are looking for – allow me to remind you, Zaki – are lyrical descriptions of the Santa Ynez Valley, penned as only you know how. In the movie it resembles heaven on earth, but all you have to say about it is that – quote – the vineyards sit on the valley slopes like the braids on Bo Derek's scalp. Who the fuck thinks about Bo Derek these days, Zaki? Not our readers, I can assure you of that. And where's the list of the ten best wineries for those readers to visit? Fucking nowhere, Zaki, fucking nowhere, that's where. The only winery you bother to describe is the Fess Parker Winery – there's a surprise – derided as Frass Junction in the movie, as I recall. And what were you thinking when you confided that its Frontier Red turned out to be liquid Viagra, and a guaranteed cure for 'cutter's slump', whatever that might be? We are a family magazine for fuck's sake, Zaki, not some fucking porno trash. All I can think is that the wine went to your brain as well as your dick. In short, Zaki, this piece of shit is an insult both to the magazine and its readership, not to mention me. Obviously I'm not paying you a fucking penny for it, but I'm also going to want some of the expenses returned. Let's say half."

Feldman elects to withhold the most significant sections of this conversation – if conversation it can be called – from his wife: most notably the fact that the honeymoon wasn't a gift after all. He knows her well enough by now to be sure that such a revelation would taint forever the memory of Los Olivos, which is the last thing he wants to happen. At the same time he'd rather not start married life with a newly acquired portfolio of secrets, things to stash away in some internal Switzerland, in the refrigerator he calls his heart, but better that (he concludes) than a ruined honeymoon. Besides, when it comes to secrets, his wife seems to have a few of her own.

He decides to assuage his bad conscience by prodding at hers.

"That stuff you told the cowpoke at the Westfall Ranch," he says, "was it all true?"

"Absolutely," she says.

"Would you mind explaining," he says, "why you felt moved to share intimacies – of which I knew nothing – with a complete stranger?"

"It all has to do with the economy of knowledge," she says. "In his case knowledge gave him no power at all over me."

"You think I'd misuse it?" he says.

"My husband did," she says.

"I'm your husband now," he says.

"I rest my case," she says.

"Was being fertile really such a big deal for you?" he says.

"Oh yes," she says. "For the both of us."

"What was the problem?" he says.

"We never really knew," she says. "Of course we both had tests, but they were inconclusive."

"Why?" he says.

"Because I stopped them," she says.

"Why did you do that?'" he says.

"Because I am a far better doctor than I am a

patient," she says, "better at delivering bad news than receiving it."

"And that's what you were expecting from your gynaecologist," he says, "bad news?"

"Enough," she says, "the balance of trade is already out of kilter. It's time for you to export a secret or two."

"Fair enough," he says.

"Why didn't you have children?" she says. "Didn't you want them?"

"On the contrary," he says, "we always thought we would."

"So why didn't you?" she says.

"Because death impregnated my wife – my first wife – before I did," he says.

Mayo corks the remainder of the Pinot Noir, and they go to bed, leaving the soiled dishes soaking in the sink.

****

Two months before the publication of *Rare Birds* – the collection of stories Feldman's been working on for over three years – his publisher informs him that he's quitting his job to become a literary agent.

Mayo goes to her medicine chest, and extracts a bottle of Jack Daniels.

"You never know," she says, "his replacement might turn out to be just as big a fan as the old."

"I'm not one of your bloody patients," he says, "so spare me your 'look-on-the-bright-side' crap."

"But it's probably true," she says, "after all the great majority of my patients do recover. Even those with diseases that, given the chance, would go all the way. Just this evening a middle-aged guy – bulky like Tony Soprano – comes to my surgery to discuss his PSA level. I tell him it's on the high side. He wants to know how high. High enough to set off alarm bells, I say. At which point, believe it or not, he starts to shake all over. Like he's been possessed by Jerry Lee Lewis. His wife is with him, and luckily for me she's not his thirteen-year-old cousin. When she's calmed him down sufficiently, I invite him to assume the position on the examination couch, and make like an alien space abductor. His prostate is certainly enlarged, hard, and non-symmetrical. None of them good signs. I mention the possibility of prostate cancer, and it's like I've donned the black cap. Before my patient has even secured his pants he starts to blub, and hugs his wife as if she were his mother. I tell him what I just told you. Most of my patients recover, and there's no reason – whatever the final diagnosis – why he shouldn't be one of them."

"Are you going to put him in your book?" says Feldman.

"Possibly," says Mayo, "but I've a far more promising candidate in Osric Hatter."

"It's a real irony," he says, "that the ticket to immortality – or at least inclusion in your magnum opus – is a mortal disease. What one's poor Osric got?"

Mayo names a condition previously unknown to Feldman. "It's a strange thing," she says, "patients present with household name diseases – the ones we all fear – and I get terribly upset on their behalf, but when an Osric shows up with something I have to double-check in the medical dictionary, I'm as excited as a birder who's just logged a dodo. There is no known cure for what ails Osric Hatter, and precious little by way of palliatives. Shall I tell you what I was thinking as – with a grave expression – I described the course of the illness and its inevitable end? I was thinking: What a great chapter this man's death is going to make!"

"My God," says Feldman, "if writers all have a splinter of ice in their heart, then you've got the iceberg that sank the Titanic."

Mayo hosts a party in her backgarden to celebrate the publication of *Rare Birds*. The erstwhile head of Feldman's publishing house shows up, but not the new one. By way of compensation the reviews are complimentary. In fact there is but one dissenting voice: writing in the *London Review of Books* Tar Paulin calls *Rare Birds* "Chekhov soft-boiled". He says all the stories come with melancholia en suite. Of the longest he asks: "Is it really worth felling hundreds of the great Russian's beloved trees in order to give the world a warmed-over 'Ward 6?'".

The answer is a resounding, "No".

Never mind, when the Books of the Year are listed in the broadsheets there are a few sightings of *Rare Birds*. But kind words alone do not shift merchandise. And in the chains *Rare Birds* is indeed a rarity. So poor are the sales that Feldman's editor lets him know that the not-so-new head of his publishing house has decided that rarity is no longer sufficient; what he's after is total extinction.

Meanwhile Mayo finishes her book and asks Feldman if he'll show it his agent.

"Beautifully written," reports the agent, "but what it lacks – that is to say, what it needs – is some sort of hook. You didn't happen to attend the death of a celebrity by any chance? That would make all the difference."

"Funny you should suggest that," says Mayo, remembering her inheritance. She unwraps the journal she extracted from the safety deposit box in Austin, Texas, and reads it for the first time. She reads it slowly because the handwriting is not always clear, and her Spanish is not as fluent as it was. But it is fluent enough for her to realize one thing. Her father was wrong about the family secret; it isn't dynamite. It's thermonuclear.

When she tells Feldman about the contents of Nunes Pereira's memoir, and that she is seriously thinking of outing Davy Crockett as lily-livered, spineless, and yellow-bellied, he is outraged.

"Not only will you be traducing the memory of Davy Crockett, and of Frank Mayo, your own ancestor," he says, "but you'll also be betraying the cherished beliefs of all your fellow Texans, including Fess Parker and Kinky Friedman. And if I cannot accuse you of betraying the man that I am, I can certainly accuse you of betraying the child that I was."

"You haven't mentioned George W Bush," says Mayo; "will I be betraying him too?"

"Do me a favour," says Feldman, "find another way of selling your book."

Mayo claps her hands, as though an occult symptom had suddenly broken cover.

"You're jealous aren't you?" she says. "Because I'm going to steal your thunder. By the time your biography of Crockett comes out the scandal will be no more than warmed-over tittle-tattle. That's the real reason you want to stop me, isn't it? Admit it! You want the glory. Shame on you, Mr Feldman, shame on you."

She calls her additional chapter, "Once Or One Thousand? How Many Times Did Davy Crockett Die?"

In it she recounts the first-hand testimony of her maternal ancestor, Dr Nunes Pereira. She reports how the doctor had witnessed the operatic arrival of General

Castrillon, all stuccoed with sand and gore, at Santa Anna's temporary HQ, hastily established after his infamous victory. With Castrillon and his men were seven foreigners held captive. One had greater stature and nobility than all the rest, and Dr Pereira (like that other eye-witness, Jose Enrique de la Pena) recognised him as being unmistakably – even without his coonskin cap – Davy Crockett. He immediately informed Ramon Martinez Caro, Santa Anna's private secretary, that one of the prisoners was untouchable, being the famous American Congressman and popular hero, Davy Crockett. But Santa Anna was neither moved nor impressed.

"Why are these men still living?" he demanded of Castrillon. "Was my instruction to give no quarter not clear enough?" "But, Excellency," said Castrillon, "when we took them the fighting was already at an end." "The fighting will only be at an end," said Santa Anna, "when the last of the foreigners is dead." It was then that Davy Crockett – may God forgive him – fell to his knees and begged for mercy, not for his companions, but only for himself.

Santa Anna looked with contempt upon America's prostrate champion. "Do you have so little respect for your honour, Colonel David Crockett, that you are prepared to beg for mercy like a slave?" said Santa Anna. "Fortunately for you I have a much keener regard for your good name, which I am determined to preserve at all costs. You may not credit me now when I maintain that in ordering your execution I am doing you a great service. For sure I cannot deny that I shall also be the cause of unendurable pain, but I beg you to consider how fleeting it will be, how short-lived, when compared to the torments of the damned. And just think what would happen if I were to hearken unto your pleas. You would be reviled as a coward among your own people, and would be counted eternally with Benedict Arnold as the worst of traitors. By taking your life – such a little thing – I shall be raising you to the status of martyr. Who knows . . . in years as yet uncounted I may be looked upon as a petty Pontius Pilate, and you as a small-time saviour." At this point Dr Nunes Pereira and most of his fellow officers turned their faces away in shame and horror, as junior officers leapt eagerly from the ranks, and fell upon Crockett and his fellow captives as cruelly as lions upon Christians. "I regret to report," writes Dr Nunes Pereira, "that the loudest screams came from Crockett himself, who sounded like a peasant woman in childbirth."

Mayo calls the episode a metaphor for the doctor-patient relationship at its most extreme.

But that is not the end of the chapter; far from it. She elects to link the death of Davy Crockett with that of her great-great-grandfather, Crockett's representative on earth during the final quarter of the nineteenth century. Like his role-model Frank Mayo flunked badly when it came to having a good death. In his later years, so Mayo read, the old boy endeavoured to sustain fleeting youth to the point of embarrassment. Apparently friends rejoiced en masse when – in the words of his obituarist – he sensibly ceased the practice of dyeing his hair. As with age, so with illness; he tried to conceal its existence, even from himself. Despite those twin evils, an elderly Frank Mayo could still turn heads as he took the air in Boston or wherever, but the illusion was sometimes hard to maintain. Walking along Washington Street with a companion (who recorded the incident) he said: "Would you mind stopping a moment with me to look in a shop window?" Once out of sight he doubled with pain, then began to thump his heart with a clenched fist, as he was wont to do in romantic roles. This time, however, love was not the cause. "When it comes to dyspepsia," he said, "this is the best cure by a mile."

Aches around the heart became particularly acute during a run of *Pudd'nhead Wilson* at Denver's Broadway Theater – very near the end of a forty-eight week coast-to-coast tour – but again Frank Mayo refused to ascribe them to anything more serious than severe dyspepsia. Even when, as happened on a couple of nights, the discomfort became so intense that he was unable to undress, he wouldn't hear of calling a physician, though all urged him to do exactly that. Did he think he could charm death, act his way out of trouble, or somehow persuade the author of all our woes to rewrite the ending? In the short term he medicated himself with liberal doses of stimulants.

After the final performance in Denver, there were just a few nights to endure at the Criterion Theater in Omaha, Nebraska, then weeks of recuperation at Crockett Lodge. On the train transporting the company over the Rockies, his body suddenly felt too riven with pain to move, and he elected to remain in his seat rather than climb into a sleeper. That's how they found Frank Mayo the following morning, stiff and cold, another victim of dyspepsia. Denial, Mayo concludes, had cost one Crockett his dignity, and the other his life.

"This is great," says Feldman's agent to Mayo, "death is always a draw, especially if it's linked with medical expertise, and laced with compassion, but now with the Crockett stuff you've got something that's really meaty. Newsworthy, even. As soon as they get a scent of it the features editors will be howling at my door. You betcha."

There's an auction: Macmillan offers more, but her agent (as he now is) advises Mayo to go with Faber & Faber.

"They've got gravitas from TS Eliot – not to mention *Cats* – and clout from Ted Hughes," he says. "With their expertise your book could turn out to be this year's *Birthday Letters*."

He's right. Faber's marketing department insist upon a bolder title: *Studied In His Death* becomes *Breaking News*. Mayo appears on Woman's Hour, Front Row, and Start the Week. One morning, a few days before publication, she telephones Feldman from the surgery.

"Something quite wonderful's happened," she says.

"You're pregnant?" he says.

"No," she says, "my little book's only been selected as Radio 4's Book of the Week."

"Fuck," he says.

"Does that mean you're pleased?" she says.

"Of course I am," he says.

She gives so many readings she even loses her voice. What she needs, she decides, is a rest. She declines all invitations for the foreseeable future. But it makes no difference, her voice remains little better than a whisper.

"This is getting beyond a joke," she says to Feldman, "my patients are beginning to complain."

She has no choice but refer herself to the ENT department of the Royal Free in Hampstead.

"What am I going to do if they find something on the vocal cords?" she whispers to Feldman, as they sit holding hands outside the consultant's office.

The word "cancer" never passes between them.

She needn't have worried, all the tests are negative, her vocal cords as clean as a whistle, not so much as a polyp in sight.

"Thank God," she says, and ascribes her condition to anxiety.

"What have you to be anxious about?" says Feldman. "You have a loving husband, and suddenly you're the most famous doctor in all England."

"Maybe that is why," she says, "maybe at some subconscious level I mistrust my good fortune, and cannot help but anticipate some mighty blow."

But instead of a KO punch she gets the George Abercrombie Award from the Royal College of General Practitioners. Their HQ, at 14 Princes Gate, looks like it's been designed to make an American feel right at home. Flanking the front door are two blue plaques; one commemorating the former presence of J Pierpoint Morgan, the other of JFK, God rest his soul.

Even more outlandish are the four handsome Red Indian heads, lodged in the voussoirs above the door and every ground-floor window, presumably because JP Morgan financed Edward Curtis's cherished project to photograph every North American tribe.

Since it is the RCGP's AGM the building is full of medicine men, some of whom – like Mayo – have come to be garlanded. The President welcomes them all. He is a big man, with a pate that looks silver-plate, and eyes as brilliant and as blue as the plaques on the wall outside. He delivers his customary address with aplomb, then announces that it's time to hand out the gongs. A parade of newly-elected Honorary Fellows is applauded, and followed by the recipient of the Fraser Rose Medal.

"Now," says the President, looking at his notes through half-moons, "it is my great privilege to present Dr Cecelia Mayo with the George Abercrombie Award – one of our most important – given for meritorious literary work in general practice."

He hands Mayo a silver medal, inscribed on the obverse with the College's coat of arms, and on the reverse with her name.

"For those of you who haven't done so already," he continues, "reading *Breaking News* is an absolute necessity. Like no book before it transports us – transports the general practitioner – to the other side of the judgement table, enables us to experience what our patients are experiencing as the breaking news – bad of course – hits home. The Greek philosophers said that it was premature to call a man happy until after he was dead. Dr Mayo maintains that you never know a man truly until you see him in his final days, facing up to the end of them. And she spares us nothing in her descriptions of humanity at the end of its tether. She shows us mankind stripped bare, with no protection but the human spirit, which can – here is the miracle – rise to the occasion. Not always, of course, but often enough."

Feldman cannot be sure, but he's willing to swear there are tears in the President's eyes as he hugs Mayo.

"*Breaking News*," he says by way of conclusion, "is probably the most compassionate book I have ever read."

Mayo – also in tears – begins her speech of thanks, but is unintelligible even before her voice falters.

"My God," says the President to Feldman, clapping him on the shoulder, "you've got a treasure there."

As Feldman returns to his wife's side, a doctor removes himself from the crowd, and approaches Mayo with unusual circumspection.

"What a wonderful book you have written," he says. "I meant to bring my copy for you to sign, but of course I forgot the thing. I'm only sorry you weren't able to talk about it tonight. By the way, I couldn't help but notice that there was more than a frog in your throat. Do you know that you are slurring your words? Have you considered that the problem may be neurological? Unlikely, I know, but worth exploring, don't you think?"

Walking back to the car through Hyde Park, Mayo tries to tell Feldman something. It is dark, and it is quiet enough, but still he cannot make sense of the words. There seem to be two of them; probably the first person singular, and a verb that ends with a hard sound, a "d" maybe.

"Are you tired?" he asks.

She shakes her head furiously.

In the car she finds a pad and a pencil and produces: "I'm frightened."

"Frightened?" says Feldman. "Frightened of what?"

"Of what that doctor just said," she writes.

****

The man formerly known as Feldman's agent is a prophet. *Breaking News* leaps off the literary pages – where it is lauded to the skies – to become the mainstay of columnists and op-ed writers from the *Sun* to the *Guardian*. A few deal with personal experience of the grim reaper, but many more gleefully seize upon the exposure of Davy Crockett as a cowardly blow-hard, a sheep in wolf's clothing. To them George W Bush is a buffoon in the same tradition. Some go so far as to call the Alamo an illegal settlement, whose defenders got exactly what they deserved, just like the American invaders of Iraq are getting at the hands of the insurgents. They shed tears for neither Davy Crockett, nor GI Joe. If there are any dissenting voices they go unheard.

But in the United States Davy Crockett has big-hitting

defenders, and Mayo's book (still only an object of hearsay) becomes yet another front in the never-ending domestic war over America's foreign policy. William Groneman, a seasoned campaigner, calls Dr Nunes Pereira's memoir a likely hoax, and demands that the manuscript be subjected to forensic examination.

Michael Lind, composer of a 350-page epic about the Alamo in the Homeric style, reminds readers of the *New York Times* that Pereira's account of Crockett's cowardice is flatly contradicted by that of Jose Enrique de la Pena, who stated unambiguously that the doomed captives all died with honour intact.

A verdict of sorts is delivered by a fashionable historian with a chair at Princeton. As far as he is concerned the appearance of Crockett in both the de la Pena and Pereira manuscripts is more or less an irrelevancy, and to concentrate upon it is a prima facie case of Texcentricity. What matters to both de la Pena and Pereira, he argues, is the amount of space they are able to place between themselves and Santa Anna, between decent officers and a war criminal, between democrats and a cruel tyrant, wicked enough to slaughter America's most beloved son in cold blood. That, says the celebrated Professor, is the real reason for Crockett's presence in the memoirs, even if he was actually absent in reality.

But such post-modern niceties are lost upon the rednecks who regard Dr Cecelia Mayo, formerly of Austin, as little short of a traitor. In their thesaurus Davy Crockett equals George W Bush, Santa Anna equals Saddam Hussein, Texas equals Iraq, and critic equals enemy. And these patriots are not ones over-inclined to sit upon their hands. Hate mail postmarked Texas begins to pour in via Faber & Faber.

And yet among the foul and impoverished language are formal letters from wealthy institutions in Austin and San Antonio offering to purchase the heirloom for six-figure sums. From Bracketville Tx Mayo gets a hand-written note signed Richard Curilla, wondering whether she really believes – in her heart of hearts – that what she has published about Davy Crockett is gospel truth.

"Your father told my father about the allegations," writes Kinky Friedman on the back of a postcard, "and together they decided to keep them under their hats. Had you asked me I would have advised you to do the same. As it is I feel inclined to advise your husband to divorce you."

Greater grounds are to be found in a fax sent by Mayo's agent, in which he informs his new client that the American rights to her book have been snapped up by a major publishing house for mega mega bucks, something Feldman has never managed in all his years as a writer. The fax is followed by a telephone call.

"Great news, eh Zaki?" says the agent. "Is the genius at home so I can give her the gory details? Is she happy so far?"

"She's over the moon," says Feldman, "but she can't speak right now. She'll be in touch."

It's not just the agent she cannot speak to. She can't speak to anyone anymore. Completely dumbstruck Dr Mayo has even been compelled to employ a locum. Reluctantly she checks herself in for scans and other tests at the National Hospital for Neurology and Neurosurgery in Queen's Square. As if to confirm Mayo's yin and yang attitude to outrageous fortune, it stands directly opposite the offices of Faber & Faber.

Being something of a hypochondriac Feldman has died a thousand times of tetanus, heart attack, kidney failure, and cancers too numerous to mention, but never of motor neurone disease. So when the consultant tells Mayo that's what she has, the gravity of the pronouncement almost passes him by. Mayo, however, looks like she's going to faint.

"Is there any room for doubt?" she writes on a pad she hands to the doctor.

"Lots," says the consultant cheerfully, "there's no definitive test. However, the balance of probability makes it more rather than less likely in your case. But I could be wrong. Let's see how you get on in the next few weeks."

Mayo has a friend who is a speech therapist. She convinces Mayo – who hardly needs much convincing – that the main impediment is not motor neurone disease per se, but the heightened anxiety triggered by the possible diagnosis.

"Your diaphragm is all knotted up and your throat constricted by hyperventilation," says the speech therapist. "No wonder the words can't get out. What you need are exercises that will relax the muscles, and set the words free."

One night Mayo falls down the stairs. She bangs her head, but does herself no further damage.

"I think it's time we started to co-habit," says Feldman.

He rents his house in St Albans to a Bulgarian couple, and takes up residence in Hampstead Garden Suburb. At dinner he notices that Mayo is taking longer to eat less. Coughing fits at the table are not uncommon. Her bones become visible, as though her flesh were shifting sand. Aware of Feldman's judgmental gaze, Mayo elects to wear pyjamas at night. They no longer make love. She does not even like to kiss, because she knows that her breath smells of acetate. She writes Feldman notes like, "What I must learn to do is put the 'I' back in MND, and regain control of my body," and, "I will not let anxiety ruin my life."

She prescribes anti-depressants for herself, but complains of side-effects such as fatigue, dizziness and nausea. With neither energy nor appetite her weight continues to decline. She takes herself off the anti-depressants, and experiences withdrawal symptoms, including fatigue, dizziness and nausea.

The speech therapist – New-York born – becomes Mayo's constant companion and – more and more – her spokeswoman.

"Your wife has become the prisoner of her own anxieties," she says to Feldman. "You must try your best to encourage positive thinking, to restore her sense of well-being."

"But she has just been told she has a horrible disease," says Feldman, "only a lunatic would respond with anything other than horror."

"For one thing it is by no means certain that she has the disease," says the speech therapist. "And even if she does – God forbid – it's obviously a very mild form. No, the pressing issues to treat are her anxiety and her soul-destroying pessimism."

"What would you have me do," says Feldman, "hire a clown?"

"No," says the speech therapist, "but you could prepare her some favourite dishes, light some candles, pour some wine, and put on some relaxing music."

Feldman resents the advice, but follows it anyway, on the off-chance that it might be good. He cooks lobster, chilli and ginger with spaghetti, opens a bottle of Ca del Solo Big House White, puts on some Ben Webster, and lights a £45 candle. He doesn't tell Mayo the price, but he does read her the cracker-barrel wisdom that comes packaged with it, which describes a scent designed to confuse the mind, and open it to the "magnetic field of the Dada movement, to the artistic dizziness and surrealist experiences". For the first time since the diagnosis his wife smiles, but Feldman recognises it as effortful and without content. And what could be more surrealistic than this scene, he thinks: a rich and seductive meal laid before a living skeleton?

Among Mayo's mail comes a letter from the National Hospital for Neurology and Neurosurgery. Opening it she reads that an appointment has been made for her to see the in-house speech therapist. A second speech therapist, and a second opinion. Unlike her friend this one takes no prisoners. She dismisses any talk of anxiety as so much mumbo-jumbo.

"I assure you," she says, "that the only thing damaging your throat is MND."

She asks Mayo if swallowing is a problem. Mayo admits that it is. The speech therapist ticks some boxes. Mayo meets Feldman after the appointment at the cafe in the British Museum. He fetches her a bowl of tomato soup.

"That woman made Ming the Merciless seem like Pope John XXIII," she writes. "According to her the depredations I have already suffered are irreversible. My voice will never return."

She puts her head in her hands. Then she writes: "Without hope what is there?"

She has more tests, and another consultation in the Neuromuscular Department. Feldman parks the car in the lot under Russell Square. Crossing Southampton Row, a mere hundred metres from their starting point, Mayo suddenly starts gasping for breath and grabs Feldman's arm. Leaning against the window of an Italian restaurant she writes with shaking hand: "I'm having a panic attack."

****

The Consultant is all smiles as he opens his door to admit both Mayo and Feldman.

"I have read your book," he says to the former. "I don't think there's a doctor worth his salt who hasn't. What an eye-opener it was. Now, whenever I have bad news to deliver – not an uncommon occurrence within these walls, alas – I pause for a moment and ask myself, 'How would Dr Mayo handle this?'" He holds his breath. "I have to tell you," he says, "that is exactly what I am thinking right now."

Mayo cups her hands to her ears, as if to say, 'Get on with it'.

"The good news," says the Consultant, "is that your extremities are unaffected. But other indications clearly confirm my initial diagnosis: you undoubtedly have MND. For the moment it is confined to your throat. And for some patients that is where it remains."

Mayo raises her hand like a traffic policeman.

"How many?" she writes. "Most of them?"

The Consultant looks at Mayo with an expression of surprise and nods absentmindedly.

"As you are aware," he continues, "the muscles in your throat control more than your voice. Without them food and drink can no longer be swallowed safely. Your dramatic weight loss indicates that this is already a problem."

Mayo raises both hands, then writes: "No, no, no." Followed by: "The problem is anxiety."

"I have no doubt that you are extremely anxious," says the Consultant, a little flustered, "but for the moment I am more concerned with issues I can address, aspiration for example."

Turning to Feldman he says: "I am not talking about social climbing, you understand, but the possibility of chest infections if food or drink ends up in the lungs instead of the stomach. Has Dr Mayo had any bad coughs recently?"

"She's just getting over one," says Feldman.

"In that case," says the Consultant, "now is absolutely the right time to introduce Percutaneous Endoscopic Gastrostomy: PEG for short. I'm sure Dr Mayo has already familiarized herself with the procedure, so I'll keep the explanation brief. What happens is that an endoscope is inserted in the stomach, a likely place found in the lining, and a small incision made from the outside. All that remains is for a tube to be fed down the mouth, through the stomach, and out the belly. What is visible is no bigger than a pencil. The whole process takes less than half an hour. Afterwards liquid feed – containing all the animals, vegetables and minerals a person needs – is delivered with a syringe, though there are other methods. Once a PEG's in use the risk of chest infections is minimized, weight loss reversed, and quality of life greatly enhanced. What do you say, Dr Mayo?"

But Mayo has been sitting for some time with her hands placed firmly over her ears.

"I know it's a Rubicon to cross," says the Consultant, turning once again to Feldman, "and I'm not saying Dr Mayo needs to do it today, or even tomorrow. But it's as well to do it soon, while her respiratory muscles are still strong. At least get her to think about it."

In the hospital's Victorian vestibule Mayo has another panic attack. "This hospital is my Alamo," she writes. "And the Consultant my Santa Anna."

Over the next few weeks the panic attacks become more frequent, and Feldman begins to fear that they are not panic attacks at all, but symptoms of weakening respiratory muscles. He becomes a proselytizer for the PEG. It seems self-evident to his layman's mind that a nutritionally sound body would be better able to ward off infections and other evils than something half-starved.

"I do not want the disease engraved upon my flesh," she writes. Or: "It will mark the beginning of the end. Is that what you want?"

To be honest, Feldman is not sure what he wants. Sometimes he worries about his lack of sympathy. Is it envy? Is there some secret pleasure to be derived from watching his wife suffer so at the height of her success? Could it be déjà vu? Has seeing it all before hardened his heart? Or is he simply relieved that it is happening to her rather than to him? Of all the possibilities Room 101 Syndrome seems the least self-incriminating.

He tries to persuade Mayo to put her experience as a patient on record.

"It seems my thesis was spot-on," she writes, "mortal illness finds you out. And I have been found wanting. I'm sorry if I've let you down, Zaki, but it seems I lack the necessary generosity of spirit to do what you suggest. I know the prognosis is good, but I cannot rid myself of an image I once saw in an episode of *Star Trek*, of a brain in a bell jar. I'm terrified that I'll end up trapped in a useless body, able to communicate only by blinking my eyelids. What compassion remains is not for sharing."

Feldman makes a ball of the communication and tosses it into a bin. He kisses his wife on the forehead. But what can he say to her? The silence is broken by the telephone.

"It was your agent," says Feldman. "He wants you to fly to New York for the American publication."

Mayo is desperate to comply, even though these days it takes all her strength to get to Crouch End, where her speech therapist lives (the friendly one). Usually she makes the journey alone, but this morning Feldman is at the wheel, for husband and wife both have been invited for Sunday lunch.

An Israeli couple are already there when they arrive. Like their compatriots these Israelis are not very good with boundaries. The subject of MND arises while they are eating their vegetarian quiches. The speech therapist, like Mayo, will not accept that a PEG is a vital necessity.

"Once we have the anxiety under control," says the speech therapist, "normality will follow."

"Sure thing," says one of the Israelis, "my father lasted for more than three years after he was diagnosed with MND, and was damn glad for most of them."

The speech therapist looks aghast.

Mayo, for her part exits the room, having first pushed the Israeli out of her way. Later that night she writes: "Three years? Was he really trying to make me feel better?"

She decides that the excitement of a trip to New York will be the perfect antidote to her morbid self-absorption.

"It will take me out of myself," she writes, "allowing the pair of us – me and myself – time apart in which to recharge our batteries."

She assures Feldman that she will return from New York a changed woman. As far as Feldman can see she already is. The youthful woman he married has been replaced by a bent, fleshless creature, barely able to climb the stairs in her own house.

And yet Dr Mayo's locum declares her fit to travel. She must have been bullied, thinks Feldman, or bribed. What else could have prompted her to declare so confidently that a week in New York would lower Dr Mayo's extremely high levels of anxiety, improve her self-confidence, and restore her vitality?

Feldman drives her to Heathrow. When he has parked Mayo writes the following: "I need a wheelchair." The demand is unexpected, but Feldman obliges. As Mayo is pushed towards the American Airlines check-in counter, her agent (already in line) is unable to disguise his shock.

"Take good care of her," says Feldman, shaking his hand.

Three hours later the agent telephones Feldman.

"What's up?" says Feldman. "Flight delayed?"

"Not exactly," says the agent. "We were already in our seats when Cecelia suddenly starts to gasp for breath. 'I'm having one of my panic attacks,' she writes. But it's me who does the real panicking. Her face – already white – has gone whiter still. Her eyes have started to roll like cherries in a fruit machine. I'm absolutely convinced she's begun to die on me. I call a stewardess. The stewardess cops one look and dashes off to inform the pilot. The pilot refuses to take off with such a distressed patient on board. I can hardly blame him or abandon her, so I get off too. The authorities want to send her straight to the nearest hospital, but I make a bit of a fuss, and now we're waiting for an ambulance to take us to the Royal Free. The best thing is to meet us there."

Feldman is horrified to see how much his wife has deteriorated in only five or six hours. She has a drip attached to her arm, and an oxygen mask to her face.

"It seems the pilot saved her life," says the agent. "The doctor chappie tells me there are so many carbon whatsits in her blood she would have been a corpse before we even reached Newfoundland. He also says that the disease is far more advanced than she thinks, and that her lungs are completely buggered."

Then the agent, who has never before displayed any kind of emotion in Feldman's presence, gasps, "The poor darling," and begins to sob without restraint.

Feldman stares at him, and wonders how he does it.

The following day Mayo improves, and even manages to shuffle to the window, which affords a view over the Vale of Health.

"Now perhaps you'll agree to a PEG," says Feldman.

A date is set, but then cancelled, because Mayo's condition has deteriorated dramatically. She lies supine, struggling – literally struggling – for breath. To Feldman it looks as if his wife is wrestling with an angel he cannot see. She manages to write: "The disease is squeezing the life out of me."

Later she scrawls a two-line note, which takes Feldman nearly forty minutes to decipher. It reads: "I don't know if there's a God, but if there is one the bastard certainly knows how to make the punishment fit the crime. Tell Kinky he was right. I shouldn't have done it."

Finally, with an effort too painful to witness, Mayo pens a sentence that – try as he might – Feldman just cannot unscramble, not now, not ever. Thereafter her strength deserts her completely, as does life itself.

Many weep as Rabbi Siskin conducts Dr Mayo's funeral at the crematorium in Hoop Lane, but her husband is not among them. He recites the Kaddish with dry eyes, nor are tears in evidence as his fellow mourners hug him and wish him – according to tradition – long life. Instead grief infiltrates Feldman's psyche in a series of horrible images, images that illustrate his late wife in misery or in her death agonies, images that he can neither control nor erase.

There are other legacies, too, Feldman discovers, such as the house in Hampstead Garden Suburb, and Dr Nunes Pereira's cursed journal. Letters demanding that it be made available for professional and public scrutiny have not diminished in number with its owner's death. Feldman responds to none, and has half a mind to make a bonfire of the bloody thing at the bottom of the garden, but cannot bring himself to join the infamous league of book-burners. Finally he secures a safe-deposit box in the vaults below Harrods, places the scandalous document within, locks the door, and considers tossing the key into the Thames.

****

"I'm looking for a date," says Rabbi Siskin's voice on Feldman's answering service many months later. "Quentin Tarantino's latest is not exactly the rebbetzin's cup of tea, but I thought it might be yours."

"I hated *Death Proof* so much I was intending to give it a miss," says Feldman, calling back, "but for you I'll take a risk."

"Good," says Rabbi Siskin. "What's not to like about Jews killing Nazis?"

They meet in the bar of the Charlotte Street Hotel, where both order large bourbons.

"Hope you won't be offended," says Rabbi Siskin, "but I've asked another friend to join us."

"It's not a shidduch, is it," says Feldman, "you're not setting me up with one of your lonely congregants?"

"Hardly," says the cleric, "it's a he, and he's a yeshiva bocher."

"It must be an unusual yeshiva," says Feldman, "that has *Inglourious Basterds* on the curriculum."

They touch glasses and chorus: "L'chaim."

"Before he shows up," says Rabbi Siskin, "why not take the opportunity to tell me how you're coping?"

"The nights are long and I think too much," says Feldman. "Among other things I think about what it means to have two dead wives. Answer me this, rabbi: which of the two am I supposed to repossess in the afterlife; the late Mrs Feldman – because she was the first – or the late Dr Mayo – because she was the most recent? Do I really have to choose, or do we all become Mormons in the next world?"

"It could be worse," says Rabbi Siskin, "you could be the Pope."

The only connection Arnon Fetterman has with the Holy Father is a skullcap. Although he sounds like he's swallowed the Bronx whole, he orders a scotch on the rocks, and gives his address as Jerusalem.

Joining in the conversation he says: "In Plato's *Symposium* Aristophanes proposes that mankind once had a third sex, in addition to common or garden men and women. These androgynous types were shaped like balls, had four arms and legs, two sets of genitalia, and moved like tumblers. Following the precedent set by Adam and Eve they got a bit too knowledgeable for their own good, found themselves on the receiving end of Zeus's temper, and ended up split down the middle – literally. Ever since they have been yearning for their other half. After the division their private parts were not compatible, which meant – as Aristophanes puts it – they sowed their seed upon the ground like grasshoppers. Taking pity on them, Zeus fixed things so that the male could generate his seed inside the female. And this we continue to do in hopes of recreating our original state, of making one of two, of healing the state of humanity. Tikkun olam, as we prefer to say. Eternity should provide you with ample time to discover which of the two ladies – assuming it is not someone else altogether – is the perfect fit."

"Are there many Jewish Platonists in Jerusalem's yeshivas?" asks Feldman.

"More than you'd think," says Fetterman. "We may be orthodox, but we are also heterodox.

It's a great pity neither Feldman nor Fetterman is a woman, thinks Rabbi Siskin, otherwise it would indeed be a perfect shidduch.

All three are crazy about the movie, and happily swallow the preposterous end in which the Nazi high command – Hitler not excluded – is incinerated in a Paris cinema.

"Have you seen Ernst Lubitsch's *To Be Or Not To Be*?" says Fetterman.

"Of course," says Feldman.

"Don't you think those last scenes in the movie theatre were almost a frame-by-frame remake of its climax," says Fetterman, "discounting the shooting and the raging inferno, of course?"

"Didn't it bother either of you," says Rabbi Siskin, "that the Basterds were led not by a fellow Jew but by an uber-goy?"

"Certainly not," says Feldman, "and I'll tell you for why. Because the Brad Pitt character my be called Aldo Raine, but deep down he's really Davy Crockett, the same Davy Crockett who was martyred by an evil dictator, and thereby converted into an honorary Jew. Why do I say Brad Pitt is Davy Crockett? Well, for a start he is described as a 'hillbilly from the mountains of Tennessee', as was Crockett, more or less. And for seconds the movie opens with 'The Green Leaves of Summer', the tune played as a requiem in John Wayne's Davy Crockett movie. You need more?"

"Hold your horses," says Fetterman. "You may think he's Davy Crockett reborn, but – unless my ears deceived me – Lt Aldo Raine announces himself as the direct descendant of Jim Bridger, a mountain man to be sure, but not Davy Crockett."

"I'll admit that little detail more than inconvenienced me," says Feldman, "it stopped me in my tracks, until I asked myself why he was called Aldo Raine in the first place. Obviously its an homage to Aldo Ray, an actor who became typecast as a tough guy, more often than not in uniform. But where does that get me? How does it further my claim? I'll tell you. Aldo Ray lived for much of his life in Crockett, Ca, where – before he became an actor – he served as town constable. In fact he is buried there, and is known – to this day – as Crockett's favourite son."

"Okay," says Rabbi Siskin, "I'm prepared to accept that Brad Pitt is Davy Crockett. But so what? Help me. What is it that I cannot see?"

"You have to study at the movie's occluded aspects," says Feldman, "as if it were a cabbalistic text. Here are two questions to get you going. One: why was Rod Taylor cast as Winston Churchill? Two: why was the Jewish heroine – Shosanna Dreyfus – given Emmanuelle Mimieux as a nom de guerre?"

Fetterman begins to nod his head.

"The answers are these," says Feldman. "One of Rod Taylor's most famous roles was in *The Time Machine*. In which his co-star was none other than the lovely Yvette Mimieux. Why does Tarantino bother with these little touches? I think he wants to tell us that Davy Crockett is also a time-traveller; born to fight dictators through the ages. One century Santa Anna, the next Adolf Hitler. But he is more than that even. He is America incarnate; its authentic spirit made flesh. The Wild Frontier's very own Jesus Christ, you should pardon the expression. In this alternative universe, in which time is a highway, it becomes possible to alter history, as Tarantino does so satisfyingly in *Inglourious Basterds.* We know it's an illusion, of course we do, but it's a grand one while it lasts. Art, for want of a better word."

"Bravo," says Fetterman, "you split hairs like a pro. But you are wasting your time in this world of shadows, where pilpul is a lost art. Better you come join us in the real world, at the yeshiva in Jerusalem."

****

The day after viewing Tarantino's movie Feldman goes to Harrods, removes the journal of Dr Nunes Pereira from the safe deposit box, and (using money from his late wife's estate) commissions a multi-lingual scribe to pen a copy of it upon the virgin pages of a blank Victorian notebook (acquired for the purpose in Portobello Road).

Even before the work is completed he accedes unexpectedly to the repeated demands of William Groneman et al to subject the document to forensic analysis, and have it authenticated or not.

The analysts will quickly spot that paper and ink do not match, declare the document a modern forgery, and rehabilitate Crockett. If Quentin Tarantino can mess with history, so can Zaki Feldman. Future editions of his wife's book will have to be doctored, as a result, but with no serious harm to its reputation.

In order to magnify its author's posthumous fame Feldman accepts an invitation to address a memorial service, hosted by the Royal College of General Practitioners. He informs Dr Mayo's peers that she faced the initial diagnosis and the subsequent mortal battle fearlessly, with all the insouciance of a true daughter of Texas. She was an exemplary patient, he says, just as she had been an exemplary GP. To the very end, he fibs, she kept notes of her interactions with doctors and nurses, as well as a running commentary on the progress of the disease, a progress that was (he adds) without mercy. To her dying breath she was determined, says Feldman, to help doctors and patients understand and appreciate one another.

"At present," concludes Feldman, "these comments are too raw and too painful to read. But I give you my word that one day soon I shall publish them as an article, if not a whole book."

He lies his head off on Mayo's behalf, and receives a standing ovation.

What good would telling the truth have done? The medical profession is better served by the image of Dr Mayo meeting the MND head-on, fighting it to the last of her strength, like Davy Crockett at the Alamo. Even so he can't help but feel a little unclean, like he had taken a bribe from beyond the grave.

****

Not only has Feldman inherited the house in Hampstead Garden Suburb, he has also inherited a portfolio of American investments about which he understands nothing.

When the tax year draws to a close, Sargent Wilder, Mayo's American accountant suggests that her widower would benefit greatly from financial advice available only in his office. "The Wilders have been doing my people's books for as long as anyone can remember," was Mayo's response when Feldman had queried why she employed an accountant in such an out-of-the-way place as Knoxville, Tennessee. The relationship had begun in New York, and had survived numerous generations and dislocations, including the final one when Old Man Wilder had sold the family business to its present owners, who continued to employ his sons.

The accountant's wife has a further inducement. She teaches in the Humanities Department at the University of Tennessee, and offers to arrange a public reading from *Rare Birds* on the campus, also located in Knoxville.

Feldman has been wondering what to do with his wife's remains, which are stored in a plastic urn with his shoes at the bottom of the wardrobe. This is like divine guidance. A few days ahead of his departure he mails the academic Mayo's ashes repackaged as a muscle-building supplement.

****

At the end of the meeting with Sargent Wilder, Feldman is none the wiser. The fault is his entirely; a failure of concentration, not of explanation. Instead of attending to the accountant, he stares at the portrait of Frank Mayo – in his prime as Davy Crockett – that hangs on a wall beside photographs of Professor Wilder, and the thoroughbreds the pair own in Kentucky. So he invests cavalierly and divests cavalierly, exactly as advised. What does it matter? He is the last of his line, a rare bird indeed.

About thirty people turn up for his performance in the McClung Tower on the Thursday. Professor Wilder introduces him by naming his books.

"What do they reveal of their author?" she says. "I'd guess that he's a man who would love to write Westerns, in which good triumphs over evil, and the boy gets the girl, but somewhere along the line the bad guys hijack the stories, forcing them to places that shock even their author. His most recent book of fiction is called *Rare Birds*. But right now he is devoting his energy to a biography of our state's most cherished native son: David Crockett. A good guy, if ever there was one. Or is there something about our local hero we don't know? If so I know I don't want to know it. Tell us it isn't so, Zaki Feldman."

"David Crockett has nothing to fear from me," he says, rising to his feet.

He reads from a story inspired by a recent sighting of a supposedly extinct Ivory-billed woodpecker in the deep forests of Arkansas. It tells of the various parties attracted there in hopes of spotting the woodpecker turned phoenix, among them a man with a shotgun, anxious to bag the last living specimen, and a disillusioned rabbi, desperately seeking evidence of the miraculous. Miraculously the audience like it. One member asks if Feldman sees any connection between the Ivory-billed woodpecker and Davy Crockett.

"You know, I think I do," says Feldman. "Both represent something noble that was lost as America progressed, and both linger in a subliminal space, forever on the edge of re-entering the world and making it a better place."

After the reading Feldman has dinner with the Wilders at a cafe on Kingston Pike. The Professor, whose area of expertise is the Victorian novel, is writing a biography of Emily Brontë.

"I've been dying to ask you this," she says to Feldman. "Do you think Heathcliff's obsessive grief is anything close to the real thing? When my father died I was heart-sick. But I also admit to wondering if it would still be all right to go to my best friend's 21st. When Cecelia passed were you as single-minded as Heathcliff, or more like me?"

"Like you, of course," says Feldman. "The mind is but the globe in miniature, a jumble of tectonic plates, pulling in all directions at once."

"Please," says Sargent Wilder, "can we think about the living for a few hours, and the sort of plates they eat dinner from?"

"Thank God for accountants," says the Professor.

"Without them we'd all starve to death," says Feldman.

Early next morning, long before her first class, Professor Wilder raps on the door of Room 352 in the Crowne Plaza. In her other hand she is holding a bio-degradable bag from Earth Fare.

"Here she is," says the Professor, handing the bag to the room's sole occupant.

Feldman accepts the bag, and removes a cardboard box, which displays the torso and boulder-like shoulders of a new-age Goliath.

****

"How could this have happened?" says Feldman.

"Nothing happened," says the Professor, naked and sweaty on the king-size. "Hotel rooms exist in a moral vacuum set apart from the quotidian. What is done within them, is immediately undone on the outside."

"Try telling that to Mike Tyson and Dominique Strauss-Kahn," says Feldman.

"Okay, it's bullshit," says the Professor, "but you're in the clear. I'm the guilty party. I'm the adulterer."

"In the clear?" says Feldman. "I fucked you in front of my wife."

"Death is to the penis, as yeast is to dough," says the Professor, who showers and departs – smelling of roses – to lecture her class on *Sense and Sensibility*.

****

Dogwood is blossoming on the banks of the Nolichucky. A few feet away stands the cabin in which Davy Crockett was born. The sun is low, the museum locked, and the place deserted. Feldman is aware that this one-room country shack isn't the original, is in fact the second replica on the site, the first having been declared too fanciful and demolished. But it will suffice. Its chimney is built of brick, its walls of logs. Dovetails join front and sides. Peeping through the door Feldman notes an authentic-looking bearskin nailed to the back wall.

Cornflowers glisten among the grasses, wet still from the downpour that nearly engulfed him as he drove the rental east along the I-40, through wood and home-stead. He unlocks the passenger door, extracts the bag containing his wife's ashes from the box, and walks back down to the river. It is so fast-flowing there are even a few whitecaps.

As Feldman stands there mumbling the mourner's Kaddish clouds begin to roil like waves in a stormy sea. Gusts of wind shake blossoms from the dogwood which fall upon him like confetti. A hailstone hits him hard on the forehead. He opens the bag, takes a handful of the ash, and attempts to cast it upon the water. Some does indeed fall as intended, and is swept away by the current, but a large part blows back, dusting his pants and shoes.

By now the sky looks as if it is rehearsing for the end of days. A fisherman comes running from downstream, holding his rod and a radio.

"Y'all take shelter," he says, "there's a tornado likely to touch-down hereabouts any moment."

Feldman tips the remainder of the bag directly into the river. Again, some reaches the water, but the greater part whirls around and smacks him in the face. Blinded he staggers towards the car. Pulses of torrential rain drench him, but also wash a portion of the ash from his eyes and his clothes. Not nearly enough, but sufficient for him to find his way.

The automobile is rocking from side to side, like a ship on the sea. Feldman's ears are popping, and his eyeballs feel as if they had grown too big for their sockets. It is as though everything, both inanimate and animate, were trying to turn itself inside-out. Feldman opens the car door, half expecting its radio and seats to fly past him, trailing wires and bolts. He gets inside and straps himself down. His wife's ashes continue to torture his bulging eyes. They are the cause of the tears that barrel down his cheeks. Lumps of mud and ash are dropping from the soles of his boots, as if his feet really were made of clay.

Maybe it's the tears, but he's never seen such a sky before. The vaults of heaven seem piled high with florets of jade, which glower greenly as though the solar system itself had turned bilious. But then the pile collapses, as if some supreme being were rotating a kaleidoscope, and the fountainheads dissolve into giddy pirouettes of malachite, which remind bookish Feldman of nothing so much as marbled end-papers. Between this overbearing verdigris and the earth is a band of sickly radiance. Flickers of electricity cross the gap, as if seeking out signs of weakness below.

Feldman decides to make a run for it. By the time he regains the Interstate the rental is being bombarded by hailstones the size of golf-balls. Bigger objects are flying through the air; branches and bark from trees, guttering from houses, fenders from autos, maybe even the very logs from Davy Crockett's birthplace. In his rear-view mirror he can see the tornado pursuing him, like a lariat spinning over the head of a stray.

STR82ANL

"HERE COMES ART," says Mrs Kingfisher, as her helmetless husband roars down the Sapsuckers' private driveway on his green-and-cream Harley Bobber. "Now we can eat".

The others continue to stand on the lawn, lazily sipping white zinfandel from flutes, which glow in their hands like electric light bulbs. Only the English couple, Zachary and Ida Siskin, regard the new arrival with curiosity, as he leaps from his bike and embraces his wife like a sailor home from the sea.

"Do you know him?" asks Zachary Siskin.

"By reputation alone," says his wife. "He's a mediocre painter. Worse even than me."

"Mr & Mrs Sapsucker would beg to differ," Zachary replies, "at least on the self-assessment."

Dedicated collectors of his wife's work, they have volunteered to host a dinner in her honour, though the true Master of Ceremonies is Ruddy Turnstone, proprietor of the Turnstone Gallery, where Ida Siskin's new show has just been hung (hence her presence in Atlanta).

Mr Sapsucker is a pain-relief specialist, and his wife a psychiatrist. Both are obviously successful, since they inhabit a mansion on West Paces Ferry Road, but neither is a good advertisement for their particular skill. Mr Sapsucker looks like a man with a bad toothache, while Mrs Sapsucker comes over as a crazy woman. Who else but a crazy woman would think of dressing like Ophelia saved from drowning, with various fresh flowers pinned to her dress, and magnolias in her hair?

One of the live-in maids comes running from the house to whisper something in her ear, whereupon Mrs Sapsucker beckons her guests to follow her into the house. She offers a brief tour, the purpose of which is to show off the five Siskins the Sapsuckers already own. Being keen to make it an even half-dozen Ruddy Turnstone has brought along a self-portrait from the new exhibit. He hangs it above the mantelpiece in the dining room (replacing an amateur effort by Mrs Sapsucker herself) so that all can admire it in situ while the meal is consumed. Hired help serve the expectant diners with cold soup. Pacific Rim Gewurztraminer (chilled to the bone) is poured.

Arturo Kingfisher, who also shows at the Turnstone Gallery, examines Ida Siskin's portrait with a professional eye. She paints herself as though she were the child of darkness and shadow, he thinks, and what has emerged is dishonestly presented. Her lips are pursed, her features pinched. Something essential has been held back, deliberately secreted in the darkness and the shadow. She looks like . . . I know . . . she looks like a châtelaine. The châtelaine of her own psyche, the jailer of improper and improbable desires. He takes a candid look at the original. For God's sake, he thinks, the woman is the double of Simone Signoret. If I were Mr Siskin I should make haste to pick that lock, lest someone beats me to it. He dips his spoon in the white soup. It tastes of custard and vanilla, and is an unpleasant reminder of the Zupa Nic or "Nothing Soup" of his detested homeland. He hears his wife asking Zachary Siskin about the flight from London.

"Entirely predictable," the Englishman replies, "even the dream I had was the sort of dream you'd expect to have at 30,000 feet above sea level. It went like this. I entered a row of ruined terraced houses turned into a Theatre of the Grotesque, and showed my ticket to an usherette, who wordlessly tore off the stub and led me up innumerable flights of steps. Reaching the top at last she switched on her torch. Its beam penetrated the darkness, and I saw that my seat was not in a row of velvet-covered push-downs, but on a narrow ledge attached to the building's back wall. Facing the bricks I shuffled along the plank, which was made of varnished wood. Not unlike a bookshelf, it occurred to me in the dream. I rotated anti-clockwise on my heels, and lowered myself cautiously, until my backside was resting on something solid, though my feet were dangling over the void. I could just make out my wife, far below in the stalls. She was obviously trying to tell me something, but I could neither hear nor lip-read over such a distance. By now I was not alone on the ledge. A young woman was sitting to my left. For the longest while nothing passed between us. Finally I said, 'Remind me not to stand up . . .' At which point a stewardess shook my shoulder, said something about clear air turbulence, and ordered me to fasten my seat belt."

Mrs Sapsucker yawns. Interpreting such a dream is clearly beneath her dignity. But Arturo Kingfisher is struck by how closely it complements his reading of Ida Siskin's self-portrait. Her husband already knows its secrets; has already divined that his wife is literally crying out for him to acknowledge and satisfy her perverse needs. But will he listen to his subconscious, and take a leap into that darkness? No he will not! Instead he meekly heeds the stewardess's advice and fastens his safety belt. The urge to deliver a warning falls upon Arturo Kingfisher.

"Fool!" he feels like shouting. "Unless you let go of your fear and stand up for yourself, you are going to lose your wife!"

No! "Fool" is the wrong word. Zachary Siskin is not a fool, he is a coward.

"Let me tell you something, Ida," says Mrs Sapsucker, "you are blessed to have a husband with such a gentlemanly inner life. Had Mr Sapsucker been the dreamer you can be sure that the unfortunate girl would have been giving him a blow-job in the blink of an eye."

Mr Sapsucker groans, as though his toothache or whatever were becoming too much to bear in private. "Your self-portrait already looks at home above the fireplace," continues Mrs Sapsucker, "and, rest assured Ruddy, will remain a friendly presence chez moi for many years to come. Believe me, Ida, I've needed one ever since my husband's super-ego jumped ship. Ruddy has called my new acquisition a 'transition purchase'. Note the 'my'. Ruddy, of course, knows why the 'my', and you (good friends old and new) also deserve to be put in the loop."

By now her husband is giving an accurate impression of Jesus on the cross.

"Well Mr Sapsucker, the world-famous pain-relief specialist, recently spent three months in Beijing extracting venom from aquatic snails for the possible benefit of humanity," says his wife. "While there he posted me a loving email every evening, and had flowers delivered every Sunday without fail. At the same time, I blush to inform you, a lab technician was extracting semen from my husband for his singular benefit. Knowing what I know I cannot believe that the deluded girl derived any pleasure from the proceedings. How did I find out about this little fringe benefit? Look at the man's face. Is there anyone here who cannot read it like a book? It didn't take me long to force a confession out of that yellow-bellied Sapsucker. I won't bore you with the sordid details. All you need to know is that they broke my heart. How does the pain-relief specialist propose to ease the pain of it? A good one would probably hang himself from the nearest tree. But not this one. This one begs me to forgive him. Forgive him? I cannot even bear to cook for him. We have to eat, so we start going to this diner where nobody knows us. We sit there in silence. One night a waitress breaks it. 'Are you folks awright?' she asks. 'Far from it,' I reply. 'What's de matta wid you aw?' she asks. 'It'll take all day to answer that,' I reply. 'Dat's awright, honey,' she replies, 'I got aw day.' Would you believe it? She lowers her bulk into the chair opposite mine, folds her arms, and rests her chins upon them. She says: 'Now, honey, you take your time and tell me what's da matta.' I cut to the chase. 'What's the matter is that I caught my husband with his pants down. And now he wants me to forgive him.' 'Forgive him?' she yells. 'Are you crazy, honey? My advice is to trow im in de road. All men is de same. They's like dogs. If they've strayed once, how you ever be sure they won't do it again?' What can the pain-relief expert say to that? He just sits there with this mortified look on his face. The one he still has. To sum up: it could be that I am in transit from being a married woman, to being a divorcee. Three things only are staying my hand. One: who will get the Siskins? Two: who will win custody of our innocent pooch? Three: there remains the remote possibility that I still love the bastard."

A flock of black hands suddenly descends upon the table and disappears as quickly with the empty bowls. The same hands return with crockery and the main course; four pheasants roast with kumquats and brandy. The aroma of the game-birds fills the dining room like a provocation, which inevitably attracts Missy, the Sapsucker's miniature poodle. She sits hopefully beside Mr Sapsucker, who finally finds his voice.

"Missy," he commands, "shake paws."

Obediently the dog raises her right paw, which he cups tenderly in his own hand and shakes. Then he says, "Kiss, Missy, kiss." At this command the dog leaps into his lap, lifts its paws to his shoulders, and licks his cheeks, not forgetting the salty tears that have begun to roll down them.

At length Mr Sapsucker rises to slice the meat. As he does so, Arturo wonders how a few molecules breathed in can so arouse his appetite. And if he is so susceptible to the invisible, then how can he be expected to have any defence against the visible? Luckily his own wife is not as censorious as Mrs Sapsucker. She would not blame him for his inability to remove his eyes from Ida Siskin's tight-fitting fisherman's top. He listens curiously as Ruddy Turnstone attempts to define her less tangible qualities.

"You are all habitués of Ida Siskin's previous shows at the Turnstone," the gallery owner says, "and are familiar with the dreamy melancholia that characterises her work. In real life she's up there with her co-religionists in demanding her pound of flesh, believe me, but in the privacy of her studio something like a Buddhist calm seems to descend upon her. She will not thank me for telling you this, but in the past year that inner calm has been severely tested. Last mid-winter a lump in her left breast was discovered to be malignant. A month later the breast itself was removed. As you can see, she has bounced right back. Nor do her new paintings show any sign of this trauma. If anything the wilting flowers and the dead animals conclude their individual struggles more gracefully than ever before. So fluent has she become that the word 'artist' is barely relevant. Better call her a medium, through whom the eternal spirit of the object under observation is transmitted to canvas."

Mrs Sapsucker claps her hands. "I always knew Ida was a remarkable woman," she exclaims, "but it seems she is even more remarkable than I thought. In my experience (which is not inconsiderable) hardly any cancer sufferers manage to avoid one or other of what I call its Sabra and Shatila, the twin evils of despair and rage. How did you do it, Ida?"

"Do I look like a sufferer?" she replies.

"No, by God," yells Arturo, banging the table, "you look like a fucking movie star!"

"Talk about serendipity!" pipes up Mrs Kingfisher. "Art just happens to be working on a series of portraits of cancer survivors – breast cancer survivors to be more precise – for ABCDF. Excuse me, the Atlanta Breast Cancer Defence Fund. All the sitters are successful women who have beaten the disease. The aim of the portraits is to provide role-models, to demonstrate forcefully that survivors don't have to sacrifice their femininity or their sex-appeal. Art has just finished the nineteenth of twenty. Who better to complete the series than our guest of honour? What do you say, Ida?"

Ida says, "No."

Not because she doesn't trust Arturo to produce an excellent likeness, she adds (claiming to be a big admirer). She says "no" because she doesn't want "cancer sufferer" or even "cancer survivor" to be her defining feature.

"I had the disease and – with any luck – it has gone for good," she concludes. "Now I want nothing more to do with it. I am sorry. I know it is a good cause, but I cannot – will not – help."

"Even though the publicity will help boost your own show?" asks Ruddy Turnstone. "You know how Americans love a fighter."

But Ida remains obdurate in her refusal, even after Ruddy has revealed that the portraits will actually be on display for a month at the Turnstone, and that she will be doing him a big favour, in addition to Arturo (not to mention all those women out there who have lost their breasts and their self-confidence).

"Let it go, Ruddy," says Arturo, "I understand exactly how Ida feels. Every time I hear someone described as an Auschwitz survivor on the TV I think, 'Is that all there is to your life?' I don't know whether Ida and Zachary have found the time to visit Atlanta's very own Jewish Museum, but when they do they'll also find it dominated by the Holocaust. An event, incidentally, that more and more historians are finding hard to swallow."

"What historians?" demands Zachary Siskin. "What are you implying? That the Holocaust was a hoax? Are you a madman?"

"Not a madman," replies Arturo, "but a Polish-born American. Having had the misfortune to grow up in Krakow I was often bussed to Auschwitz for educational purposes. As you know our teachers and our leaders lied to us with such regularity that even schoolboys ceased to believe a word they uttered. We assumed everything they said was the opposite of the truth, including what they told us about Auschwitz. In America I have come to realise there was some truth in what they claimed, but just how much I do not yet know."

Zachary Siskin stands up.

"I am very sorry," he says, "but I cannot sit at the same table as a Holocaust-denier." He looks at Ida. "Are you coming?" he asks.

She looks at Ruddy Turnstone, who shakes his head.

"You take the car back to the hotel," she says, "someone will give me a lift."

Why has she elected not to accompany me, he wonders, feeling embarrassed by her defection, if not actually betrayed? At the same time he reminds himself that they had flown to Atlanta for one reason, to advance Ida's career, and he had seen Ruddy Turnstone shake his head, which he interpreted to mean that there was yet more pressing business to be conducted before the night was out. Thus he rationalises his wife's behaviour.

For her part Ida is also asking herself the same question. All she knows is that the decision had nothing to do with Ruddy Turnstone's wishes or needs; of them there are none so urgent that could not abide till the morrow. She is in no hurry to hear him contradict in private what he has just said in public. He has warned her more than once that her canvases were becoming too dark, and that she would have to work with brighter colours if she wanted to sell to anyone other than depressives with disposable incomes.

As Zachary Siskin backs clumsily towards the door a woman does arise after all; but not his wife.

"Poor Zachary," says Mrs Sapsucker, "perhaps tomorrow will be a better day. Do you have any plans?"

"I'm not sure," he mumbles, "maybe the Botanical Gardens."

"May-be the Bo-tan-ical Gar-dens," she echoes, while shaking her head slowly from side to side like a donkey. "Why are you such an Eyeore, Mr Siskin?" But having said that, she embraces him with more intimacy that their brief acquaintance warrants, and whispers in his ear: "You are my hero. I love you."

****

After some slices of pecan pie, and a mint julep or two, Arturo Kingfisher offers Ida Siskin a ride to her hotel on the back of his Harley. But she has not drunk sufficient to accept, and instead jumps into the brand-new Luther King alongside his wife. Whereupon Arturo abandons his bike, informs the Sapsuckers that he will collect it in a day or so, and hitches a ride in the black SUV with the two women.

"Tell me, Mrs Siskin," says Mrs Kingfisher, as she waits for the wrought-iron gates to swing open, "what would you do if you were in Mrs Sapsucker's shoes?"

"Well, if I were in her shoes I should certainly forgive Mr Sapsucker," Ida replies, "but whether I would let Mr Siskin off the hook is another matter entirely."

She watches as the Luther King's headlamps play upon the assorted trees of West Paces Ferry Road like the sticks of a xylophone.

"And what would you do, Mrs Kingfisher?" she asks.

"In my case the question is not hypothetical," comes the reply, "in my case I have learned to be as forgiving as the

Pope. My husband is not handsome, but women cannot help but do his bidding. And he cannot help but bid."

"It seems that my legendary powers have no effect upon Mrs Siskin," comments Arturo from the backseat, "two times already she has rejected me tonight. I doubt my self-esteem will survive a third rebuff."

Ignoring him Mrs Kingfisher takes a right on Northside Drive, which is as straight as a Roman road.

"Have you heard of the Battle of Peachtree Creek?" she asks Ida.

Needless to say, Ida has not.

"It happened but a few miles from here," Mrs Kingfisher continues. "Since the cottage into which we moved as newly-weds is also but a few miles from here – on Peachtree Battle Avenue – I suppose I ought not to have been surprised when I started to unearth cartridge cases, tunic buttons, and even cannon-balls in our back-yard. One of the men who helped with the heavier spade-work was a local historian. Thanks to him I discovered that the foundations of our marital home rested upon the bones of Hooker's XXth Corps, which had defended our plot of land as if it had been the pass at Thermopylae. As it turned out it was the gateway to Atlanta. Being a Southern Belle with the standard sensibilities I was horrified, and filled with dread that discord and disunity would seep into our house like rising damp. Art was not sympathetic. He looked only to the future, and poured scorn on all those – including his new bride – who remained in some way wedded to the past. I guess he was right because – twenty-five years on – we are still living in the same house."

"Afterwards I did a little reading on the subject," adds Arturo, "and learned a valuable lesson. The original Confederate plan had been based upon that time-honoured strategy: the best form of defence is attack. As it marched upon Atlanta the Union army was stretched to the limit. General Johnston of Tennessee decided that the best place to drive a wedge between its two flanks was at Peachtree Creek. Had he done so – as he might well have done – Atlanta would probably have been saved. But on the eve of battle he was relieved of his command by President Davis. His reluctant replacement fucked things up. Men died on our doorstep because he lacked self-belief. In this country self-doubt wins you no battles. Or anything else, for that matter."

"My husband learned his lesson well," says Mrs Kingfisher, as an illuminated sign announcing the approaching turn for Peachtree Battle Avenue jumps out of the darkness, "no one has ever accused him of self-doubt."

"Look," he says to Ida, "I respect your reluctance to sit for me, and will make no effort to persuade you to do otherwise. But I would be very grateful to have your opinion on the works I have completed so far. What do you say?"

This time Ida says, "Yes."

She knows the word is not innocent, but for the life of her she cannot see any harm in it. Burdened with greater foresight, Mrs Kingfisher suddenly swerves to the left. As the Luther King begins to descend Peachtree Battle Avenue, Ida can hear the hooting of Barred Owls over in Atlanta Memorial Park.

****

Mrs Kingfisher says "Goodnight" cheerfully enough as Ida follows Arturo's Maglight down the garden path to his studio at its furthest end. He unlocks its door, switches on its lights, and points towards an easel at its centre, to which a canvas is secured. The first thing Ida notices is that the model is naked (save for a discreet scrap of white towelling).

"You didn't mention anything about me having to take my clothes off," observes Ida.

"That's because it's not obligatory," replies Arturo.

"How many have kept them on?" asks Ida.

"None," replies Arturo, "but that's because they are determined to demonstrate that no mutilation can stop them remaining objects of desire."

"Bollocks," laughs Ida, "they strip because you're a bully."

"You are suggesting that I threaten them with my fists, or put a gun to their heads?" he asks in mock outrage.

"Don't be an idiot," says Ida. "You know as well as I do that the relationship between painter and sitter is a form of wrestling. In the end one has to submit to the will of the other. Which is why – despite the entreaties of Ruddy – I have declined to accept commissions from the likes of Elton John. I fear that his very presence in my studio would force me to produce a representation, something that would be much more to his liking than mine. So I stick with sunflowers, anemones, and anonymous models. That way I can make paintings."

"I am not blind," says Arturo, "I know that your paintings are a thousand times better than mine, that you have true greatness in you. I can also see that you are not impressed by my work, that you think it is shit. Of course you are right. The example you are looking at is more soft-porn than portrait. My only real interest in the sitter was to show that women can have mastectomies and still have great-looking breasts. But you are far too English to tell me so yourself. Perhaps that is why your paintings still fall short of their potential. Some vestige of that Englishness stays your hand at the last moment, prevents you from delivering the coup de grâce. I have the temperament, but lack your divine gift. If only I knew how to teach, I would teach you how to strike without fear, how to take without guilt."

"You are absolutely right," she replies, "I need to learn how to take."

"And to give, and to give your all," cries Arturo, "damn it Ida, let me paint your portrait. Fuck the other women with breast cancer. Let me do it for my own enjoyment. Sit in that chair over there."

And Ida sits, like Missy the poodle.

She watches as Arturo dismisses Breast Cancer Survivor No 19 from the easel and replaces her with a blank canvas. How is he going to prepare it, she wonders, watching him open an earthenware jar and tip something that resembles red-brick dust on to a marble work top. Of course she identifies it immediately as Armenian Bole. Who would have thought it, she muses, he is going to prepare the canvas exactly as I would have done?

"I see we are going Dutch tonight," she observes. "I am surprised. I had you down as a German Expressionist."

"That is because my other sitters were flighty things, women of the air. Whereas you are an earthier creature."

Like some magician he conjures up an egg out of nowhere, cracks it, expertly isolates the yolk, and drops it bomb-like upon the powder. He grinds the two elements with a glass muller until they are bound as one. Finally he thins the paste with lighter fluid (which makes Ida a little high), and smears it all over the canvas. While the glaze rapidly dries he squeezes first raw umber, then (in rapid succession) burnt sienna, yellow ochre, vermilion, cerulean blue, ultramarine, terre verte, and zinc white onto the kidney-shaped palette.

Ida notes that Arturo moves quickly, but not hurriedly, as though confident that she will not change her mind (which she won't).

He blocks in the shadows with a big brush, dipped in burnt sienna and turpentine, then studies Ida's face to see exactly where the light falls, and wipes clean the equivalent spaces on the canvas with an old cloth, allowing the original surface to shine through. He discards the rag, picks up a smallish sable brush and begins to pick out her features with raw umber, and vermilion (for lips and ears). Her eyes he marks with cerulean blue.

"It is at this point that a mediocre painter like me begins to destroy the painting," he says.

Disregarding his reservations he works at it non-stop for the best part of an hour. When he turns it around to show Ida she is astonished to see a crude facsimile of the self-portrait so recently acquired by Mrs Sapsucker.

"That's not very original," she says.

"That's because you pulled an Elton John on me," he replies.

"How could I do such a thing," she protests, "when my will is such a featherweight?"

"False modesty does not become you," says Arturo. "So fierce was the resistance that I felt more like a member of the Gestapo than a portrait painter. It was my benign intent to shine a little light on the shadows that surround you – yes – to illuminate the darkness of the heart. But all I got to see was the public face. Did you come here simply to humiliate me? To demonstrate that you are the stronger? If so you have succeeded admirably."

Is this a shot in the dark? Or does Arturo Kingfisher somehow intuit that just as Kryptonite makes Superman buckle, so accusations of strength turn Ida to jello? To counter the accusation she has no choice but to feign meekness.

"What do you want of me?" she asks.

"Privileged access," he replies.

"To what?" she asks. Arturo pauses.

"Your breasts," he replies.

Ida laughs. Without a second thought she lifts off her sweater and uncouples her brassiere. For a woman who has had a mastectomy such exposure is no big deal; she is used to having her breasts prodded, probed, squeezed, and weighed – even photographed – by any number of strangers. Arturo scrutinizes her breasts no less candidly than the nurses, the oncologists, and the surgeons.

"If the right breast is any guide the loss of the left one was something of a tragedy," he observes, "though the plastic surgeon has done an excellent job. I only hope I can do his work justice."

Breast Cancer Survivor No 19 had been a tall, angular woman, with breasts to match, so he had ordered her to sit as if posing for Rodin's Thinker. Because Ida is shorter and rounder he asks her to stand.

"The skirt makes you look like one of Gauguin's Tahitian whores," he remarks.

So Ida removes it.

"Why keep the knickers?" he asks.

This time Ida does hesitate. Even Breast Cancer Survivor No 19 had preserved some modesty. Could complying with Arturo's request be construed as infidelity? Ida does not subscribe to the notion that conventional morality ends at the studio door. She would no more think of fucking one of her models (of either sex) than she would of walking on water.

In her studio the boundaries between painter and painted are always respected. She doubts that Arturo is equally fastidious. Would he consider the discarding of her panties to be an invitation? Probably. Even so she knows that she is not at risk. Arturo is hardly a rapist, and she can always say, "No". If he gets aroused let him divert the unspent passion to the canvas, as she always does when on form. Having satisfied her conscience she makes the mistake of removing her knickers.

To be standing stark naked before a virtual stranger is certainly unusual, but not unprecedented. What is without precedent is the feeling of being entirely exposed. Even on the first night with Zachary the persona he saw (or so she believed) was her own creation. In fact all anyone ever saw of her was a carefully wrought self-portrait, a membrane of imaginary paint, behind which her secret self cowered (and sometimes raged). How she knows not, but somehow Arturo has stripped away that patina, has revealed the unretouched Ida Siskin. She feels vulnerable, but not scared. If anything it is a big relief to be off duty for once, to turn a blind eye upon herself. She wonders what Art will do with the control he has wrested from her.

He decides to pose her belly-down on a rug, head resting on an elbow, bottom a little raised. He touches her as he pleases; in order to raise a shoulder, to shift an arm, to spread her legs ever-so-slightly. Ida proves to be a quick learner. Before long she is responding accurately to every command issued from the easel. It certainly makes a change from the strict democracy of modern matrimony. No "would you mind" or "if you please", just "do this" or "do that". And how willingly she does his bidding.

So when (after thirty minutes or so of concentrated

silence) he suddenly barks, "Kiss!" what can she do but approach his kneeling form on all-fours, place an arm on either shoulder, and kiss him on the mouth?

One day historians will question Arturo Kingfisher's intentions. Some will maintain that he was already planning this assault when he drove a wedge between husband and wife at the Sapsuckers. Others will insist that he was merely taking advantage of an opportunity that unexpectedly presented itself. For the moment all that can be said with any certainty is that the second Battle of Peachtree Creek (unlike the first) will be a victory for the home side. Ida's lips have already betrayed Zachary, as has her tongue. Instead of turning away in disgust, her neck can't wait to do likewise. A commando raid secures her bosom. After that her unprotected belly falls. And then in slow degrees her sturdy thighs and her bended knees. These well-shaped but cowardly joints quiver at the victor's approach, and threaten to overturn the body politic. Close to toppling anyway, Ida prepares to assume the supine position. But cunning Arturo slips behind, and buttresses her hips. He then applies gentle pressure to her back, until she understands that he wants her rumpside up.

Standing at the easel, Arturo had laboured valiantly in the manner of Rubens, recreating that same posterior with swatches of zinc white and a hog's-hair brush. He mixed in a dab or two of raw umber to add shape to its shadowy flanks, and burnt sienna to show where the light warmed its twin cupolas. For the crease itself he dipped the tip of a sable in vermilion, and delivered the paint like a fencer. Looking at his handiwork, he saw that it was good. But where was the anticipated rush of satisfaction?

Kingfisher's mind turned to Chloe, a woman he had only

read about in a magazine. Some details stuck; she lived in the San Fernando Valley, she was a porno star, and she drove a Mustang. He did not recall its colour, but he remembered its licence plate all right: STR82ANL.

Now he finds himself thinking about it again. He is still thinking about it as he prepares his penis for banditry with a Trojan, and scoops the remaining raw umber from his palette with an index finger. Ida gasps, but raises no objection when he inserts finger and oily paint as far up her rectum as possible. Ridiculous as it sounds he wishes his wife could be there to applaud his achievement as he slowly feeds his penis into Ida's little anus, which expels some bubbles and a small wake of raw umber. It is difficult to say which of the pair is the more astonished as it inches into her. Ida, who has never been buggered before, can hardly believe she is voluntarily surrendering her anal integrity to a stranger. If, on arrival, she had been asked to compile a list of a million things that might happen to her in Atlanta, that would not have been one of them. Arturo, for his part, cannot get over the fact that this exemplary artist, this gentlewoman, is permitting him a liberty never before taken on a first date (except with whores).

Uncertain as to what is expected of her in such a situation, Ida groans, grunts, and shakes her head like one possessed. As the act progresses to full-blown buggery she simply amplifies her mummery, until she is unexpectedly seized by she knows not what, and begins to babble in tongues. Who can interpret what she is saying? Not even Arturo. He hears his name, and extravagant words of devotion, but the ecstatic woman could equally well be referring to her vocation. Either way, he feels fully entitled to commission a third party to produce a commemorative canvas, provisionally entitled: The Triumph of Art over Zachary's Wife.

****

Meanwhile, alone in their 7th floor hotel room, Zachary Siskin is beginning to pine for Ida. When the phone rings sometime after midnight he assumes – not unreasonably – that she is calling to explain her absence.

"Where are you?" he says.

"Perhaps I should tell you who I am," a man answers, "before I tell you where I am. Hickory Waxwing at your service. Ruddy Turnstone's right-hand man. That's the who. The where is downstairs in the lobby. Now for the why. When he got home from the Sapsucker's soirée – which he said had developed into the dinner party from hell – my lord and master immediately dispatched me to guide you through Atlanta's demi-monde. "Leave no stone unturned in the pursuit of pleasure," were his instructions. I am here to carry them out to the letter. Am I to understand that your wife has not yet returned? Meet me in the bar, and we'll wait out her coming in the company of good ol' Jim Beam." Hickory Waxwing adds that he is easy to spot, his hair being the colour of a Georgia peach (though not naturally so).

Sure enough Zachary Siskin spots him easily. Both men order their bourbon neat.

"Have you noticed," says the blond-haired one, "that our names are practically homonyms? Though we don't look much alike. And probably don't act much alike either. What is it you do, Mr Siskin?"

"I'm a rabbi," replies Zachary.

"Jesus," exclaims Waxwing, "a Jewish one?"

"Most of us are," replies Zachary.

Hickory Waxwing whistles.

"I would never have guessed," he says. "Does it bother you to be seen with someone like me?"

"Someone like you I do not know about," replies Zachary, "but with you I have no problem."

"I was under the impression that your God took a dim view of Sodom and its eponymous perversion," says Hickory.

"Fuck my God," says Zachary Siskin, "I am a rabbi not because I believe in Him, but because I believe in man."

"I believe in men, too," counters Hickory, "but not to the extent that I worship them."

"I don't worship man, either," says Zachary, "I simply maintain that he has the capacity to do harm, and the capacity to do good, and that it is my duty to encourage the latter proclivity."

"Encouragement is perfect," says Hickory, "the problem with religion over here is that it's all about control."

Is that what I am doing, wonders Zachary, trying to control Ida? Nevertheless he calls up to their room three times during the course of the next hour, to check if she has returned unobserved, or at least left a message to ease his worried mind.

From Hickory he learns that his wife had left the party with the Kingfishers. Although it is close to 2.00 am he phones their home. Mrs Kingfisher picks up. He makes his apologies, and is assured that Ida is fine.

"She's with Art in his studio," the woman adds. "Been there for a couple of hours at least. I can only assume that he persuaded your wife to sit for him after all. He can be a very persuasive man."

Zachary downs another measure of Jim Beam (his sixth)

and says to his new bosom buddy: “Okay, Hickory, let’s go turn over a stone or two.”

Waxwing does a double-take. He knows how to burn the candle at both ends, but doesn’t know how much of this knowledge he should share with a rabbi.

“What is it you’re hoping to find under them?’ he asks.

“Naked women,” replies Zachary.

“What sort?” asks Waxwing, beginning to wonder if his companion really is what he said he was.

“Not whores,” replies Zachary, “dancers.”

“You want to see a titty show?” exclaims Waxwing.

“Exactly,” says Zachary. “One of my congregants, an employee of Coca-Cola, and a frequent visitor to your great city, informed me of its claim to be the lap-dancing capital of the world. I may not be able to prove the existence of my CEO, but I can certainly test the truth of that proposition. With your assistance, of course.”

The real reason Zachary wants to go to a lap-dancing club – the one he won’t admit to himself, let alone Waxwing – is old-time jealousy. Although he trusts his wife, he actually feels like a cuckold, and can too easily picture that swine Arturo Kingfisher feasting his bulbous eyes upon Ida’s breasts.

Anyway Waxwing hails a cab, and tells the driver to transport his passengers to Spring Street, which turns out to be blocked by an accumulation of mechanically-enchanced Hummers.

The interior of Sheena’s is more barn-like than palatial, more cattleman’s club than a structure befitting the Queen of the Jungle. Either way it is rectangular in shape, with a long bar to the left, and an equally long bar to the right. Placed prominently at each corner are giant screens broadcasting basketball matches. In front of the bars are long runways, raised just above head-height. There are three dancers on each, some naked, others not quite. Another trio is cavorting on a stage at the far end, also naked, or in the process of becoming so. The space which the nine girls border is filled with round tables. More girls – all of them stark naked – are jungle-jiving at some. Yet more naked women are wandering around looking for employment. One of them spots the newcomers, and offers to find them a table.

"Kinda sweet," says Waxwing, as they follow her fleshy behind, "puts me in mind of a painting by whatshisname . . . Ingres."

It turns out that Waxwing's interest in the showgirl's excess fat is professional. On the days when he does not slave for Ruddy Turnstone, he works as a nurse in the clinic of a well-known plastic surgeon. Many of the girls at Sheena's are his clients, including the blonde bringing them their umpteenth Jim Beam.

"Miss Liberty Bunting here is our masterpiece," says Waxwing, "Dr Shrike himself took care of the titties, but that great derrière is a Waxwing special."

Miss Bunting shakes it on cue, but only halfheartedly.

"Sweet thing, you look real down," says Waxwing, "tell ol' Hickory what's bothering you."

"I'm in mourning," says Miss Bunting, as bitter tears fill her eyes, "for my chihuahua."

"What are you thinking?" asks Waxwing of his pensive companion, when Liberty Bunting takes her great ass elsewhere.

"That if Mrs Sapsucker were to throw out her husband and keep the mutt," replies Zachary, "your Miss Liberty might find someone with whom to share her grief."

Hickory Waxwing claps his hands. “Let’s hope Mrs Sapsucker does both,” he says. “Miss Liberty could do with a bit of romance. Her new titties and ass don’t seem to have brought her much, unless you count pussy hunters.”

They drink to Liberty Bunting’s future happiness.

“We seem an unlikely couple,” says Zachary, “but in fact we’d make an excellent double act. I improve the soul, while you perfect the body.”

“You may think you’ve got the harder task,” says Waxwing, “but actually it’s me who’s got the short straw. It bein’ a lot easier describin’ the torments of hell than inflictin’ them. Every time I enter Dr Shrike’s surgery I am reminded of the fire and brimstone preachin’ I heard as a boy. Anyways I am in charge of liposuction. The type Dr Shrike favours is known as ‘tumescent liposuction’. Probably because it’s performed with just a local. You’d be amazed at how brave the girls are when I perforate them around the tush. They do not even cry out as I insert tubes into the gaping wounds, and introduce a cocktail of salt water, epinephrine, and lidocaine. The mixture flows until buttocks and thighs are so pumped up the skin looks fit to pop. You can tell from their faces that it hurts like hell. And that’s just for starters. The worst bit comes when the cannula are inserted and the fat vacuumed out. This is when the Michelangelo of liposuction comes into his own. Alas it is also the point when dollars as well as dolour become an issue. Because the fat is collected in bottles. And the more bottles the more dollars. This means that sometimes my contouring falls short of perfection.”

Miss Tiffany Thrasher, another of Waxwing’s near-perfect living sculptures (wearing a little gold dress) comes to inquire whether he and his friend would like a “hot dance”. Waxwing declines, but Tiffany sits with them anyway. When she hears that Zachary's wife is an artist she gives a little yelp, and tells how she once wanted to study art, but was forced by her parents to do something with greater economic opportunities. Now she is a supply nurse by day, and a stripper by night.

As soon as she stands up to leave, the men at the next table demand an exhibition of her entrepreneurial skills. There are six of them, all dressed in cheap suits. Their ringleader has prematurely grey hair. He addresses Tiffany Thrasher in English, but his colleagues in German. Zachary decides they are dentists. Tiffany shucks off her dress and tosses it towards the table. The grey-haired dentist catches it in mid-air and places his trophy on his head, as if it were a blonde wig. Ignoring the insult Tiffany leans over the man, and begins to sway, so that her surgically-enhanced breasts are passing back and forth before his undeserving eyes.

All this is happening about an arm's length from Zachary. He realises that watching Tiffany perform is a bit like reading a neighbour's newspaper over his shoulder, but who can resist when the story is so interesting? Zachary soon wishes that he had, because he suddenly finds himself confronted with a variant text, in which his wife has replaced the lap-dancer, and Arturo Kingfisher the German dentist. As if that were not torture enough, Tiffany (or Ida) executes an elegant turn, bends until her backside is in a position to have a chin-wag with her employer, and then exercises a talent new to Zachary. Apparently of their own volition her buttocks begin to open and close like the gills of a fish, exposing the interior right down to bedrock. Observing Zachary's bug-eyed interest the grey-haired dentist opens his mouth wide, not in order to show off his gleaming teeth, but to make an obscene gesture with his gargoyle-length tongue. A gesture which is both mocking and proprietorial. Assuming these taunts come from his nemesis, and concern the evil one's corruption of Ida, Zachary begins to seethe. How he wishes that he had belted Kingfisher when he had the opportunity, instead of retreating like some fucking turn-the-other-cheek milksop. Now he has been given a second chance to remedy the omission, and punch that big-beaked, wife-stealing, Holocaust-denying, Polack smack in the kisser.

This time he doesn't intend to let it slip. He rises to his feet, makes a fist of his right hand, and slowly lifts his arm, as if somewhere deep inside a rubber-band were being cranked. Fortunately Waxwing recognises the stance of a bar-room boxer and snatches the flailing arm before the blow can be landed, and the damage done.

"I know your people still have issues with the Germans," he cautions, "but it surely ain't right to go attacking every one you see."

"But that one called the Holocaust a myth or a hoax, I forget which. And I took offence. Excuse me, Hickory, but I did. As I'm sure you would if I called the burning of Atlanta a fiction. And how do you think that black blimp over there would react if I were to inform him that his life-long alibi was nothing but a big fib, nothing but a con-trick dreamed up by some smart-ass shvartzers to make whitey feel guilty?"

As it happens the 300 lb bundle of heavenly joy is heading in their direction, giving Zachary the opportunity to find out. Despite Waxwing's frantic efforts to prevent him, he catches the man's brocaded cuff as he passes.

"Pardon me, sir," he says, "but my friend and I are having a little spat which you seem ideally suited to settle. I am contending that institutionalized slavery never existed. My evidence for such an unfashionable claim? Let's imagine for the sake of the argument that I've totted up the cubic capacity of every vessel that made the Atlantic crossing in the relevant years, and found the figure wanting. To be blunt it is insufficient to accommodate all the Africans supposedly brought to Dixie as slaves. Meaning that the majority came as free men. But being work-shy they failed to prosper, and invented the myth of slavery, in order to obtain reparation, repatriation, and a big slice of Africa. My friend accuses me of being a racist. But I maintain that he's the racist. He's the one who won't accept that shvartzers can be as cunning as Yids. I say that if the Yids are able to sell the world a bill of goods, why not the shvartzers? So which of us is the racist? You be the judge."

The verdict is immediate and unequivocal. The outraged citizen gives Zachary a black eye, and continues on his way.

****

At the same time Arturo Kingfisher is driving Ida back to her hotel in the Luther King, the silence only broken by the *hoohoo-hoohoo . . . hoohoo-hoohooaw* of owls. Ida is embarrassed by what she has done, and fearful of its consequences, but above all she is confused. The confusion arises from the elation she is continuing to experience. Her unexpected orgasm had come from deep within, from a place she hardly dares name. Others less reticent might suggest that Kingfisher had penetrated her body and soul, and fucked them both. In which case Ida's biggest problem is what to do with the unprecedented feelings the invasion has awakened? And how to conceal them from her husband. So apprehensive is she of facing Zachary that she almost cries for relief when she enters their hotel room and finds it unoccupied. Instead of locking herself in the bathroom to avoid the third degree as she had planned, she undresses rapidly and goes straight to bed. With any luck I'll be fast asleep when Zachary returns from wherever he's gone, she thinks. Failing that she intends to fake it.

Within minutes the all-embracing warmth of the blankets renders any pretence unnecessary. Unfortunately the warming process also has an effect upon the evidence of adultery, much of which had evaded Arturo's cursory wipe with a kleenex. It begins to leak from Ida's anus while she snoozes, and is quickly absorbed by her knickers.

Sozzled and bruised Zachary carefully opens the door and is relieved to hear the regular breathing characteristic of untroubled slumber. At least she is safe, he thinks. His head aches so much he decides not to awaken her, and to postpone any accusations until room service delivers breakfast. But as soon as he lifts the covers his reeling senses are assailed by the pungent aroma of oil and earth, a smell which instantly brings to mind his wife's studio. Zachary knows that she has travelled with her paints in order to restore any canvases damaged in the transit from London to Atlanta, and quietly scans the room with his one good eye for any uncapped tubes. There aren't any. Conclusion? His wife must be the source of the eye-watering smell. But he can see all of her body (save for that small part covered by her knickers) and it is spotless. Closer inspection reveals that the same cannot be claimed for the said underwear. Because Ida is sleeping in the fetal position Zachary has a clear view of a dark and reeking blemish on the backside of her panties. Its shape is that of an overturned heart.

As her husband slips his hand between knicker elastic and skin, Ida awakens but immediately decides it more prudent to counterfeit sleep. She feels his fingers grope for clues, and hears him sniff the gathered evidence. He will sniff it more than once, thinks Ida, hoping against hope that it is nothing worse than menstrual blood, but will have to conclude that he can smell a rat. And when that happens, thinks Ida, I will be in big trouble. Why had Art not warned her that he had used oil paint to assist his entry? Was it because he wanted Zachary to find it? If so his ploy has worked. The enlightened cuckold looks about ready to call for his chariot of fire. This is not evidence, he fumes, looking at his fingers, this is proof positive of my wife's comprehensive betrayal. What other explanation can there be for the presence of a lubricant – however unconventional – in her back passage? During the remaining hours of darkness Ida does her desperate best to think of one. Rising shortly after dawn, she seeks sanctuary in the bathroom, where she uses every available unguent and perfume to wipe away the near indelible stain.

Over breakfast she notices her husband's own mark of Cain – his shiner – for the first time, and goes on the offensive, demanding an explanation of her own. Getting one she accuses Zachary of alcoholism, sexism, racism, and conduct unbecoming to a rabbi. He offers no defence. In fact he says nothing. He doesn't have to. The words j'accuse, j'accuse are everywhere like a plague of locusts. The unwelcome insects float on the meniscus of her orange juice, they stand on the pats of butter and pots of honey, they even cover the croissant she puts in her mouth. They stick in Ida's craw.

"After you left the dinner party," she croaks, "Ruddy Turnstone suddenly jumped up from his seat in obvious distress, and began a long lament, to the effect that he was a martyr to his haemorrhoids. Mr Sapsucker, grateful for the opportunity to show off his professional skills, produced a tub of evil-smelling ointment, which Ruddy applied to the affected parts in private. He reappeared all smiles, and delivered a ringing endorsement. As you know I have been constipated since our arrival in Atlanta, so I asked if the same ointment could be used as a preventative, and was given a tub of my very own. Sorry it made such a pen and ink." It is a credible story, with only two flaws; it isn't true, and the tub doesn't exist. Amazingly the locusts all buy it and vanish anyway, which means that her husband has bought it too – or so Ida assumes.

In Zachary Siskin's ancestral lands there were basically two kinds of rabbis; you were either a hasid or a mitnaged. If you were a hasid you believed in miracles and wonder-workers, if you were a mitnaged – literally an opponent – you didn't. You were a rationalist. Zachary is also a rationalist, though he has sympathy (even a little envy) for those who aren't. He would like to be able to swallow Ida's cock and bull story, but he can't. He considered calling her bluff and demanding to see Mr Sapsucker's panacea, but decided against. Failure to produce it would have just brought forth more lies, and left him no nearer certainty.

Instead he asks Ruddy Turnstone about his haemorrhoids while promenading through the parterre at the Atlanta Botanical Garden. Turnstone denies any knowledge of them. A clean bill of health confirmed by Hickory Waxwing. Ida's expression indicates that she considers the question a clear breach of trust. Zachary's face is a mask. The gallery owner, his catamite, the artist, and her heart-sick consort all enter a hot-house brimming with palms and other tropicana. Turnstone has led Ida here in hopes of inspiring her to switch her floral preference from the temperate zone, towards these more flamboyant shapes and displays. Georgia is booming, he explains, and householders want scenes of exuberance, abundance, and overnight growth.

"Withering is not their thing," he says by way of conclusion.

Artfully placed among the exotics are the even more exotic exhalations of the prodigiously lunged glass-blower Dale Chihuly. Zachary and Waxwing pause before a group that resembles extra-terrestrial plant-life from a *Star-Trek* episode. The so-called Tiger Lilies rise vertically from the humus like tumescent phalluses; ribbed, red, and far larger than life. Kingfisher's prick would have looked like one of them, thinks Zachary, had the Polack bastard used vermilion instead of raw umber to redecorate my wife's insides.

He gives Waxwing's arm a squeeze.

"Thanks for getting me back to the hotel in one piece," he says.

"You would have done the same for me," replies Waxwing. He asks what Zachary's injured eye looks like under the shades. Zachary lifts them, and shows him. Waxwing whistles.

"Slavery's still a touchy subject in Georgia," he notes.

"The big issue for me this morning," says Zachary, "is the 7th commandment." Suddenly the effort of dealing with it overwhelms him. He makes his excuses and heads for the exit.

He waits for the others beside a fish-tank filled with radiant blue fish that sparkle like chips from one of Chihuly's larger works. Above the aquarium is a notice-board. Having nothing better to do Zachary reads all the items pinned to it. Among them is an article someone has clipped from the

Atlanta Journal-Constitution. Its subject is the resurrection of the late Ivory-billed Woodpecker, known to expert birders as *Campephilus principalis*, and to non-expert Southerners as the Lord God bird (that being their exclamation on the rare occasions when they were vouchsafed a sighting). Godly it certainly was (judging from the accompanying illustration); larger than a raven, with a fiery red crest, dazzling white wing patches, and the eponymous bill. Throughout the latter half of the 20th century it was thought that this singular divinity was dead, extinct, to be seen only stuffed and mounted on dead trees (strangely like the crucified Christ, thinks Zachary). However, a few true believers held fast to the hope that the Ivory-billed Woodpecker had somehow survived undetected amid the swampy bottomland forests of the Deep South. And – what do you know – the true believers were right. Recently a lordly woodpecker of extravagant dimensions was spotted by a kayaker on Bayou de View in the Big Woods region of Arkansas. Getting wind of the sighting an ornithologist from Cornell University – a damn Yankee – and a local photographer went out together to see if they could identify the bird. Upon seeing it for himself the photographer put his face in his hands and began to sob, "I saw an Ivory-bill, I saw an Ivory-bill."

How Zachary envies him. Finally another kayaker caught the bird – albeit for only a few fleeting seconds – on video. That clinched it.

If she had been buggered by Picasso, thinks Zachary, I suppose I would have learned to live with the shame. But Arturo Kingfisher? A self-confessed antisemite, and (in Ida's own estimation) an insignificant painter. What possessed her to offer herself to such a mediocrity? A man not fit to clean her brushes.

****

As he enters the Turnstone Gallery alongside its guest of honour he cautions himself not to make a scene during the reception to celebrate his unfaithful spouse's big night. The presence of the Sapsuckers – especially Mrs Sapsucker – is another reason to keep his lip buttoned. God forbid he should end up like her.

"Have some champagne," says Waxwing, handing him a flute of merry-making bubbles.

"Hickory," replies Zachary, "you are turning out to be my guardian angel."

As the gallery fills many new voices sing the praises of Ida's latest work. Some even purchase the paintings they praise. One goes to a woman wearing a toga fastened at the shoulder with a golden scorpion, another to a lesbian carrying two babies (not twins) simultaneously. Within the first hour it becomes clear that the exhibit will be a success. Still Atlanta's artistic elite pours in. Even so the crowd is not sufficiently large to conceal from Zachary the horrid fact that his wife is hobnobbing with the man who turned up like a thief in the night and carelessly stole her away. Her lips are moving, but (as in his dream) he cannot read them.

"My husband knows what happened in the studio," she is saying, "what happened while Mrs Kingfisher was waiting Penelope-like in the house, and the owls were hooting outside."

"How?" asks Arturo. "Did he torture you? Or did guilt do the trick?"

"Neither," she replies, explaining about the tell-tale paint.

"Whoops," gasps Arturo, and begins to laugh.

At the sound of which Ida gently places two fingers upon his lips, as though slipping an invisible cigarette between them. This intimate gesture is more than Zachary can bear. Unable to control his passions he homes in on the sinners like a heat-seeking missile.

"Hello Zachary," says Arturo, "may I congratulate you on your wife's remarkable performance? What an original woman she is! Everyone else travels from A to Zee. Only she begins with Zee, and ends up with A."

"A downhill journey, I fear," replies Zachary.

"On the contrary, she's been taken to heaven and back," says Arturo, "while you look like you've spent a season in hell. Was it Beelzebub himself who blackened your eye?"

Ida sets him right.

"Did he hit him back?" inquires Arturo. "I have heard that your lot believe in an eye for an eye."

"No," says Zachary, "I was saving my revenge for a more deserving target."

So saying he launches his right fist in the direction of his over-confident tormentor's face and connects. Down goes Arturo, champagne flute and all.

"Take that you antisemitic cocksucker," Zachary bellows. "That'll teach you to stick your uncircumcised dick into my wife's Jewish arse!"

Ida regards her husband with astonishment, seeing not the familiar rabbi, but a pint-sized Muhammad Ali. For a second or two she leans in his direction, but is then drawn irresistibly back towards the magnetic Pole, whom she helps to his feet.

The long silence in the gallery is broken by Mr Sapsucker, who lets out some sort of primal scream and pushes over his wife.

"You self-righteous, frigid, ball-breaking cunt!" he shouts as she hits the hardwood floor.

Needless to say, Mrs Sapsucker does not take the insult lying down. She flings herself at her husband's knees, and fells him with a ferocious tackle.

"You adulterer!" she yells. "You two-faced piece of shit!"

Hers is an example Mrs Kingfisher elects not to emulate. Having tipped the contents of an ice-bucket into a napkin, she presses the freezing poultice against her husband's fast-swelling eye. Half-a-dozen other women (including Ida), form a protective shield around their beleaguered sheik, to protect him from other vengeful spouses, who are beginning to circle them like Hollywood Indians.

Elsewhere a gent sporting a silver toupee places his hands on the bare shoulders of the woman with the golden scorpion and hisses: "Compared to you the goddamn Whore of Babylon was a fucking nun!"

"And compared to you," she replies, "the Pope's a stud."

Even the woman with the two babies joins in the mêlée. "Screw your perfect body," she says to her partner. "Next time I'll donate the eggs, and you can carry the fucking baby."

"The party seems to be going with a swing," says Ruddy Turnstone (not without satisfaction) to his assistant, Hickory Waxwing.

As he passes the couple, Zachary says to Hickory: "Enjoy life, my friend. But don't fly too close to the sun."

Reaching the door the Menelaus of Atlanta takes time to look back upon the strife he has accidentally occasioned.

While the refined feelings of Ida's delicate portraits and natures mortes remain serene and secure within their carefully chosen frames, the emotions of their potential purchasers have broken out of their cages and are running amok, proving yet again that unfettered nature really is red in tooth and claw. All my working life I have been a kind of a picture framer, he thinks, a man who has imprisoned (or tried to imprison) the emotions of my congregants within borders imposed by God's ancient spokesmen. The need for such restraints is obvious, but I am no longer the right man to impose them. What my congregants need is a believer, a man (or woman) prepared to turn a blind eye to the incontrovertible evidence that God (if He exists) does not have the best interests of humanity at heart.

Ida is shouting something – perhaps at him – but he cannot make sense of what she wants, and anyway no longer cares. Recalling his dream (yet again) he realizes that the ledge upon which he sat was no ledge but a perch, and that he had been looking in the wrong direction; not down, but up. And so he turns away from his wife, his congregation, his God, away from everything he once held dear, and walks out alone into the warm Georgia night.

****

"Fuck art," he thinks as he starts the rental. He takes Interstate 20 going West in the direction of Birmingham, Alabama. From there he drives to Tupelo, Mississippi. At Memphis, Tennessee, he buys a map of Arkansas. His destination, he discovers, lies mid-way between Memphis and Little Rock. He exits I-40 just a few miles east of Eden.

"Welcome to Brinkley," says the sign, "home of the Ivory-billed Woodpecker".

He checks into the Ivory-bill Motel. First there was Wild Bill and Buffalo Bill, he thinks, and now there is Ivory Bill. A holy trinity of American heroes. For $5.95 he has an Ivory-billed cheeseburger at Gene's Bar-b-Que. He observes that he is not the only pilgrim in the place. What marks the others out are the binoculars that bounce – like a high priest's pectoral – on their breasts. Zachary has yet to declare his allegiance so openly. An omission he makes good the following morning at Ivory-bill's Treasure Chest. Looking through a pair of Lite-Tech 10x25s it occurs to him that the instrument serves both science and faith; not only facilitating the study of what is already there, but also encouraging hopes of observing things as yet unseen.

Elsewhere, Zachary quickly learns, faith and science are not in such harmony. Already sceptics have begun to question the video evidence. They say that the fugitive bird – so briefly seen – is not an Ivory-billed after all, but its common cousin the Pileated Woodpecker. There are disputes about wing-markings that resemble the hair-splitting of biblical scholars over the exegesis of arcane injunctions. One of the faithful says, "The woods are my church." To which a sceptic responds by accusing him (and those like him) of "faith-based ornithology."

If they were rabbis the first would be a hasid, and the second a mitnaged. Although a former mitnaged himself Zachary cannot bring himself to join their camp. Not when he becomes conversant with the Ivory-billed Woodpecker's persecution at the hands of money grubbers and worse. In the 1880s Yankee logging companies felled much of its natural habitat (the forests of the erstwhile Confederacy), turning the hardwood logs into railways sleepers.

By 1944 the Ivory-billed Woodpecker was confined to one place, a swathe of virgin swamp in Louisiana, known as the Singer Tract, on account of the fact that its trees were destined to become sewing machine cabinets. For a time it seemed that the presence of the bird might save the cypress and the tupelo, but it turned out that the stay of execution was because of economics not ecology. As soon as felling the trees became a profitable enterprise down they went. What made it so was the arrival of German prisoners of war, whose labour was more or less free. It was these captive Nazis who destroyed the last remnant, wiped the Ivory-billed Woodpecker from the face of the earth. What choice does Zachary have? How can he do other than side with those who now believe otherwise?

But he does remain enough of a mitnaged to require proof, preferably supplied by his own eyes. How to find it? That is the question. What he needs is a canoe, with which to explore the Bayou de View, and its adjacent waterways. He makes inquiries at Gene's Bar-b-Que, and is informed (by Gene himself) that Pippa Longspur may have one for rent. Zachary knows the name, has seen it attached to paintings for sale at Ivory-bill's Treasure Chest. All the canvases are variations on the same theme; the return of the legendary woodpecker. Most are playful, showing the bird in a variety of comic situations, but a few touch something deeper than the funny bone. One in particular presents a breeding pair on a dead log, at ease in some ghostly cypress swamp. The painting (or so it seems to Zachary) is full of longing for a world that once was, and – by some miracle – may yet be. Pippa Longspur's art may not be art in the same way that Ida Siskin's art is art – it knows nothing about painting, or the achievements of earlier practitioners – but at its best it gives expression to what Zachary is longing to see.

It takes him five minutes to walk across Brinkley to Pippa Longspur's little wooden house, the back of which is decorated with a painted garden, an arboretum, and a menagerie. Its owner opens the door. Her perfume is turpentine and oil. Her lovely face is marred by a broken nose. One day I shall be told of its cause, thinks Zachary. One day I shall be permitted to do unto her what Kingfisher did unto Ida. But not today. Today he asks if she would be willing to rent her canoe on a weekly basis. They agree a price. She invites him in for a Bud. They talk about the Ivory-billed Woodpecker.

Zachary learns that Pippa Longspur was born in Rapid City, South Dakota, where early on she started to draw the birds of the prairie. Her role-model was Alexander Wilson, the first recorder of North America's varied avian population.

"Reading his description of the Ivory-billed Woodpecker changed my life," she says. "His usual method was shoot, skin, paint. But one of the Ivory-bills he shot wasn't dead by a long way. So he rents a room for him and his bird, meaning to paint it from life. But the bird is what you'd call a reluctant sitter. First he attacks the artist with beak and claw. Then he destroys the table to which he is tied. Finally he heads for the window frame, and reduces that to matchwood. Wilson said his eye was brilliant and daring, and that his spirit was noble and unconquerable. I fell in love with that bird as a teenager, and love him yet. Searching for him is what brought me to Brinkley."

"You'll be the first to know when I find him," promises Zachary.

Thereafter he spends every day, from early morning until twilight, paddling quietly among the giant trees of Bayou de View. Gradually he learns to call the birds by their names.

"A Great Blue Heron," he says to himself (like Adam on the sixth day of creation), as a huge bird glides towards the water. Nor is he now in danger of ever mistaking a Pileated

Woodpecker for an Ivory-billed, either by sight or sound. He can tell their wing markings apart, and their cries. Indeed he often hears the *kuk-kuk-kukkuk* of the former emerging from the mysterious interior of the forest.

But only once so far has this happened: *bam-bam*!!! The sledge-hammer notes of an Ivory-billed at work. Zachary immediately places the binoculars to his eyes, and scans the trees where he guesses the sound originated. Zilch. After the initial excitement has worn off, he is forced to consider the possibility that the sound was not of the present, but the echo of a long-dead specimen, replayed by a volunteer from Cornell in hopes of enticing survivors into the open. Who knows? And so it goes, day by day, until the arrival of that blessed moment when all uncertainty will be removed, and he will cry – on finally seeing the bird – "Lord God!"

THE VENUS MOSAIC

TIME WAS WHEN I laid claim to be the finest portrait painter in the USA, by which I mean the University of St Albans of course. That preeminence came to an abrupt end when Professor Nightshade took over the Art Department, and announced that Life Drawing was an artisan craft, unworthy of university study. Besides, he added, what use is portraiture in an age when selves are fragmented and personalities multiple? If I wished to retain my position I would have to embrace Conceptual Art.

The process of making thought visible had no appeal. Instead of Conceptual Art I embraced life itself in the shape of Connie Hanks, Connie Hanks of Malmesbury, a member of the Wiltshire family which had gifted the New World the great Abe Lincoln (mine had blown in from elsewhere, like an easterly).

Oh for the balm of Malmesbury, that most ancient of cities. Most English too, if I may say. How its very name rolls around my tongue like a boiled sweet, leaving a taste of marmalade and mulled wine. My wife's dowry was a house on its High Street, which in a previous existence had been the Bear Inn. After our marriage she resigned her post as head of history at Beaumont, and together we sought a new life in the west.

By 1981, the year our only child was born, we had stripped away most of the soiled patina of the fifties – linoleum, false ceilings – to reveal the pine floors and oaken beams beneath. Our bedroom, located in the former attic, filled with dawn light on summer mornings. No sleeper I, it was my delight to watch the sun butter my wife's face. As it rose higher her hair turned as golden as ripening wheat. Her eyes – when she opened them – were as blue as cornflowers. It was the very picture and image of my happiness. However, my wife was not always comfortable with the intensity of my gaze. Once she even went so far as to say: "That look of yours feels like a pillow on my face."

In those early years we lived off the income that came from commissions I received to portray the ladies of the Beaufort Hunt. It was from Lady X herself I learned that Prince Charles was going to bring his new bride to Highgrove House in neighbouring Tetbury. Though sworn to secrecy I passed on the news to my wife, whose indifference matched my own. Even so, the presence of the royals, invisible to us, began to exert a significant influence upon our own lives. Strangers began to stare at my wife in the street, especially when her pregnancy began to show. One even sneaked a photograph. Only when a tabloid ran a story labelled "Exclusive", and headlined, "England Expects", did the penny drop. My wife was Princess Di's double. And the hapless paparazzi had snapped and sold a photo of the wrong twin.

Urged on by her friends my wife joined the books of an agency which specialised in celebrity look-alikes. Why not? The extra money paid for our child's nanny, and for our annual trip to Italy, where my mother-in-law owned a villa on the Amalfi coast.

It was a sight more substantial than the ruin we helped unearth in a field outside Kingscote, on the Cotswold escarpment, just a few miles beyond Tetbury. A shared love of Roman history meant that my wife and the dig's director soon became as thick as thieves. Me he called “the miserable sod”.

We turned what seemed like tons of the stuff and were eventually rewarded with a mosaic pavement at the centre of which was a medallion featuring a female bust assumed to be Venus. Her head was tilted to the left, the better to examine her reflection in the oval mirror she was holding aloft.

An entrance to a hypocaust, more or less intact, was found beside an adjoining room. The director claimed the privilege of being the first to enter. Someone handed him a flash-light, and he penetrated the narrow aperture on his belly. Soon only the soles of his shoes were visible, and then they too were swallowed by the underworld. He returned breathless with excitement. My wife insisted upon seeing what he had seen. He did not discourage her.

Within moments the space once occupied by Connie was transparent. All that remained was the echo of her voice calling enthusiastically: “I must be below the Venus mosaic.”

And the rest, it seemed, was silence, until from deep beneath our feet: “I cannot breathe!”

The director pulled her out, feet first, like a country vet.

Our growing child, I'm glad to say, preferred the living thing, his grandmother's villa over in Italy. Unlocking the door, after our return from the twelth consecutive visit, I heard the telephone ring.

"Bring up the cases," I said to the teenager who was following in my footsteps, and unencumbered ascended the stairs at a run.

"Hello," I said, snatching up the receiver. A man with an over-pronounced French accent asked to parler avec ma belle femme.

"Connie," I called, "it's your lover."

"That was the Deputy Head of Security at the Ritz in Paris," she reported afterwards. "He wants me to check into the hotel at the end of the month, when Diana is due to spend one night there with her Dodi. My role will be to act as a decoy to keep the paparazzi off the scent of their real quarry."

The Ritz. Now the word sticks in my craw like a broken cracker. But at the time I advised her to take the job. My wife telephoned but once from France.

"You should see what they've done to me," she said. "Even I can't tell the difference. If there is such a thing as a perfect counterfeit I am it."

They said it was Princess Diana they were burying that August, but since that day my wife has been officially listed as a missing person.

PRISONERS OF THE SUN

NOT LONG BEFORE she died my mother wrote a brief autobiography. It is brief because it concludes abruptly with my birth. To her I was not a beginning but an end. Not a source of joy, but an object of terror. An unruly creature sent by the Almighty to advertise her failings as a mother, failings her gruesome relatives sought out with malicious eagerness. What notions my mother had on the subject of child-rearing were imported from an obscure shtetl in Poland. They were not designed to produce well-adjusted adults.

My formative years were spent in a semi-detached on the Watford Way, between Hendon and Mill Hill. Instead of a sibling I was presented with a highly-strung pooch. Only recently has it occurred to me that my parents may have fibbed about his bollocks, or lack of them. They always maintained that he had been born that way. But who's to say that they didn't order their surgical removal? Too late to confront them now.

Nor can I enquire of the breeder, who may well be still alive (for reasons that will become apparent). His name was Ray, and he raised Scotties as a sideline (his real purpose in life being to manage the factory founded by my father and two of his brothers, in the wake of the Second World War). Had my pup been black I would have named him Sooty. But he was white, so I called him Snowy. Notwithstanding the absence of testicles he attempted unnatural conjunction with every visitor to our house. If I innocently sought to prise him from the newcomer's leg he would furiously bite the hand that fed him. I endeavoured to civilize him, but his animal instincts kept fracturing the veneer. Finally my parents were forced to knock him out with doggy tranquilizers whenever guests were anticipated.

By the mid-fifties Londoners were at last feeling confident enough to re-decorate their homes. They flocked to department stores and ordered new carpets, new curtains, and – praise the Lord – new furniture. As a consequence the family business – which manufactured dining tables and chairs – began to thrive. The brothers acquired larger premises. And before long my father was going to the new factory six days a week. I accompanied him on the Sabbath, driving from London's North-Western suburbs to its Eastern End, a great improvement on attending the local synagogue.

One Saturday, as we waited to turn right from Commercial Road into Hague Street (where the factory was located), I observed a trio of broad-shouldered beefcakes, with Brylcreamed hair and cut-throat razor creases in their trousers, light up their Woodbines. Blowing smoke they formed a conspiratorial huddle on the corner. To my amazement they all saluted our car as it passed.

"Who are they?" I asked.

"The Kray Brothers," my father replied.

"You know gangsters?" I exclaimed, mightily impressed.

"I prefer to call then rough diamonds," he replied. "They have never been anything less than respectful to me, as you have just witnessed."

"Do you have to pay them protection money?" I asked him.

"Don't be daft," he replied, "they own a dive called La Condor, that's where they make their money."

Maybe that was another evasion, like the denial of poor Snowy's castration.

Our increased prosperity enabled us to move out of the semi-detached into a villa, also in Hendon, swap the Humber Super Snipe for a metallic blue Jaguar, and start taking holidays on the Continent. We could even afford a Mediterranean cruise aboard the SS Iberia, which sailed out of Southampton in the summer of '59. My father took an 8mm movie-camera with him, and every so often I run the fragile film through the old Bolex. My mother must have shot the opening sequence, because it features my father leading me up the gangplank. Both of us are smiling and waving. I showed the film to my son in 1992, when I was the same age as my father, and he was the same age as my younger self. My father and I were like twins, but my son bore no resemblance to me. He has inherited his mother's good looks, which are no longer of any use to her.

****

After a brief visit to Madeira, with its colossal blooms and sea-borne beggars, we approached the North African coast. Pilots sporting turbans boarded the ship, and threw cables to the tugboats which, like a pair of bridesmaids, led the great white liner to its berth in Casablanca. Already the air smelled differently; a mix of the unknown perfumes of Araby, and pesticide.

Once the ship had docked we trooped down the gangplank, swept past the port officials in their red fezzes, and made straight for the awaiting guides. How my father managed to find a Jewish one is a mystery. His hair was black, his complexion swarthy. He wore a brown suit, with a cream-coloured shirt beneath. The trousers were baggy, and the jacket hung asymmetrically from his sloping shoulders. His grin was equally lop-sided.

"My name is David Perez," he said, extending his hand, "late of Toledo."

"How late?" asked my father.

"1492," he replied.

He raised his right arm, and clicked his fingers. One of the taxis broke ranks and glided across the tarmac towards us.

"I still have in my possession the ancient key to our former house," he said, as he opened the car door.

On the steps of an ancient synagogue in the mellah, David Perez said: "I am a good Jew, but I am a better Moroccan. I am proud of Israel, but I love my homeland more. Long live King Hassan."

It was in Casablanca that I went missing for an hour. You can see the moment of my disappearance on my father's film. One minute I am brandishing the curved dagger I had acquired in the casbah, the next I am nowhere to be seen. The camera begins to move around, slowly at first, then with ever greater speed, as if increasingly anxious to find me again. You don't have to be a lip-reader to appreciate what my mother (in close-up) is shouting: "Where has that child gone?" Now I can appreciate my parents' anxiety, but then I didn't give it a second thought, as I wandered back into the casbah alone. Little did I know it, but I was about to meet the boy who has influenced my life, from that day to this.

The fateful encounter took place in a tiny bookshop, whose name I have long-since forgotten.

"Entrez," said the proprietor, waving me in with his hand.

So I did.

Spread on a central table were several Tintin albums, a character unknown to me until that moment. What irresistible covers they had. It was as though their creator possessed an intimate knowledge of my inner life; knew that I was crazy about cowboys, space exploration, and treasure hunting. I picked up an album called *Objectif Lune*, and was immediately captivated, even though my French was rudimentary. Only when I reached the very last frame – the rocket is heading for the moon, but no one within can respond to earth's despairing call: "*Allo, allo ... J'appelle fusée lunaire ... Allo, allo!*" – did I recollect that I also had been out of contact with mission control for too long.

Once away from the shop, and all alone in that alien bustle, my fear began to match that of my parents. It was our guide, David Perez, who eventually found me and reunited us.

My father's first reaction was to shout, "Never worry your mother like that again!", and to slap me around the face with his open hand. His second was to hug me. As he did so he made a terrifying sound, which I eventually identified as crying.

When we returned to the ship at the day's end David Perez passed me a thin package. He had returned secretly to the bookshop and purchased *Objectif Lune*, as well as its sequel, *On A Marché Sur La Lune.*

"I too love Tintin," he said.

I still have the book, as well as every other volume Hergé ever published.

****

In 1973, as a result of the machinations of Bab El Ehr and his ilk (vide *Land of Black Gold*), there was a four-fold increase in the price of timber, with catastrophic consequences for my father's business. By that time the factory's other two founding fathers were dead, and Ray had been made a partner in their stead, in spite of my mother's dire warnings.

"I don't understand your objections," my father had said. "Ray has been with the firm for years. He knows the business inside out. What's more, our customers trust him."

"That's exactly what I don't do," said my mother. "There's something about his face. He looks . . . he looks sly."

She was spot on. Behind my father's back Ray had established a series of satellite workshops, which were immediately given contracts to supply the parent company with upholstered seats, formica work-tops, and numerous other parts not manufactured in situ. Although demand did not fall, nor production falter, profits plummeted, until it became obvious that the factory could not sustain two directors. Whereupon Ray revealed his hand: not only did he own half of the business, but he also held a controlling interest in most of its suppliers. He offered to purchase my father's fifty percent at the market price (which was considerably depressed).

Otherwise he intended to resign and open a factory of his own, which would – of course – bankrupt his ex-partner. He had mooted the possibility with a number of their largest customers, most of whom had promised to give their next orders to him. My father had no choice but accept Ray's offer.

Nor did his humiliations end there. Negotiations took several weeks, during which time my father continued to go to the factory, as if nothing were amiss. If the outward journey was grim, the return must have been hellish. For no comfort awaited him at home. My mother could not forget that he had ignored her advice. And she was determined to ensure that he did not forget it either.

She cooked dinner every night, as usual, but served it with bad grace. No pleasantries were exchanged as we ate. Silence would have sufficed, but my mother was incapable of suppressing an emotion. Before we left the table she was guaranteed to say something unforgivable.

One night, seeing Snowy (now elderly) dozing on the mat, she broke her silence thus: "What Ray once did to that dog, he has now done to you. All because you didn't believe me. Or were too cowardly to do anything about it if you did."

"I've been betrayed by my business partner," responded my father. "A man who owes everything to me. Isn't that enough?"

My mother clearly thought not. She would not be denied her revenge.

"You think you've been betrayed?" she cried. "What about me? My advice scorned by my own husband, who chose to put his faith in a shaygets. And has made us all paupers as a consequence. What do you want me to say? Mazel tov?"

She pushed her plate away, its contents more or less untouched. My father rose without a word, picked it up, and carried it to the kitchen sink, where he dispatched the debris down the waste disposal. The noise of the blades, as always, distressed Snowy. My mother, however, did not move a muscle, just sat there like fury personified. Her behaviour disgusted me; even so I couldn't deny the righteousness of her anger. I left them to it, and retreated to my room. Snowy, ever faithful, followed.

You may be wondering why a fellow in his twenties was still living with his parents. Well, I had gained my BA in a remote part of England, and gained my Masters on the West Coast of America. After that I had returned home temporarily, in order to complete my doctorate as quickly as possible.

Its subject owed everything to the thoughtful gift David Perez, our guide, had given me in Casablanca.

On first attending university I had assumed that Tintin would be among the childish things I would be required to put aside. Boy was I wrong. The place was swarming with hip academics who actually wrote learned articles about my childhood obsessions, Tintin included. Indeed, one of them became my mentor, and subsequently helped me find a subject for my doctorate: Tintin and the Art of Political Engagement.

I sat at my desk and immersed myself in the texts, hoping to blot out the disturbing sounds rising from downstairs. I opened *Tintin au Pays des Soviets* (yet to be translated), and turned to the sequence that shows English fellow travellers being duped by the sight of factory chimneys belching black smoke. Tintin is not fooled, however (any more than my mother was by Ray). He peeps inside and discovers nothing but stage effects; one man is burning bundles of straw to create the smoke, while another hammers metal to mimic the sounds of machinery in action. I compared that right-wing exposé to Low's *Russian Sketchbook*, a contemporary volume, in which similar Englishmen journey to the Soviet Union in expectation of finding an economic miracle.

Unlike Hergé, Low always gave the Soviets the benefit of the doubt. His hopes were not foolish, they were simply misplaced. Hergé was too quick to assume the worst. Even though he turned out to be justified. He was not yet thinking for himself – his vision was founded on prejudice not observation – which meant that his alter ego was too ready to tell his readers what they wanted to hear.

Meanwhile my mother continued to pursue an opposite course of action in the kitchen. Try as I might I couldn't ignore the commotion.

"Listen, Snowy," I said, "Captain Haddock and Bianca Castafiore are going at it hammer and tongs."

****

My father got a job as a rep for a company that marketed pillows and quilts. Every day he shuttled from department store to department store, doing his best to peddle its wares. He no longer drove a Jag.

As for me? I got my doctorate, and a job at the University of St Albans. It didn't last, and I moved to Wiltshire, where I created a family of my own. My father adored his new grandson. Soon it became apparent that the feeling was mutual. My father worked as a salesman for fifteen years. During all that time he never uttered a word of complaint. He liked his boss, though not his politics.

In particular he disagreed with his uncompromising views on Israel. They had many arguments on the subject, usually during otherwise amicable games of bridge. On one occasion my father voiced the opinion that the recent election of Binjamin Netanyahu was a disaster.

"Four years the settlement freeze lasted," he said, "and now he ends it overnight. That's not what I call giving peace a chance."

"The man is Prime Minister of Israel," said his boss, "don't you think he knows better than some shmendrick in Hendon what's good for his country?"

"As a matter of fact I don't," said my father.

But as he argued his case with increasing passion, dizziness overcame him, and an ambulance was summoned. I did not receive the news until the following morning, whereupon I drove directly to my son's school in Chippenham, withdrew him from his class, and – once we were on the M4 – floored the accelerator. At the Royal Free I was assured by a nurse that my father's condition was not life-threatening. She was dead wrong. Like Yitzhak Rabin before him my father died a martyr to peace.

The day after we buried him at Bushey I decided to raise my son's spirits, and took him to see a new exhibition at the Chelsea Town Hall; Tintin: 60 Years of Adventure. Of course my son was already well acquainted with the boy reporter, his eccentric copains, and their numerous scrapes, but the exhibition prompted questions he had never raised before: "Did Tintin have a mother? If so, what happened to her?"

Questions I couldn't answer, any more than I could explain what had become of his own. As we progressed through the exhibits hand-in-hand I gradually became aware that I no longer identified with Tintin (who had not aged a day in those six decades). No, my new role-model was old blistering barnacles himself; Captain Haddock.

My son's question continued to nag at me: did Tintin have

a mother? So I asked colleagues around the world, who shared my enthusiasm for Hergé, if they knew the answer. Some imagined that Tintin had been born – like Superman – on a doomed planet (not earth). Others mooted the possibility that he was the orphan child of missionaries to the Congo.

But I liked the suggestion of Gabriel Benveniste, Professor of Comparative Literature at the Universidad de Lima, best: "Maybe he is the offspring of Marrano Jews, the modus vivendi of whom is forgetfulness. And so it was natural that when his parents were murdered in a pogrom he immediately suppressed all memory of them."

Benveniste alone backed up his theory with textual evidence, referring to the scene in *Tintin au Pays de L'Or Noir* when our hero is mistaken for his double – a Jew.

At which point someone – maybe it was even me – proposed that we constitute our informal bonds into a Society. And so was born Les Amis de Tintin. It seemed only fitting to hold our first conference in Brussels.

Thereafter we picked a city associated with one of the adventures. Two years ago it was Shanghai. Last year it was Sydney. Next year it will be Haifa. This year it is Cusco, Peru.

My son has agreed to accompany me yet again, though for the first time he has set conditions: he must be back before August 10, so that he can be in Cornwall by the eleventh, to witness the total eclipse of the sun.

"No problem," I say, remembering how I stood in the playground, and viewed the partial eclipse of '54 through a pad of black & white negatives, "I'm delivering my paper on the fifth, and the conference wraps up on the seventh."

I book the flights; departing July 26, returning August 8.

Today is July 22, the last day of term. For the past seven years I have driven my boy the fifteen miles from our home in Malmesbury to his school, before starting my own working day at Corsham College of Art. Usually we make the homeward journey together as well. But no more. Today I am doing the school run for the last time. It is the final summer of the 20th century, and my son has just completed his secondary education.

"Fuck school," he cries triumphantly, when we reach home, "fuck homework, fuck exams!"

He tears off his shirt, and stretches out on the uncut grass like a slice of white bread under the grill. Always the concerned father I extract a tube of factor 30 sun block from the bathroom cabinet.

"Dad," complains the boy, as my shadow falls across his face and chest, "you're obstructing the light."

"More like saving your life," I say, as I spread the cream over his torso.

"You're beginning to sound like your mother," replies my son.

"On the contrary," I say, "my mother was convinced that sun bathing was good for the body. Every fine day she would say to me, 'Why don't you go outside and start a tan?' Of course no one had heard of skin cancer in those days."

More than a decade ago I took a photograph of my wife on that same lawn. I look at it sometimes, but not too often, because she is naked. Sometimes it seems so cruel not to be able to stop time, to arrest the development of one's child so that they remain fixed in that moment when the bond between you is unbreakable.

****

On idle afternoons I have patiently observed spiders spin shrouds of silk for their trapped prey. The light within must be similar to that which falls upon the city of Lima from April to December, when the sun is hidden by the dismal garua, or coastal fog. And its citizens, like the doomed insects, seem mindful of a terrible enemy. Everywhere pedestrians are outnumbered by armed guards, and even the concierge, who runs to open the door of the taxi that has delivered us to our hotel, is not only wearing a flak-jacket, but also packing an Uzi. The threat, if it exists, is invisible. Possibly the fabrication of a bad conscience.

"You are wrong," says Gabriel Benveniste, who was waiting with the driver at the airport, "it exists all right. Once it was political, but now it is mainly criminal. And a lot deadlier than a bad conscience. You must have more sympathy for the ill-starred residents of Lima, my friend. Ahead of them lies the vast Pacific, behind them are the mighty Andes. The very sky seems to be pressing down upon their heads. As if that weren't bad enough murderers stalk their streets. It seems to me that they have two possible responses; they can become emasculated by fear, or they can espouse hedonism."

There seems little doubt which of the duo our louche host favours. If I were Hergé I would give him the sort of mane a lion would die for, and goatish hairs on his chin. He looks like a man who devours life raw.

On exotic holidays my parents would eschew all the local delicacies and plump for cheese omlettes or grilled fish. Even so my mother was sure to end up bent double. What would she have ordered at Pantagruel, the restaurant to which Benveniste has taken us? Probably tamalitos verdes, just like her son. My son, however, is bolder. His choice is brazuelo de alpaca.

"What is the meat like?" he asks.

"Very suave," replies the waiter.

"Suave?" says my son.

"Yes," says the waiter, "very suave."

"He means it's not over-spiced," says Benveniste, "and quite tender, like lamb."

The three of us sip pisco sours while we await our food.

"Pantagruel is only the second restaurant serving novoandino cuisine to open in Lima," says Benveniste. "It's proven hard to shake the prejudice that people who eat guinea pigs are savages. But Bernado Roca-Rey, the newspaper magnate, is doing his best. If the cause of comidas peruanas has a god-father: he's it. As a matter of fact, this restaurant is run by his daughter."

By the time we have finished our main courses it seems that Bernado Roca-Rey's campaign may be bearing fruit: the restaurant is full. A smartly-dressed party, led by a patriarch wearing a blazer and sharply creased slacks, enters and ostentatiously gestures in our direction.

"Do you know him?" I ask.

"Not personally," replies Benveniste, "but I know the type; top-end mafioso."

The smooth-faced villain summons our waiter, points to our table, and hands over an indeterminate number of dollars.

"Shouldn't we go?" I ask.

"Without sampling their world-famous espuma de quinua!" cries Benveniste. "Are you crazy? Let the bastard wait for his dinner."

The poor waiter looks like he is signing his own death warrant as he writes down our dessert order; soufflé de chocolate, espuma de quinua, piramide de limon.

Hedonists seem few and far between, as we trail after Benveniste, along the Jiron de la Union. It is the exploited of the earth who fill the dark streets and the plazas, flocking to the numerous churches, begging for miracles, while vultures take off from their roofs like warmed-up gargoyles. I keep an eye on my boy. You can't be too careful. In this year's text there's a scene in which a condor rises aloft bearing Tintin in its talons.

The next morning we are transported high into the Andes by other means.

"I hardly need tell you," says Benveniste, as Les Amis de Tintin congregate in the lobby of our hotel in Cusco, "that *The Prisoners of the Sun* was originally called *Le Temple du Soleil*. But what you may not know is that our splendid hotel stands alongside the real Temple of the Sun. It is an auspicious omen for what will be the scene, I trust, of a memorable conference."

To call the Hotel Libertador palatial is to do it justice, for it was originally built for Pizarro by Inca slaves, and called the Casa de los Cuatro Bustos. Its walls are decorated with paintings from the Escuela Cusquena, which mixes colonial and local styles. The synthesis is unproblematic in all save one; a nativity scene. Here the Madonna and child are off-centre, ceding pride of place to a native woman, who looks defiantly at the viewer, as if to say: "A curse on your house." Sure enough a handful of our compadres keel over, poleaxed by altitude sickness. The rest of us gulp mate de coca to ward off the evil eye. My son, who exhibits no ill-effects anyway, is tickled by the fact that the leaves suspended in his glass are the source of cocaine.

Even without the benefits of stupefying narcotics he stoically endures the conference papers, including a pedantic effort by an indigenous scholar who contrasts the *Prisoners of the Sun* with a later adventure, also set in South America. In the first, we are told, Hergé clearly privileges the Incas over the hybrid mestizos, implying that these naturales are the only authentic Peruvians. Unfortunately this infatuation with the exotic – which the speaker calls "occidentalism" – blinded him to the political realities. By the time he came to produce *Tintin and the Picaros*, however, the scales had dropped away. In this adventure the naturales are background figures, while the foreground is filled with cynical politicos, who care for nought but power. Hergé, it seemed, was echoing the observations of William Miller, an English fighter for Peruvian independence, who noted how the same Cusquenos who had formerly cheered the Spaniards, now feted the nascent republic.

"Your boy appears to be very patient," says Benveniste, "but I suspect he is quietly straining at the leash. Today, for a reward, I shall buy him lunch at Peru's best restaurant, where they will cut your throat if you speak of novoandino cuisine. You are welcome to join us, of course."

At the appointed hour he leads us through narrow passages lined on either side with perfectly fitting blocks of volcanic rock, through the Street of Seven Snakes, through dark alleys where Quechua-speaking women hawk papas rellenas. Finally he arrives at a battered door hanging on broken hinges, the sort you might find on a rabbit hutch. It opens upon a pitch black room with glowing embers at the far end.

Benveniste squeezes through the narrow gap, and beckons us to follow. As our eyes adjust we behold a filthy crone, resembling one of Lucifer's lesser minions, dismembering chickens. We skirt around this devilish scullery-maid, who remains oblivious to our presence, and enter an ill-lit corridor, full of fire-wood and sleeping dogs.

We step gingerly over the under-nourished beasts and find ourselves in a cramped court-yard, which is (in effect) an al fresco kitchen. Here cooks are at work: one stirs a large black pot; another squats before a stone slab, upon which she slices herbs with a blade the size and shape of a small Viking ship. Beyond these underlings is the dining room itself, if room is not a misnomer. Shafts of sunlight pour through the fractured roof, illuminating three or four refectory tables. Other members of the conference are conspicuous by their absence.

"As you see," says Benveniste, "this is a place for campesinos only."

He orders fried guinea pig. My son follows his example, though favouring the roast version. I prefer grilled trout with cumin and corn. Two blind musicians, led by a street urchin, enter and sing of unrequited love. Suddenly a man bursts in. One look and you know that "unrequited" is not part of his vocabulary. His features are those of a campesino, but his proportions are those of Charles Bronson. He swaggers as if he has spurs on his boots. You can almost hear them jangle. His hair is dark, greasy, and long. Shades protect his eyes. A black cloak covers his shoulders. Beneath is a purple shirt, split to the waist, exposing a massive silver crucifix and matching chain. His expansive smile of greeting reveals several gold teeth.

"Try not to stare, my friends, but you're now in the presence of Irbesartan, the local Mr Big," whispers Benveniste excitedly. "He controls the drug trade hereabouts. And everything else."

Bodyguards overtake the charismatic brute, so that they

have time to dust his chair, and wipe clean his knife and fork. His jeans are so tight it's a wonder he can sit. In his wake comes his woman, barefoot, blonde, bra-less, a ravaged beauty in her early twenties; probably an ex-hippie who came from the North, and stayed to bear his children (one of whom is in evidence), and get hooked on his production line.

Irbesartan ignores our presence until the guinea pigs are served. Benveniste's looks like road-kill, but my boy's stands upright on his plate, bald but otherwise intact.

Intact but dishonoured, having been penetrated by a bundle of pungent herbs. Everyone (not excluding Irbesartan) stares at my son, waiting for him to turn squeamish and ask a waiter to decapitate his lunch off-stage. Instead he rises to the occasion and (not without panache) performs the beheading himself.

"How is it?" asks Benveniste.

"Excellent," replies my son, "somewhere between a mallard and a rabbit."

The fish, I must say, is unexpectedly delicious.

"I have just made an unfortunate discovery," announces Benveniste, when we are ready to leave, "this establishment does not accept credit cards. Do you happen to have any cash?"

As I prepare to pay the bill I sense Irbesartan's malign concentration shift from my son to my open and very full wallet.

****

On the fourth morning of the conference, Les Amis de Tintin rise early in order to catch the first train to Machu Picchu. We assemble outside the Estacion San Pedro. The air is chill.

There is frost on the tiles, and white top hats on the heads of village women, already stocking the Mercado Central with their purple potatoes.

Benveniste distributes our tickets. For some reason he insists upon sitting next to my son. I take the only remaining space, beside our guide for the day.

"Buenos dias," he says, "my name in Benjamin Perez."

The exit from Cusco is so steep that the train is required to perform a series of switchbacks. My neighbour looks at me quizzically as the engine shunts back and forth.

"I know what you want to ask me," he says, "all Americans ask the same question as soon as they hear what I am called."

"But I'm not an American," I say.

"Nevertheless, you were plucking up your courage to ask, 'Are you Jewish?' Is Benjamin right?"

"Benjamin is right," I concede.

"The answer is no," he replies, "though your suspicion is not unjustified. After all, my name is half Benjamin Netanyahu, half Shimon Peres, candidates in Israel's last election but one. And it is also true that Benjamin is a very unusual name in Peru. My father was called Benjamin, as was his father, and his father before him. Who knows? Perhaps Benjamin the First was indeed a Jew. But, alas, not a brave one. Perhaps he saw the Inquisition burning his co-religionists, a practice that did not cease in Lima until the 1740s, and decided to change sides (unlike Professor Benveniste's forefathers, who never renounced their faith). Anyway, for better or worse, I am a Catholic now."

"But with Jewish roots," I add, "just as many of the houses in Cusco have Inca foundations."

"As I say," replies Benjamin Perez, "perhaps."

The train traverses mountainous panoramas, descends into the sacred valley of the Incas, then follows the fast-flowing Rio Urubamba all the way to Aguas Calientes.

"I always knew I'd end up in hot water," I say to my son as we disembark.

"My friends," says Benjamin Perez, as we stand amid the ruins of Machu Picchu, "Benjamin, your guide, will now inform you about this famous place, which the all-conquering Spaniards never found."

"Tell me," I say to my son, "what was so important that Benveniste had to monopolise you for the entire journey?"

"Nothing special," he replies.

Unlike me he has no fear of heights, so can venture places I dare not follow. Consequently I do not immediately register his extended absence. When I do the tumultuous gorges and towering peaks no longer seem objects of wonder, but deadly traps designed to swallow the beguiled wanderer.

"Have you seen my boy?" I ask Benveniste.

"Not recently," he replies.

"Have you seen my boy?" I ask Benjamin Perez.

"About an hour ago," he replies.

I know that my panic is unreasonable, but it is not irrational; opportunities to stumble and fall are legion. I begin to call his name.

"Don't worry," says Benveniste, "he'll show up. In fact, if you follow me, I've an idea where he might be."

We ascend a. steep stone stair-case, at the summit of which is a semi-circular building, much like the Temple of the Sun in Cusco. However, our destination is only half-way up; a meadow, upon which stand three wooden stakes, the sort that gave our guide's ancestor the willies. The grass is peopled, I note, with Les Amis de Tintin. To the left is a trapezoidal door, out of which emerge ersatz Incas leading two prisoners; none other than Captain Haddock and Tintin (not to mention Snowy). Haddock is represented by the most nautically bearded Ami, Tintin by my son.

"You bastard," I say to Benveniste, who slaps me on the back.

"Where better than Machu Picchu to restage the climax of our chosen text?" he says. "If you look closely at the relevant frames, you'll observe that Hergé's location bears a more than coincidental resemblance to this very spot."

Like *Explorers on the Moon*, *Prisoners of the Sun* is a sequel. At the end of the first volume scatty Professor Calculus is abducted by South American aborigines, and spirited away to Peru. In the second Tintin (accompanied as ever by faithful Snowy and Captain Haddock) tracks his missing friend to the Incas' last stronghold, only to be captured (along with his friends). All three (four, if you count Snowy) are accused of sacrilege, and sentenced to death by fire. As a concession the condemned men are permitted to nominate the day on which they are to die. Today, it seems.

Captain Haddock and my son are bound to the outer stakes. The middle one awaits the third captive.

"Captain, there's Professor Calculus," cries my son (who makes a convincing Tintin). "Old Cuthbert, after our long search! Here he comes. They're going to tie him up beside us."

What the Incas do not know is that a total eclipse of the sun is predicted at any minute. Knowledge available to Tintin, of course.

"O God of the Sun, sublime Pachacamac, display thy power, I implore thee!" cries his stand-in. "If this sacrifice is not thy will, hide thy shining face from us!"

At this point we are required to use our imagination, and accept that the excitable extras are apparently fleeing darkness at noon.

"It's a pity you couldn't have performed the show on August 11," I say to the star on the journey back to Cusco. I am still astounded that my son could have been involved in such an extravaganza behind my back; astounded, proud, but also betrayed.

****

"Are you nervous?" asks my son.

"Not really," I say.

"Good luck, anyway," he says.

"Where are you sitting?" I say.

"Over there," he says.

"See you later," I say.

Benveniste summons me to the platform. I acknowledge the audience, and place my paper on the lectern.

"Tintin an antisemite?" I begin. "Perish the thought. If only . . . But we are scholars, here to turn stones, not to brush unpleasantries under the carpet. Georges Remi – whom the world knows as Hergé – was born into the bourgeoisie, the Belgian bourgeoisie, compared to which other bourgeoisies are bohemian. Strange mutant off-shoots wore its uniform, and subverted it from within. Hergé was never one of those. Far from being an iconoclast, he remained too loyal to a sinister eminence grise; Father Robert Wallez. This sworn enemy of Freemasons, Bolsheviks, and Jews, (declared a 'friend of fascism' by no less than Mussolini himself), was the man who launched Hergé's career as a cartoonist, making him (in effect) Tintin's god-father. He also doubled as a surrogate father-in-law; pairing his protégé with his secretary. It is hardly a surprise to find the cleric's hatred of Bolshevism reflected in the young reporter's first adventure, *Tintin in the Land of the Soviets*, just as his views on colonialism are apparent in the second, *Tintin in the Congo*.

"Nor was Father Wallez Hergé's only unfortunate influence. He became friendly with Leon Degrelle, Belgium's home-grown dictator manqué, and (I regret to say) even illustrated one of his political pamphlets. In later years Degrelle fancied himself as Hergé's inspiration, and wanted to call his memoirs, 'Tintin chez Hitler'. Need more? There is plenty, alas.

"*The Shooting Star* was serialized in *Le Soir* (a collaborationist newspaper) in 1942. You are all familiar with the plot, but let me remind you of a few frames that have been excluded from more recent editions. As the eponymous meteorite hurtles towards earth (destined to destroy it, according to some astronomers), two Jewish shopkeepers (you can guess what they look like) find a silver lining; at least they won't have to pay their creditors. (In real life they would soon be forced to wear the yellow star). The prophets of doom turn out to be wrong; the star misses the earth, though a fragment breaks off and plunges into the sea. A race to recover it ensues. Tintin sails in one ship, accompanied by German scientists. The other flies the Stars and Stripes, and is financed by a crooked banker named Blumenstein (you can guess what he looks like).

"As if all this weren't bad enough, it is alleged that Hergé drew antisemitic cartoons for the *Brusseler Zeitung*, which he supposedly covered up by having the offending pages ripped from the national archive. I stress the word alleged. Be that as it may, at the war's end Hergé was accused of collaboration, and was fortunate to spend only a day in jail."

I pause, taking time to wink at my son.

"Once, in a fit of rage," I continue, "my mother said to my father: 'You'd have co-operated with the Nazis, if only they would have let you!' She was understandably exasperated by his conciliatory ways, but she was being unfair. My father was an old-fashioned liberal, not an appeaser. When it really mattered he stood up to be counted. He was one of those who held the line when Oswald Mosley and his Blackshirts tried to march through London's East End. In brief, he knew the difference between good and evil. The question we must now ask ourselves, ladies and gentlemen is: did Hergé?

"There are indications – even before the war – that he was toying with the idea of breaking free from the oppressive influence of Father Wallez. The evidence may be found in *Tintin au Pays de l'Or Noir*, which began to appear at the end of the '30s. Seeking to solve the mystery of unstable petrol Tintin sails for Haifa (location, I need hardly add, of next year's Congress), where he is promptly arrested by the British authorities (who think he is a spy), and immediately snatched from their grasp by Jewish terrorists (who appear – with unwitting irony – wearing gas masks). However, the faces beneath are hardly antisemitic caricatures. They belong to muscular fighters, who look comfortable wearing holsters. These Jewish tough-guys have rescued Tintin from the military police, because they think he is one of their own; a certain Finkelstein (later to be redubbed Salomon Goldstein). An understandable error, given that Finkelstein is Tintin's double, not excepting the trade-mark quiff. A coincidence first pointed out to me – I am pleased to add – by our conference chairman, Professor Gabriel Benveniste.

"What is going on, mes amis? How can an alleged

antisemite allow his favourite to be mistaken for a Jew? Impossible! So let us consider the opposite proposition; that Hergé was actually a philosemite. In which case he would have seen Finkelstein and his co-religionists as role-models, and their revolt a metaphor for his own. What other explanation is there for the strange equation? Unfortunately the new adventure – and his own bid for freedom – was curtailed by the invasion of Belgium. Whereupon Hergé meekly submitted to the zeitgeist, thereby doing great harm to his reputation, and his psyche. Israel gained its independence in 1948. It took Hergé several more years, not to mention a personal crisis, and a period of Jungian analysis, to achieve effective adulthood, to be his own man."

I look to my son for applause, but his seat is empty.

My son's defection is a disappointment, even a blow. Soon it becomes a cause for concern.

"What are you planning this time?" I ask Benveniste. But he denies any knowledge of my son's whereabouts.

"I enjoyed your talk," he adds, "very piquant."

But I am not interested in compliments, false or otherwise.

"Are you sure you don't know where he is?" I ask.

"I would tell you if I did," he says. "Permit me to offer you some advice instead. He is a young man, with a young man's curiosity. And there are many women in Cusco who would be happy to satisfy it. Let him discover them for himself. You must allow him more – what's the word? – more latitude."

I know that Benveniste is right, but my fears refuse to curl up and slumber. I check my son's room, the restaurant, the bars, even the toilets (perhaps he has diarrhoea, not unknown hereabouts), until I am more or less certain that he is not in the hotel. I retrace our usual route to the Plaza de Armas, and make straight for his favourite haunt, a cosmopolitan cafe, from where he loves to watch the world go by.

Trotamundos is full of noise and excitable adolescents, but not the one I am looking for. I turn back, trying to convince myself that he will be waiting for me in the hotel. There is a welcoming committee, but it consists only of Benveniste and the hotel manager (clutching a glass of pisco). Both are white-faced.

"You were right to be concerned," says Benveniste. "There has been a phone call. It is catastrophic news. I'm afraid that Irbesartan has kidnapped your boy."

I can clearly visualize the cruel words in a speech bubble above Benveniste's head. I long to reach out with an eraser and replace them with kinder sentiments. But I am unable to move. For a moment I fear that I am losing control of my body.

"Drink this, señor," says the hotel manager, holding the pisco to my lips.

I am guided to a sofa in the hotel lobby.

"Altitude sickness?" asks the sea-dog who played Captain Haddock at Machu Picchu. "Don't fret. It could happen to any of us."

I don't respond and he eventually wanders away.

"Has anyone informed the police?" I ask at length.

"It is not a good idea, señor," cautions the hotel manager. "Most are in the pockets of the desperadoes. The exceptions are often trigger-happy, and many get hurt as a consequence; both the good and the bad."

"So what is to be done?" I ask desperately.

"Listen," says Benveniste, "like many in this god-forsaken country I have an insurance policy to cover such an eventuality. It is underwritten by Lloyd's of London. With your permission I will contact them immediately."

I nod assent. Benveniste returns from the manager's office beaming triumphantly.

The following night an outlandish figure shows up in the dining room, where I am sitting with Benveniste (needless to say I can't swallow a thing). A trio of diminutive musicians in ponchos is playing El Condor Pasa on flute and pan-pipes. Others feel wistful, and imagine the giant bird hovering amid Andean peaks; I can only see my helpless boy in its clutches.

There is no mistaking the identity of the newcomer. Benveniste beckons him to our table.

"How do you do," the man says, extending his hand. "My name is Thompson – with a p."

"Please be seated," says Benveniste.

Am I going crazy, or is our visitor really wearing a bowler hat, and does he really have a toothbrush moustache?

"First things first," he says, opening a notepad. "Which of you is the boy's father?"

I raise my hand.

"What is your son's name?" he asks.

"Abie," I reply.

"Does his mother know what has happened?" he asks.

"I doubt it," I reply. "She is dead. As is mine. In fact there are no women in our lives, unless you count Bianca Castafiore."

"Who is she?" he asks.

"No one," I say, "it's a joke."

"It would be better if you confined yourself to the facts," he says. Obediently I tell him Abie's age, describe his appearance, and try to remember what he was wearing when he was taken (was it only yesterday?).

"There are a few things you should bear in mind when the kidnappers contact you again, as they surely will," says Thompson. "Before anything else you must demand some proof of life. Get them to ask your son a question only he can answer. His mother's maiden name, something like that. The reason is simple; you want to be sure that you are dealing with the right gang. Also – there is no pleasant way of putting this – you need to know that you are not haggling over a corpse. Unfortunately, there are times when the evidence of possession can be a little gruesome. Usually a minor body part; an ear, a toe, a finger or two. If you are required to pick up a packet containing any of the aforementioned, never do so alone. Always travel with a companion, who must remain in the car and keep the engine running. Kidnappers have been known to strike twice."

An image comes to mind unbidden; a painting by that other famous Belgian, René Magritte, which also features a hand in a box. I wonder why no scholars have remarked upon the obvious similarities between Hergé's incompetent detectives, Thompson and Thomson, and his eccentric co-national. There is definitely something surrealistic about the dim duo's modus operandi. I pray that the real life Thompson is more efficient.

"As to the negotiations themselves," continues Thompson, "it is vital to set limits before you start; to establish a financial strategy, if you prefer. Since you do not actually have a policy with us, it is up to you to decide how much you can afford to pay. In any case open with a much lower offer. The kidnappers, of course, will demand the earth. Don't panic. Always remember, you are the only buyer in the market. In time they will come down, and you will go up. As soon as you have reached an agreement I shall facilitate the payment and co-ordinate the exchange. All that remains to be done is to elect a go-between, a chappie you can trust. A Cusqueno if possible. What is essential is that he be slow to anger. He must be polite to the kidnappers at all times, whatever the provocation. In no circumstances should he try to trade insults with Irbesartan."

"Look no further for your champion," says Benveniste.

He certainly seems the obvious candidate; proud descendant of a family that had kept the faith through centuries of vicissitude. Like his ancestors he is stubborn, unyielding, and – I'd guess – heroic.

"I am honoured by your offer," I say, "but I must look elsewhere. Benjamin Perez is the one who will save my boy. Precisely because he lacks all your fine qualities. He is the man the moment demands; a man of compromise, not confrontation."

****

Benjamin Perez is a reluctant hero. Not because of fears for his safety, but because he dreads the consequence of failure.

"I shall be at your side day and night," I say, "the responsibility will be mine alone."

Irbesartan kidnapped Abie on 5 August. Thompson arrived on the sixth. On the seventh, the last day of the conference, Benjamin Perez receives the first demand from the bandits.

"What are they saying?" I ask.

"They are obviously using a public telephone," replies Benjamin Perez, "which means that there is much extraneous noise. But if I have heard correctly they are expecting one million dollars."

"They are crazy," I say, taken aback, "they must think I've found Red Rackham's Treasure at the bottom of my garden."

Remembering Thompson's advice I instruct him to offer two hundred and fifty thousand. By 10 August, the day my son was expected in Cornwall, the sum of three hundred thousand dollars has been agreed.

"If all goes well," says Thompson, "the swap will take place tomorrow, the day of the eclipse."

****

Hergé died while working on *Tintin and Alph-Art*, making it the ageless journalist's last adventure. The manuscript was published just as it was; unfinished, twenty pages short of the inevitable 62.

Suspicious of the goings-on in a darkened villa, Tintin decides to investigate with the aid of a flash-light. In a vast room he discovers works by Léger, Renoir, Picasso, Gauguin and Modigliani. The paint on the Modigliani is still wet. It is a fake, as are all the others. But before Tintin can report his discovery, he is surprised by the villa's owner and two gun-toting henchmen.

"Well, my friend," says the villain, "we're going to pour liquid polyester over you; you'll become an expansion signed by César and then authenticated by a well-known expert. Then it will be sold, perhaps to a museum, or perhaps to a rich collector . . . You should be glad, your corpse will be displayed in a museum. And no one will ever suspect that the work, which could be entitled 'Reporter', constitutes the last resting place of young Tintin."

The final frame shows Tintin being marched at gunpoint

to his execution: "On your feet! Get moving. It's time for you to be turned into a 'César' . . ."

Can it be that Tintin will really end up like a fly in amber? Or will Snowy find Captain Haddock, and the pair of loyal helpmates arrive in the nick of time? The reader, aware of the conventions of the comic-book, knows which of the two possibilities is the likelier. But the incomplete nature of the work leaves a nagging doubt; salvation is not inevitable. And so Tintin takes his bow, forever poised on the cusp of redemption or eternal youth. And as night falls on Cusco I picture my son in the same tight spot, wondering what the morrow will hold.

SHYLOCK MUST DIE

WHEN MARCO POLO sailed home from the East, he returned with many novelties. Among them were manuscripts written in unreadable pictograms on strips of palm leaf. Each strip was about a metre in length, and as wide as a thumb from tip to base. They were bound together by cord, which was threaded through holes on either end of the leaves. On the top and the bottom were thicker slats of wood, which served as protective covers.

As soon as merchants began to trade with China, they brought back many more of these manuscripts, some twice the size of Polo's originals. Poor Venetians hung these impenetrable stories on their walls in place of tapestries. My father had a brighter idea: he hung his over the windows. Later he devised a way of altering the angle of the leaves, so that he could control the amount of light that entered his office. He liked the chiaroscuro effect that this created. It resembled life, he said, in which some things are revealed and others hidden. He called his invention a Venetian blind. When friends asked him how they too could make a Venetian blind his answer was always the same: You poke his eyes out.

"As far as our family is concerned," he said to me, "the

more blind Venetians the better." He made his living by seeing what they could not see, by penetrating darkness and mysteries on their behalf. He was their private eye.

When I was nineteen he passed on one of his cases to me. He said it would be easy, and would provide an instructive introduction to the profession.

It is a commonplace that a man never forgets his first time with a woman. I remember my first client in the same way. Signora X was not a beauty, but I retain the image of her sitting in my office in the late afternoon. It hangs in my memory like a portrait by Titian. The sun squinted through the blinds my father had fashioned, and transformed her body into a staircase of light, which my impolite eyes ascended. I vowed inwardly to defend her against all enemies. The foremost of whom turned out to be her husband.

She told a sad tale of betrayal and obstinacy, while tears slithered down her cheeks like glass snails (an effusion she ascribed to the sun). In short she had married a pig. Of course he did not regard himself as such. On the contrary, he thought of himself as a pious Jew. He did not beat her, but every morning after prayers, he cursed God for giving him such a shrewish wife. He claimed that was why he no longer lay with her. But she was convinced that he was keeping a mistress somewhere in the Ghetto. She confronted him with her suspicions, which he did not deny, and yet he refused to offer her a divorce, to grant her the infamous get, without which she would be unable to remarry. In despair she commissioned me to find irrefutable proof of his infidelity.

I laughed when I set eyes upon this Romeo. He was as bald as a ball of mozzarella. It seemed to me that he was lucky to have found a wife, let alone a mistress. But he did have one. And to prove it was childishly simple. The cleric I chose as my witness was Rabbi Leone Modena. We stood together beneath the woman's casement, which she made no attempt to shutter, and watched as she entertained my client's unfaithful spouse. He turned out to have as little backbone as he had hair. When confronted by the rabbinical authorities he burst into tears. His wife got her get. I believe she has since remarried. My father congratulated me on the success of my initial investigation, but cautioned me against over-confidence. Of course I did not heed his advice, and came to bitterly regret it.

****

My next client was none other than Rabbi Leone Modena himself, a man of wisdom, and some ten years my senior. He had been impressed, he said, by the exemplary discretion I had shown in my dealings with Signora X. He took a seat. The light wrapped itself around him like a prayer shawl.

"Imagine me a Sicilian ruffian," he said, "quite prepared to cut out your tongue if you should gossip about his predicament."

I replied that such imaginings were redundant, since the code of my profession counted the office of a private eye on a par with the confessional of a priest.

"Are there many private eyes in Italy?" said the Rabbi.

"At least two," I said. "Tubal Sr and his son. To the best of my knowledge."

"My predicament is this," said the Rabbi: "I owe money to a loan shark. You are thinking such a creature is as kosher as a lobster. But to whom else could I turn? To a member of my congregation? Usurers are always Jews, loan sharks are anything but. This was their advantage to me. But they have drawbacks too: usurers are talmudic in their appreciation of contractual obligations, whereas loan sharks favour muscle and steel. One is hated, the other is both hated and feared. And I am greatly afeared."

I asked the obvious question: "Why did you need the money?"

"I have a weakness, which my wife calls an addiction," said the Rabbi. "I am a gambler. But a very poor one, alas, and my losses multiplied. Thanks to the loan shark I have paid off those creditors. Only to find myself in deeper waters. The loan shark has bigger appetites, which I cannot satisfy. Last week his myrmidons took my son – the apple of my eye – and threatened that I would not see him again unless I cleared my debt – which increases by the hour – within the week."

"The loan shark is acting outside the law," I said, "why not report him to the authorities."

The Rabbi laughed: "I should report him to himself?"

"Can you meet his demands?" I said.

"Only thanks to Shylock," he said. "He is one of us. His profession may stink like yesterday's fish, but he is a mensch."

"What do you want of me?" I said.

"To help redeem my first born," said Rabbi Leone Modena.

Two nights later we met again by the Ghetto's locked gate, and bribed the guard to let us trespass. Calle Vallaresso, our destination, was full of gambling dens, out of which rakes and prostitutes tumbled like dice. Our rendez-vous was at its darker end, deserted and dead-quiet, save for the sound of the water gently slapping the banks of the stinking canal.

"Young Tubal," said the Rabbi as we waited, "you must prepare yourself for a shock. After I collected the money from Shylock, I begged the Eternal One for the strength to resist temptation. But in his wisdom he turned a deaf ear."

"How much remains?" I said.

"About half of what is needed," he said.

"In which case your boy is in grave danger," I said.

"I trust that the Almighty will spare my son, as he did Isaac," said the Rabbi, "perhaps with your assistance."

Out of the darkness three figures emerged; two men nearing thirty, flanking a boy not yet thirteen: Zebulum. The man on the right was holding a lantern, which paved the canal with cobbles of gold. Because they were dealing with Jews they did not bother to hide their faces.

"Here is your boy," said the man with the lantern. "Where is the money?"

"Here is one half," I said.

"And the other?" said the man with the lantern.

"You will have that tomorrow," I said, handing over the satchel.

"Antonio," said the man without the lantern, "these Jews take us for fools."

So saying he silently slipped a stiletto from its scabbard and sliced open the boy's belly, as if he were a trout. I will not describe the Rabbi's lamentations, which I hope one day to forget.

"Bassanio," said his partner, "what have you done?"

"I have taught the Christ-killers a lesson," said the murderer. "For half the money they get the boy, but drained of blood; that is forfeit, for this earthly and that other eternal debt."

Shylock, on the other hand, immediately wrote off the ducats he had advanced the Rabbi. "What," he said, "I should slaughter another of his chicks?"

From time to time I heard of Rabbi Leone Modena, who

had become a wanderer; some claimed that they had seen him play the fiddle at a wedding, others that they had seen him preach a sermon. Some claimed to have read books that he had written, among them an autobiography, and a polemic against gambling. Readers may have been converted, but not the writer: he gambled away his daughters' dowries. There were rumours that his wife had gone mad. "If tragedy strikes, if fortune turns ill," he was reported to have said. "What can I do? Let me imagine I lost it at play."

I could never forgive myself for what happened to the Rabbi's boy, though I did not know what I could have done to prevent the butchery. But if only I had done something, I would not have felt so bad. The murderer acted with impunity, because he guessed – correctly – that the Rabbi's bodyguard was unarmed. So I took to carrying a dagger. The weapon sent out a message: If you prick us, you too will bleed.

****

Years passed. I was no longer Young Tubal, but Tubal proper. I married, and – thank God – we had sons. Others, like Shylock, were not so fortunate. Near my father's age, he was blessed with only one child, a daughter, before his beloved wife, Leah, had been taken from him. She died of the influenza. If she had lived she might have saved him from the folly that destroyed his good name. But she was not spared.

It began one Saturday, after services in the synagogue.

"Shabbat shalom, Shylock," I said, kissing his cheek.

He looked me in the eye. "Business is good, is it not, Tubal?" he said.

I nodded: "Sinners are never in short supply."

"In which case you will have no problem in lending me three thousand ducats," he said.

"Has the world turned upside-down?" I said. "Have lenders all become borrowers?"

"I have such a scheme, Tubal," he said, "that should it come to pass will make good an ancient grudge. But to finance it I need not credit, which I have in plenty, but gold to raise up the gross." Seeing that I was not yet convinced he added: "It will be an act of healing, a tikkun olam."

"The Ghetto is full of usurers," I said, "why have you come to me?"

"Because you are one of those who suffered the wound," he said, "one of those who are not yet fully healed."

Then he told me his plan.

"You are familiar with Antonio, of course," said Shylock, pacing back and forth, "that honourable man, that saint among merchants. When I pass that paragon on the Rialto I always step aside, to evade his phlegm, or the kicks he aims to clear unclean dogs like me from his path. But yesterday was different: in place of kicks there were handshakes. It was as if I had suddenly become human in his eyes. Of course there was a reason: he needed three thousand ducats. His best-beloved Bassanio is to go a-courting, and must fit out a ship. I agreed, Tubal, I agreed. Said that I only wanted his friendship, and his love. Said that I would let him have it without a minim of interest. Then I said, as if in jest, that all I required, should the bond become forfeit, was a pound of his flesh."

I said that he was mad, and that I would not advance him so much as a ducat.

"Listen carefully, Tubal" he said, grabbing my gaberdine

in both his hands. "We both know that Antonio is a murderer. We also know that no judgment will ever be passed against him in Venice. Nor is my scheme likely to alter that. For he has three or four argosies on the high seas, any one of which will make good the debt three-fold. But if it should happen that all four are destroyed, then surely we can detect God's hand at work. It will be a sign that I am acting with His blessing, that His hand is guiding mine as I finally extract justice for Zebulum. Ha! With the court's permission! Can you not acknowledge the beauty of it? And, yes, the irony, the blessed irony of it. They will curse me as a blood-thirsty Jew, as I cut out Antonio's heart, little knowing that I am the agent of divine justice. Ho, Tubal, to hell with them all."

What else could I do? I promised him the money.

****

Shylock collected the ducats on Monday. On Tuesday he handed them to Antonio. By Wednesday he was my client.

Also on Tuesday – the night of his departure for Belmont – Bassanio organized a farewell dinner, to which he invited Shylock. Why did he invite Shylock? Perhaps because Shylock's money – actually my money – had enabled the whole enterprise; because he was the key, the sine qua non. But why – in God's name – did Shylock accept the invitation, that is the bigger mystery? Had he not, by his own account, rebuffed a previous invitation with the words, "I will buy with you, sell with you, talk with you, walk with you, and so following: but I will not eat with you, drink with you, nor pray with you"?

"What changed your mind, Shylock?" I said.

He was sitting in the client's chair. There was no sun to

offer light – it was after midnight – only a single flame that danced on the head of a candle. But it brought no illumination. As shutters make private the secret life of a room, so Shylock's hands concealed his face, and the emotions that showed upon it.

"Stop torturing me with your questions, Tubal," he said, his voice emerging through the bars of his fingers. "Do you think I have not asked myself the same question a thousand thousand times? Why did I go to the house of that prodigal son of a pig? Why did I not heed my dream that seemed particularly ill-omened? It prompted me to warn Jessica to lock all doors and casements, and not to show herself at any window. But it did not persuade me to stay. My last words to her still ring in my ears, 'Do as I bid you, shut doors after you, fast bind, fast find'."

His hands formed fists and banged upon his forehead.

"But of course when I came home she was nowhere to be found," he said. "I ran through the streets, half hysterical – a man turned mother – but found no help from onlookers, only insolence and mockery. What did Lucan call our children? Hostages given to fortune, or something like. Then it struck me that the invitation to dine with Bassanio was but a ruse to draw me from the house, leaving my daughter – my Jessica – alone and unprotected, easy prey to his minions. And then I remembered what he and Antonio had done to poor Zebulum."

The chair could no longer contain him.

"They will hold her until the day that Antonio's debt comes due," he said, as he staggered to the window. "And if – by some miracle – it should be forfeit, they will offer to sell my daughter back to me for three thousand ducats."

Parting the Venetian blind, he looked down upon the

Fondamenta di Cannaregio, and at the oases of light beyond. "She is out there somewhere, Tubal," he said. "Can you find her for me? She's all I have left of Leah. Tubal, you must find my little girl."

"I will do my best," I said. "I will promise you that. But it is no good running from door to door like an unhoused lunatic. There must be method in our madness. Have you informed the authorities of Jessica's disappearance?"

Shylock groaned, and slumped back into the empty chair. Then he laughed. "Think you otherwise?" he said. "Am I not a man of the law? I went straight to the Duke. He looked at me, as if I were a land-rat strayed into his palace, but he did agree to accompany me to the port, where Bassanio's vessel was docked. Too late, too late. It was already under sail. Antonio was still at the quayside, watching it diminish. He swore to the Duke that Jessica was not on board. Then he said – with a smirk, I swear – that my amorous – that's the very word he used, 'amorous', as if my daughter were a common whore – that my amorous daughter had been seen in a gondola with a knave called Lorenzo. But they could not tell me where to find her. Nor why she had not come home. Could it be true, Tubal, that she has abandoned her father, and her faith for a creature like that?"

"God forbid," I said.

Shylock arose again, and – in his misery and despair – hit the wall, not with his fists, but with his head.

"Instead of knocking your brains out," I said, "perhaps you could use them to recall anything out of the ordinary that may have occured yesterday."

"Not a thing, not a thing," said Shylock, "except that my man, Launcelot, left my service to enter that of Bassanio."

"You call that nothing?" I said. "He could have betrayed

the secrets of your house to Bassanio's men, and even provided them with a key."

"The man is a clown, Tubal," said Shylock, "who thinks with his stomach. That is why I let Bassanio have him, so that he would eat through his purse, as a horse eats through a nose-bag of hay."

"The fact that he played the clown for you, does not mean that he is a clown for others," I said. "I'll wager he knows something."

Shylock was ready to storm Bassanio's residence at once, but I persuaded him to remain patient until sunrise, at which time the gates of the Ghetto would be unlocked.

We made ourselves known to Bassanio's man, and Launcelot was summoned. He had brains, but no skill in dissembling. When he denied any knowledge of Jessica's disappearance, it was evident to us both that he was lying. With his new master absent on matrimonial business, there was no authority to prevent us from frog-marching him back to the Ghetto.

He was a big man, but he was built of fat, not muscle, and he lacked the strength to resist us. He kept calling upon his father to come to his aid, but his father was either not in earshot, or unwilling to take the risk. The hardest part was persuading him to mount the stairs to my office. I think he feared for his life. Once there we bound him to a chair. As soon as breath returned to his body he begain to wail: "God protect me from the Jews!"

Shylock was in no mood to comfort him.

"If you don't want to die," he said, "tell me what Bassanio and his band of thieves have done with my daughter."

"Your daughter was kind," said Launcelot, "ergo she could not have been yours."

Shylock, in a rage, began to box Launcelot's ears.

"What good will that do?" I said.

Shylock stared at me, the ungutted candle reflected in both eyes, as if his very soul were aflame within him. "Tubal," he said, "I fear you will never unsheath that dagger you wear so boldly, even when your blood is hot. So give it here. Mine is near boiling."

"Do you hear that Launcelot?" I said. "Shall I do as he demands?"

The fat man began to bawl, as a baby does when it is hungry.

"Spare me, good sirs," he cried, "for all I did was act the go-between. Jessica – I mean your daughter – handed me a letter and a ducat, and bade me give the former to a fine fellow named Lorenzo, who was to dine with you at Bassanio's. Lorenzo, for his part, ordered me to deliver an immediate reply. I was to tell your daughter that he would not fail her. In what I did not know, though it is no secret now."

"So it is true," said Shylock, "my daughter has eloped with a Christian?"

I approached Launcelot.

"Wither did they flee," I said, "if not to Belmont?"

He remained silent. My hand snatched at the hilt of my dagger. It was an involuntary act, which frightened me almost as much as it frightened Launcelot.

"Genoa," he said. "I overheard Lorenzo boast to his cronies that he was taking his new bride there."

I lifted the dagger meaning to sever Launcelot's bonds. But he did not arise, or even thank me, for my gesture had caused him to faint dead away.

"Bride?" said Shylock. "Woe piles upon woe." But he ever was a practical man. "Why Genoa?" he said.

I shook my head.

"You must go there, Tubal," he said, "and redeem my daughter."

I explained that I was not now – nor ever had been – in the redemption business. I was a private eye, pure and simple. I handed Shylock the usual contract.

"It'll cost you two hundred ducats a day plus expenses," I said.

****

My wife packed my bag. My children – bless them – begged for presents. I put on my hat, made of rust-coloured felt, wrapped an orange kerchief around the crown, kissed my wife and my children, then quit the house, the Ghetto, and – within the hour – Venice itself.

How pampered are its citizens, who travel everywhere by gondola. It is true that putrid smells often arise from the canals, but their waters are mostly placid, and a cooling breeze is frequently in evidence. I was soon to discover that the experience of a traveller on land is very different. My chaise was cramped, the road uneven, the air more dust than ether. If the blinds were lowered the heat within grew one degree short of Gehenna, but if they were left raised foul odours – discharged at regular intervals from the rear ends of over-worked and ill-fed horses – found entry.

I recognised my travelling companion as the very merchant who had gleefully broadcast Shylock's public distress, when my friend first discovered that his daughter was missing. He recognised me too, if not by name, then as a Jew, and acted as if the only visible part of me were my hat, which advertised my tribe.

At Verona, the first of countless stages, the horses were replaced; likewise I exchanged my tell-tale hat for a non-descript barrette noire. As soon as our journey resumed, Solanio – for it was he – suddenly became affable, and began to converse with me as if a different person were now seated beside him. He observed that the digestion of the new horses was no improvement upon that of their predecessors, but took pains to assure me that his suffering – he used the word "suffering" – would be well-rewarded, when he finally presented his merchandise from the Far East before the cities of the West. Every time the vetturino failed to properly navigate a half-buried boulder he winced, not from discomfort, but from fear that his precious Chinese porcelain should come to grief, and with it his expectations. I cursed my bones, but could not find it within myself to wish him ill. He too was travelling all the way to Genoa: the further from Venice, the higher the prices.

After several days of unlooked-for intimacy the chaise crested a summit, and we beheld a sight. The prospect was not serene, as the prospect Venice is serene; but it was superb in a way that Venice is not superb. From our vantage point we beheld an amphitheatre of civilization, a vast city that plunged towards a great bay, into which molos extended like the pincers of crabs. Between these jettes ships rocked at anchor; most single-masted skips, but some three-masted galleons, provisioned for voyages of discovery.

The city itself seemed to consist entirely of palaces and churches. What made the sight so stupendous was the vertiginious quality of the ground upon which the buildings were constructed. They seemed to stand proud in defiance of all known natural laws. It appeared as if the city of Genoa was not the product of architects and engineers, but was dreamed into being by the collective will of its inhabitants. Without their concentrated energy Genoa would be nothing more than rubble and dust.

On a promontory at the far end of the Cape del Faro, the ancient lighthouse pulsed like a heartbeat. The Gulf was a deep ultramarine, upon which wavelets sat like fringes of icing sugar. From our lofty mountain peak all looked beautiful and good, as the world had seemed to God on the first days of creation, but I knew too well that closer inspection would reveal repetition of behaviour that brought down the Great Flood upon humanity. I knew too that somewhere in that tumultuous city was Jessica. Perhaps a captive, more likely a willing convert. What I didn't know was how to find her.

Soon the chill and resinous air of the heights was replaced by more maritime odours, and not long afterwards we spotted white-washed cottages spaced amongst orchards of olive trees. As we descended further we entered a sweet realm of orange groves and villas, and then the gates of the great city itself.

We ran parallel with what can only be described as a palisade of palaces, and then disembarked at our final stage, where porters vied for our business. Solanio had plenty of employment to offer, while I had nothing to carry but a single bag. We took our leave of one another, not without some regret. He proceeded to a well-lit auberge frequented by other merchants, while I made my way down darker alleys.

The inn I happened upon was accessed by a steep flight of ill-made steps. Reaching the top I discovered a trap-door, which opened upon a public room. I entered head and shoulders first, and immediately put an end to all conversation. Eight men were seated at a long table. All stared at me as if I were a demon newly discharged from the underworld. I asked if the proprietor was present, and thereby acquired accommodation. It would have been better for me if I had not, but so much worse for the bedbugs.

After dinner – a crime against the palate – I wandered back to the auberge on the Via Dante where Solanio was bedded, in hopes of catching him afoot. I was not disappointed. He was clearly well-acquainted with the city, and he all but ended my surveillance on two or three occasions, but I managed to stay on his trail until he reached his goal in the Piazza Embriaci.

Once the square had been dominated by a castle decreed by the knight, Guglielmo degli Embriaci, whose seige-engine was supposed to have facilitated the capture of Jerusalem in 1099. But time and neglect had delapidated its mighty walls, and all that now remained of it was the Torre degli Embriaci, at the foot of which was a rectangle of light. Solanio strode boldly into it, like a Christian entering heaven, and I slipped in behind, like his shadow.

As I had always suspected, heaven turned out to be a gambler's paradise. Candles were everywhere, like ghosts with burning hair, their passion multiplied a thousand-fold by well-placed mirrors. In this temple of fortune – both good and ill – dice were rolled, cards dealt, wheels spun, and purses cut. The saved emitted whoops of joy, while the damned groaned as only the damned know how.

Among the latter, arm-in-arm like newly-weds, were Lorenzo and Jessica, he slicked and oiled, she flushed with wine and hot-blood. I slithered through the crowd until I happened upon a dimly-lit niche, from where I could observe Jessica unobserved. Solanio, meanwhile, approached his friends, both of whom embraced him as if he were a hostage new-released from a distant captivity. Solanio must have asked if luck were with them, for both shook their heads vigorously. Then this third party placed his hand on Lorenzo's arm, and drew him slightly aside, perhaps to advise him that a Venetian Jew had been his travelling companion.

At the same time Jessica waged fourscore ducats on a roll of the dice, and was instantly divorced from them all. She turned over her purse, and became desperate when no coins tumbled out. Seeing her behave in so petulant a manner I recalled some remarks of Rabbi Leone Modena, to the effect that there is no better test for human character than the way the gambler reveals himself – or herself – at play. Jessica was also revealing herself in other ways, I could not help but note. Her gown was cut low, after the fashion of gentile courtesans, so that each of her breasts was seen to be in possession of a roughed eye-brow, petulantly arched.

I reckoned the possibilities of wresting her away from Lorenzo and his ally, and considered them remote. Made remoter still by the fact that Jessica showed no inclination to be elsewhere, or any sign that she would welcome my intervention. On the contrary she would probably scream blue murder, whereupon her companions would likely denounce me as a Jew, and I would be hung from the nearest perpendicular by the mob.

Patience seemed to be my only weapon, and I spent the following day trailing Solanio as he disposed of his oriental wares. When night fell he returned – as anticipated – to the Torre degli Embriaci, a far richer man than he had been when he arose. Lorenzo was awaiting him there, but of Jessica there was no sign. It was apparent that Lorenzo was also richer than he had appeared yesterday, or had recently become one of fortune's darlings. But where was Shylock's darling? Her absence was beginning to alarm me, and I comforted myself with the supposition that she had renounced gambling, or feeling unwell, had taken to her bed.

At the close of proceedings I chose to follow Lorenzo to his lodgings on the ill-named Via San Lorenzo; an undertaking hampered by clouds that obscured the stars, rain that curtained the streets, and ground that had grown treacherous underfoot. I offered the proprietor of the establishment – a man who seemed built out of blubbery quoits – a respectable bribe, and learned in return that the pair had left in the morning, but that only one – the signor – had returned in the afternoon. This was not good news.

In my frustration I decided to return to Solanio's auberge, and do what I did not yet know. With each step I took, I cursed the very notion of patience. Why had I not acted last night, when I had Jessica within my grasp? I swore at prudence. I poured scorn upon my cowardice. Infuriated and blinded by self-loathing, I over-stepped the auberge, even though it was advertised with crucibles of fire, and found myself at the very end of the Via Dante, outside an ivy-clad house, dimly lit, and far from palatial.

****

I thought myself well-cloaked by the darkness, but someone with a practised eye picked out a solid shape amid the insubstantial night. Without introduction he began a minor oration: "You do well to pause and wonder, signor, for in that modest abode once lived our state's greatest son, and the world's most daring navigator. You know his name already, but I shall pronounce it anyway, for the very sound of it – like soft winds hissing in the sails – gives me ease: Christopher Columbus."

From which I quickly deduced that the speaker was a mariner without a berth, a seaman gone to seed.

"Ah, signor," he continued, "if only Genoa had been willing to supply him with the ships and men he so earnestly requested, then the New World would have belonged to us, not Spain, and all the riches thereof. And you and I, signor, you and I would have been princes, a Pizzaro or a Cortez. Instead of broken men who wander the city dreaming of voyages that never were."

Obviously he thought that I too was a vagabond. But before I had the opportunity to disabuse him I was distracted by a great internal illumination. Of a sudden I was privy to it all; to the plot against Jessica, and her present whereabouts (more or less). Without even acknowledging the garrulous stranger – who had all unconsciously unlocked the mystery – I turned my back upon him, and began to run as fast as I dared in the direction of the molo vecchio.

My thoughts were these: as Venice traded with China, so did Genoa with the Americas. Among the products it dealt in were slaves; black slaves for the mines, and white slaves for the men. Is it any wonder that I ran?

But just as abruptly I stopped. What did I know of ships, who had never been on anything larger than a gondola? I hurridly retraced my steps up the steeply ranked cobbles, and reached the Via Dante breathless, where – thank God – the old salt was still cataloguing the many luxuries that had eluded him.

"Signor," I said, "I bring you an offer with no promise of reward. A lady has fallen prey to wicked men, and her life is at stake. Are you willing to help me mount a rescue? Do you have the stomach for one more bold adventure?"

"Thundering typhoons!" he bellowed like old Boreas himself. "You have breathed life back into my deflated spirit. If there are wenches to be saved, I'm you're man."

He was not fleet-footed, but he knew the path. Our passage was further assisted by the moon, new-burnished by clouds that streamed across its face like sheets of shammy-leather. It also made visible four full-rigged ships anchored in ragged formation around a man-o'-war.

"She'll be on one of those, for sure," said the old salt. "The man-o'-war gives it away. The last flotilla that approached the Americas with a cargo of women was boarded by pirates, and every last one of those unfortunates was raped fore and aft. No respect was shown to virgins either. By the time the ships made land the merchandise had lost the best part of its value. To prevent a repetition of that tragedy the owners have commissioned a guardian angel."

"How will I know which one of the four hides Jessica?" I said.

"I have the nose," he said, "and as I now can observe, you have the purse."

Even from where we stood we could see there was much activity on the molo; torches by the dozen were dancing through the darkness like so many drunken fireflies.

"Signor," said the former sailor. "The wind has changed course, since the rain ceased. It is now set fair. Look how fore and main sails are being unfurled. After that the halyards and the braces will be belayed. Finally anchors will be weighed and catted. And then this lady of yours will be lost to you forever."

At the entrance to the molo my companion spotted an old soak, perched upon a milestone.

"Half-a-dozen voyages I made with him as my first mate," said the ex-seaman. "He'll have the answer. For a price."

Which I gladly paid on Shylock's behalf.

Seeing his former commander's approach, the man removed the clay pipestem from his mouth, arose, spread his arms, and exclaimed: "Captain Merluzzo, is it really you?"

The two old companions hugged for several moments, after which words were exchanged, money deposited, and a name given.

"She's on the Santa Lucia," said the man I now knew to be Captain Merluzzo.

The Santa Lucia was, of course, the furthest ship on the molo. Her name was chiseled on her stern, under the captain's mullioned windows, and again on the bow beneath a bare-breasted figure-head. Captain Merluzzo figured the vessel's weight to be in the region of two hundred tons. A fo'c'sle and a poop towered above her main deck. Between them were three masts, whose sails were already lapping the briny air. Frayed ropes creaked with the strain of keeping them land-locked. The night smelled of things to come.

"The gangplank has not yet been raised," noted Captain Merluzzo. "Also in our favour is the fact that the crew is preoccupied with making final preparations for the long voyage. Once on board we must proceed with confidence, as if we were their ship-mates."

The noise on the main deck was an orchestra of discord, what with the waves, the wind, the whip-crack of sails, and the crew chorusing shanties. Enough, you would have thought, to drown the sound of Captain Merluzzo splintering the door to the companionway with a carpenter's maul, carelessly left nearby. But, alas, the hammering alerted an idle sailmaker, who quickly realized our intention.

For the first time in my life I drew my dagger, and pointed it menacingly at another human being. He stepped back, not in fear, but only to better unscabbard his cutlass. He thrust at me without discipline, obviously uncertain whether he favoured disembowelment or beheading. His second swing came closer to my neck. Who knows? His third attempt might well have succeeded in separating my head from my shoulders, and sending the orphaned comet on a bloody orbit across the deck, if Captain Merluzzo had not laid him out with a blow behind the ear.

Now the way was clear to midships where – we had been told – seventy girls were hammocked. I tumbled down the ladder, raised myself to my full height, and walloped my own scalp on a cross-beam. Regaining my senses I saw that I had fallen into something like a chapelle ardente. Whereas most were high-vaulted, this was low-ceilinged. What light there was came from guttering candles. Instead of a Doge or other great personage lying in state, there appeared a bivouac of overweight chrysalids suspended in mid-air.

I threw a name into that obscurity: "Jessica!"

And out of the obscurity came the reply: "Thank God, Tubal. Did Lorenzo send you?"

A head emerged from one of the cacoons, then another, and a third. The braver materialized fully and placed their feet upon the rough timbers. Splinters entered their soles, and drew blood; a presage in miniature of what would befall them if they did not seize the opportunity lately provided of flight.

Instead they screamed. The man who finds a gentle way

to end female hysteria will quickly rival Croesus. I am not that man.

"Quiet, ladies," I pleaded. "We have come as rescuers, not ravishers."

They did not credit my words, and screamed all the more. Some of these banshees were clothed in white smocks, others in fleshings, or – in some extreme cases – the very flesh itself.

But when they saw Jessica unharmed in my arms, and of her own volition, they calmed sufficiently for us to usher them up the steps to freedom. Captain Merluzzo led the party. I followed the naked buttocks of the last.

Surveying his small kingdom from the poop deck, the captain of the Santa Lucia spotted the departure of his raison d'être, and ordered his crew to stop it. Those who heard his command above the general commotion, took position between our troop and the gangplank. They numbered twenty or more, and were armed to the teeth.

Captain Merluzzo shook my hand. "You have given me new life," he said, "but even if it ends on the night it began, I shall die a happy man."

I advised Jessica to jump overboard when I met my end.

My bold companion raised his maul, and prepared to sell his life dearly. I unsheathed my dagger for the second time, and recited the Shema: "Hear, O Israel, the Lord is God, the Lord is One".

But as it turned out, we did not lead the charge. The advance guard came from the ranks. As Jessica later explained, not all the women were virgins, and not all were prisoners. Some were already prostitutes. Others were ready to whore themselves in exchange for passage to the New World. They actually wanted to sail with the Santa Lucia, but

– God bless them – were prepared to sacrifice themselves in order to assure the escape of those who did not. They flung themselves upon our astonished antagonists, who – forgetting themselves – first dropped their weapons and then their breeches.

Once he had assured himself that my path was clear, Captain Merluzzo elected to change sides, and commenced mortal combat with one of the ungirdled Amazons, who employed whorish tactics to first inflame and then subdue.

"I never thought to see such a night as this again," he gasped as we parted. "Tell me, did God send you?"

"No," I said, "only Shylock."

A simple fact that Jessica refused to believe. Counting her twenty women were restored to terra sancta that night, but I only had an interest in one of them.

My immediate concern was to escort her to my inn. The sky was now clear but the air was chill, and Jessica stood shivering in her shift. She was barefoot too. Although she sometimes called me Uncle Tubal, it was my father who was Shylock's contemporary, not me. I was her senior, to be sure, but only by a dozen years, and was certainly not insensible to the attributes that would have made her such a valuable commodity in the bordellos of New Spain.

To carry her would not have been beyond my strength, but would have taxed other powers best monopolized by my wife. So I gave her my cloak, and told her to mind where she stepped.

We discussed the night's excitements, and spoke of the great battle we had won. I told her the news from the Rialto.

Back in my chamber the spiders had woven a welcome mat. But Jessica only wanted to know why her beau had not busied himself in some like manner.

"Where is Lorenzo?" she said. "Why is he not here?"

"Because he has no idea that you are," I said.

"But he comissioned you and the brave captain with my rescue, did he not?" she said.

"He did not," I said. "Shylock did."

Jessica shook her head.

"But Lorenzo said that my father had disowned me," she said, "and shown the world that I was dead to him by sitting shiva – of course he did not use that word."

"Then he lied," I said. "Your father is angry, but he is also broken-hearted. He badly wants you back."

"But he cannot have me," said Jessica. "I belong to another."

The room was not furnished with chairs, or any other comforts, so I motioned for her to sit on my pallet, thereby awakening a whole continent of verminous life.

"Are you Lorenzo's wife?" I said.

"In the eyes of God," she said.

"What does that mean?" I said.

"He has known me," she said.

"Like Adam knew Eve?" I said.

She hesitated.

"It would be better to say, 'I knew him'," she said. "To save him from committing the sin of Onan, I swallowed his seed."

Dear God, I thought, already he has begun instructing her in the arts required to please those who will be paying for their pleasure. But I was curious to know how he had guiled her into such a pastime.

"Lorenzo persuaded me that it would be preferable for us to commence new lives in the New World," she said, "since we were both orphans, and had no ties in the Old. He secured our passage on the Santa Lucia, and explained that he had best reserve his full marital rights for the other side, lest I fall pregnant. Seasickness, he said, was curse enough."

I could forebear no longer.

"Foolish girl!" I said. "There is but a single reason Lorenzo did not split your hymen, and it is not the one he gave. You were spared because virginity is valued higher than rubies in the stews of the Americas. Do you not understand, Jessica? Lorenzo sold you into white slavery."

She rose from the infested cot and began to beat me with her little fists.

"Lies," she cries, "lies, lies, lies!"

"Now I know why they say the truth hurts," I said, as another blow landed on my nose, "but nothing you do will change the fact that Lorenzo was in the Torre degli Embriaci gambling away his new-found wealth, while you were a prisoner on the Santa Lucia."

"More lies!" she cried, but her protestations were beginning to lack conviction.

"Think, Jessica," I said, "can you explain why Lorenzo was not counted among your redeemers?"

She laughed, as if my question were the question of a simpleton.

"His face was known to the crew," she said, "and would have betrayed your intentions."

"But he knew nothing of our intentions," I said. "Why would he when his were the opposite?"

"At last I truly believe that my father sent you, Tubal," she said, "to poison my mind against Lorenzo."

I blew out the candles, but neither of us could sleep. Jessica stretched restlessly on my mattress, waiting only for the morn, when she could return to the arms of the very man who had betrayed her. While I lay open-eyed upon the floor, rehearsing arguments designed to prevent this act of amorous folly. Then there was the question of retrieving the glittering dowry Jessica had so carelessly – and illegally – bestowed upon her worthless paramour. Above all, how was I to convince a love-struck girl to abandon the object of her desire, and accompany me back to Venice, and her father's house? In the topsy-turvy world she now inhabited, her enslaver had become her liberator, and her protector her jailer.

Neither of us spoke. The only sounds were of our irregular breathing, and of rodents scratching their way from wall to wall.

When the sun rose I knew she could be restrained no longer. Arising also, I elected to escort her back to Lorenzo myself, in the hope that his discomfort would become apparent even to her, and act as antidote to the venom he had already poured into her ear.

"See how Apollo still blushes," said Jessica, "for all the sins committed while his back was turned."

Her mood had lightened as soon as we stepped out into the street; it was as though anticipation had usurped reality, and she was already in the arms of her lover.

"Come, Uncle Tubal," she said, placing hers through mine, "we must not keep Lorenzo waiting. Let us hurry and catch him at his toilet. I cannot wait to see the joyful expression when he realizes that I am safe, and restored to him."

Fool that I was, I felt guilty, even cruel, for the method I was employing to crush her trusting nature, to make a laughing-stock of her idealism. I foresaw her despair, and the comfort I would offer, and the opportunity I would take to spirit her away.

Walking briskly we turned on to the Via San Lorenzo, which was already as over-crowded as hell's inner circle. A few of our fellow pedestrians took cognisance of Jessica's outlandish appearance – her shift was concealed by one of my lighter cloaks, and her feet by a pair of my black boots – but most let her pass unremarked. Even the proprietor of the inn where her seducer lodged barely gave the silly girl a second glance. He was the same fellow I had bribed but yesterday, and he afforded me a sly smile.

Jessica bounded up the stairs, and without troubling to knock, opened the door to her erstwhile room. My best hope was that Lorenzo would be abed with a local trollop. Failing that I hoped to discover him packing his bags in preparation for flight. What I had not expected was to see him on bent knees apparently at his orisons.

Turning to face Jessica, he said unblushingly: "Have my prayers been answered? Is it really you?"

In desperation I attempted to ground Jessica as she took flight in his direction.

Encircling her possessively, he began to shout: "A Jew! A Jew! A dog Jew has come to murder my wife; to end her life for deciding to abandon the wicked faith of deicides."

Downstairs I heard the sweaty proprietor haul himself from his chair, and summon armed men.

"Oh Jessica," I said, "such a mistake you are making."

"Not as big as the one you will be making if you do not leave now," said Lorenzo.

The last thing I saw as I backed into the Via San Lorenzo – my dagger once more pointed at my enemies – was Jessica's head framed in the casement above, and the last thing that I heard as I raced along it, was the sound of her laughter.

****

And the last person I wanted to encounter when I returned to Venice was her father. Needless to say, he was the first. And he saw me before I saw him.

"How now Tubal!" he said, "what news from Genoa? Hast thou found my daughter?"

I could not bring myself to tell him the bare fact that I had arrested his daughter, only to lose her again. God help me, I lied: "I often came where I did hear of her, but could not find her."

"No news of her? Why so!" he cried. "And I know not what's spent in the search: why thou – loss upon loss! The thief gone with so much, and so much to find the thief, and no satisfaction, no revenge, nor no ill luck stirring but what lights o' my shoulders, no sighs but my way o' breathing, no tears but o' my shedding."

Although my untruth had occasioned this outburst, I felt absolved by Shylock's anger. How dare he question the cost of my investigation? Had he forgotten so quickly that the Tubals had financed his loan to Antonio? I decided to pay him back in kind.

I said: "Your daughter spent in Genoa, as I heard, one night, fourscore ducats."

"Thou stick'st a dagger in me," said Shylock, clutching at his chest, "fourscore ducats at a sitting, fourscore ducats."

Nor was that the conclusion of my revenge. I told Shylock that I had returned to Venice in the company of one of Antonio's creditors.

"He showed me a ring," I said, "that he had of your daughter for a monkey."

"Out upon her! – thou torturest me Tubal," cried Shylock.

"It was my turquoise, I had it of Leah when I was a bachelor: I would not have given it for a wilderness of monkeys."

The sight of his misery undilute caused me to repent of my indignation, and I reminded Shylock that other men had ill luck too. I told him that I had also heard in Genoa that one of Antonio's argosies had come to grief, and that the same creditor who had shown me Leah's ring, had assured me that Antonio was certainly undone.

"I thank thee good Tubal," said Shylock, "good news, good news: ha ha! heard in Genoa! I will have the heart of him if he forfeit, and Zebulum will have his revenge."

****

And his plan might even have succeeded if Bassanio's new wife hadn't entered the court at the last minute, in the guise of Balthazar, a lawyer's apprentice. At first, with honeyed rhetoric, she prosletysed the cause of mercy, but Shylock rebuffed her pleas, insisting upon justice; justice for him, and – all unspoken – for Zebulum too. Counterfeiting surrender Balthazar – rather Portia – counseled Antonio to lay bare his bosom. Would Shylock really have plunged the blade through flesh to beating heart? To this day, I do not know the answer. But I suspect – judging from my own experience – that he was by then a passenger of the drama, and would not have been able to stay his hand, even if that had been his dearest wish.

In any event, Shylock never got the chance to strike, for just then Portia introduced a conceit, the like of which I had not heard since I stood with Rabbi Leone Modena on the Calle Vallaresso: "Take then thy bond, take thou thy pound of flesh, but in the cutting it, if thou dost shed one drop of Christian blood, thy lands and goods are confiscate."

This pronouncement was the end of Shylock, and his vision of justice. Now it was Portia's turn to demand it, all thought of mercy gone; for the Jew there was to be no hint of mercy, no gentle dew, merely justice. In the end the court stripped Shylock of everything, even his Jewishness. How he passed empty days as one of the new baptized I do not know, but on the sabbath I often saw him standing outside the synagogue, silently mouthing the prayers that were being declaimed within.

And what of his daughter, what of the girl I had failed to restore unto him? Even though Jessica was known to have returned to Venice, she made no effort to contact Shylock. There were even reports that she had been seen with Lorenzo at Belmont, home to the woman who had destroyed her father, and to the man who had robbed Zebulum of threescore years.

Like Zebulum, Jessica tugged at my conscience, caused me to lay abed but awake, reliving my defeat, and seeking strategies that – if pursued – would have altered the course of events. Insomnia was bad enough, but sleep was worse, for with sleep came dreams, out-of-control dreams that had me do things I repented upon awakening.

****

Then one fine day Jessica flounced into my office. Seeing her in the alternate light and shade created by the Venetian blind, put me in mind of that graceful but strange creature, the zebra. But as she drew nearer I noted that she was in fact dishevelled, and that her composure was a fragile thing.

"Oh, Tubal," she said, and dissolved into tears.

I jumped from my seat and clasped her to me, thinking to

offer her comfort, and in so doing felt at last the body I had deemed too tempting in Genoa. My embrace had been temporary in intent, but it seemed she did not want to let me go.

"Uncle Tubal," she said, so that I could feel her moist breath buttering my cheek, and fogging my brain, "I owe you an apology. You were right about Lorenzo. As was my father when he said: 'I have a daughter – would any of the stock of Barrabas had been her husband rather than a Christian'. But I took no heed of either of you, and now I am the wife of one."

"Apology accepted," I said, managing at last to untangle myself. "Is there anything else I can do for you?"

"You remember that paper Antonio forced my father to sign?" she said, walking back and forth, like a captive beast in a cage. "The one that made over all he possessed to the 'gentleman who lately stole his daughter', and to the ingratiate herself, in the event of his death? When he signed that document, Tubal, he signed his own death warrant. You think that maybe I am exaggerating? That this is all the imagining of a troubled conscience? Well listen, Tubal, listen well."

So saying she sat at last, and delivered an episode from life at Belmont.

"Last night," she said, "as they arose from the dinner table, Lorenzo began to speak about my father with Antonio and Bassanio. Knowing their destination I excused myself, hurried along a torch-lit corridor, passing tapestries that depicted scenes of hunting and battle. Reaching the library I concealed myself behind an arras. The three merchants followed, and seated themselves close to the log fire. The flames cast grotesque shadows, making them look as hellish as their thoughts. For it was in that spot, surrounded by books of law, that I over-heard their plot to hasten my father's end.

"After they had toasted the success of the enterprise, Bassanio inquired of Lorenzo why he had married a Jewess.

"'For the same reason you wed Portia,' he said; 'to become heir to her father's wealth.' With those words all the dreams – all the hopes – of my youth were turned to ash. If Lorenzo married me with a cold heart, what else might that cold heart have him do? Do you think he will rest when he has killed my father, Tubal, or think you that am I in danger too?"

"I think you are in danger too," I said, "but first things first. I must start to watch over your father. And you must become a spy in your own house, listening until you know for certain the very time and place of the sticking point."

She hugged me again before we parted.

"You are a good man, Tubal," she said.

The following week she sent me a note, via Launcelot, who had returned to her employ.

"The conspirators have found that tomorrow Shylock will be visiting an establishment on the Calle Vallaresso," it read. "Lorenzo has elected to strike the fatal blow as the clock chimes midnight."

****

And it came to pass at midnight, just as Jessica had predicted. From my vantage point in the shadows I observed Lorenzo as he began to overhaul a stooped figure in a black cloak. I kept thinking of the last words Shylock had uttered in court: "I pray you give me leave to go from hence, I am not well." That was how he looked now, not well. I called upon Lorenzo to stop, which he did. Only to turn with his stiletto already to hand. I unsheathed my own dagger, and closed upon him. He thrust, I side-stepped, and without forethought lunged at him. The blade struck him between the ribs, and did not cease until it had stopped his heart. I shall not easily forget the look of astonishment upon his face, as his corpse slipped through my arms to the ground.

Ahead of me Shylock was on his knees, but when he turned to thank me, I beheld neither beard nor wrinkles, but skin as white as a lily; for the face beneath the hood belonged not to him, but to his daughter. Realizing then the truth of the matter, I began to shake. I was no saviour, but an assassin.

"Why do you look so horrified, Tubal," she said, "when you have just saved my life?"

My mind – all unbidden – began to test horrid conjectures: what if she had stitched together her story, what if it were as mythical as a scene on one of Belmont's tapestries, what if Jessica not Lorenzo had been the only begetter of Lorenzo's plot?

"You have not been honest with me, Jessica," I said, "so how can I be confident that Lorenzo really said what you said he said."

"Was the blade in his hand not proof enough?" she said.

"It is equally possible that he took the man who challenged him to be a murderer – correctly as it turned out – and looked only to defend himself," I said.

"You may call yourself whatever comforts you," she said, "but as far as I am concerned, you are my champion. I doubted you once, Tubal, as you doubt me presently. But now I am sure."

She arose from her kneeling position, and embraced me.

"No," I said, but she persisted.

"How you are shaking, Tubal," she said, "like a man in need of succour."

"Not from you," I said.

"Do not be so obstinate, Tubal," she said, "unless you want the authorities to find you here. What do you think they will make of a Jew standing over the body of a Christian?"

"Much the same as I do," I said.

Nevertheless, I allowed her to lead me down deserted alleys, all the way back to my office. I unlocked the door and saw – or rather didn't see – that only black light slid through the Venetian blinds.

"Tubal," said Jessica, "where are the candles?"

When a few were lit she noticed, for the first time, that the left sleeve of my doublet was heavy with blood.

"Why, Tubal," she said, "you are hurt."

It was a matter of indifference to me, but I did not stop her from removing my jacket and the blouse beneath. The blood was still wet, but no longer flowing freely. The wound itself was in the upper arm, where an observant Jew winds his phylacteries every morning.

"This was a thrust meant for your heart," said Jessica.

It occured to me that I was now standing just as Antonio had stood before the Duke, awaiting judgment, his life seemingly in the balance. In which case my Portia was Jessica, and the portion at stake – or so it felt to me – was not my life, but my very soul. And I feared that I was an irresolute guardian.

"You must think me a poor nurse," said Jessica, whose own hands were as bloodied as my arm, and whose bodice had become as stained as my doublet.

"I am as indifferent to your skills, as I am to my injury," I said.

"In which case I must act for the pair of us," said Jessica, making a bundle of my clothes.

Then she began to remove her own.

"Why do you stare so, Tubal," she said, "have you never seen a woman's breasts before?"

They were perfect in every detail, and drew me to them as if I were a suckling babe, but they were unclean, dyed crimson by my own blood. With an effort I stepped back. Sensing the cause, Jessica laughed.

"Ho, Tubal," she said, "you act as though you had seen the devil in person. Permit me to demonstrate that you are in error."

She snatched my right hand and placed it on the hidden under-carriage of her left breast.

"Do you feel scales, Tubal?" she said.

I do not know what I felt, any more than a dog knows what it feels when it mounts a bitch. All I know is that it was not my seed she sucked into her womb, when we copulated upon the floor, but my will, and – yes – perhaps my soul with it. Did I reason with myself, did I argue thus: 'Tubal, you have already committed murder this night, so why not add adultery to your bill?' I cannot say.

"Are you married, Tubal," said Jessica, when I was still lying all spent atop her.

"I have a wife," I said.

"And I always imagined you a bachelor," she said. "My father never spoke of her."

"I would prefer if you did not speak of her either," I said.

"I understand," she said. "I too have cause for guilt. After all it is not very becoming for a woman, newly widowed, to consort with the very man who put her in that state. If I wished to absolve myself I could call you 'rapist'."

She paused to make an observation.

"Poor Tubal," she said, "you have begun to shake all over again."

"What do you want of me?" I said.

"Foolish man," she said, kissing me. "I already have what I wanted."

"You mean Lorenzo dead?" I said.

"That too," she said. "Was it not you, Tubal, who first tried to convince me of his treachery, and his greed? When I finally accepted that you were right, I resolved that he would never live to enjoy my fortune. I am not a second Portia, Tubal. I would never willingly have called him my lord and my master, and ceded to him all the treasure that my industrious father had accumulated. Maybe your suspicions are correct, and he never uttered the words I put in his mouth, but do you seriously believe that he never thought them? And – knowing what you know – do you think he would not have wished me dead too? Think what you will, Tubal, but to my mind you saved my life tonight."

Perhaps the desire for her was in me from the beginning, but once ignited it knew no bounds. I had supped at Jessica's breasts, and tasted not mother's milk, but my own blood. The evidence was on my lips, which were now painted like a whore's. All restraint was gone. My heart and my kidneys were speckled.

We wrestled all night upon the floor like Jacob and the Angel – except that I was no patriarch, and she no angel – and were still contesting the space when I felt light from the new day lashing my back. No, I was no Jacob. I was not even an Esau. Esau was hairy, but I was hairier still. As I disengaged from Jessica's privates for the last time, I recognised that I was cousin to the monkey that had been had for a ring. It was true! I was no better than a beast, my commandments reduced to a couple: to gratify my appetites, and to survive.

"They will have found your husband's body by now," I said, "and you must be at home when the news comes."

Like it or not, I had become a co-conspirator.

"You know that we have completed but half the job," said Jessica. "The ducats and the jewels are still in my father's possession."

"Where they belong," I said.

But I realized, even as I spoke, that never again would my soul know rest, that the remainder of my life would be plagued by remorse for what I had already done, and what I was yet to do.

"Is it not true that my father would rather have them than a living child?" she said. "Is it not true that he said to you: 'I would my daughter were dead at my foot, and the jewels in her ear, would she were hears'd at my foot, and the ducats in her coffin'? Or were his words misrepresented?"

"Those words were wicked," I said, "but they were words spoken in anger."

"Every breath he draws is drawn in anger," she said. "He knows no other emotion. Sooner or later I am bound to feel the full force of it. Unless . . ."

I knew what was coming next, and no longer had the strength or the will to stop it.

"Tubal," said Jessica, "you must kill my father. Shylock must die."

A BAD END

RABBI GOLDFINCH WAS a swine. About that, if nothing else, all his congregants agreed. Every shabbat, after the holy scroll had been returned to the Ark, he took his place on the bima and accused the worshippers of all manner of sins; of embezzelment, of fornication, of driving to the synagogue instead of walking. Nor was he hesitant about naming names. And yet there was never an empty seat in his synagogue. There was no mystery to this. What was the point of a rabbi who did not strike fear into the heart of a sinner? And who amongst them had clean hands and a spotless soul? Their God was quick to anger, and they expected no less of their rabbi.

His son, little Joshua, knew all about that. His lively ear, and uncanny cordination, made of him a musical prodigy. His father, the rabbi, did not deny him lessons with the émigré violinst who lived in the next street, but when it came to the matter of higher education, the rabbi lifted his flaming sword and barred the way. Instead Joshua was diverted to medical school, where he learned to play the veins and arteries, the muscles and sinews of the human body, as if they were so many violin strings.

After seven years it came to pass that the rabbi was able to boast, "My son, the doctor."

Needless to say, Joshua soon earned a reputation as a great surgeon, a virtuoso of the operating theatre. But when the Angel of Death tapped his father, the rabbi, on the shoulder, none of his innumerable skills could save him. And so the rabbi, his father, was buried by another rabbi in the traditional manner.

When Rabbi Goldfinch opened his eyes again it was not in heaven, but in a pigsty.

"Oh my God," he thought, "the Buddhists were right. I have been reincarnated as a pig."

At first the idea of being devoured by gentiles filled him with horror. But after a while he was able to console himself with the consideration that – due to the laws of kashrut – he would never be eaten by his own flesh and blood, and that his own son could never become – albeit unwittingly – an incestuous cannibal.

After some days the rabbi began to suspect that his pigsty was no ordinary pigsty. It was indoors, for one thing, and the farmers all wore white coats, for another. And where was the filth in which swine loved to wallow? On the contrary, this place was spotless.

Meantime, the Angel of Death was abroad hunting new quarry. He began to stalk an old fat man with a bushy white beard. Although the man lived in the city he maintained a small herd of reindeer. He fed them oats, but himself only mince pies and port wine. With his x-ray eyes the Angel of Death was quick to diagnose diabetes, which in turn was hastening end stage renal failure. The old man in the red dressing-gown was clinging to life by a thread, even though he didn't yet know it.

But the Angel of Death, being eternally busy, had failed to keep up with the latest developments in medical research: the word "zenotransplantation" was not yet in his lexicon.

In truth the technique was only in its rudimentary stage, and Joshua, the rabbi's son, happened to be its chief practitioner. When the word got out that Santa Claus was about to die for want of a suitable kidney, he offered his services and those of his experimental laboratory. The powers-that-be had no choice but accept.

Back in the pigsty, the rabbi was beginning to enjoy his new life. It was a huge relief not to be burdened with daily responsibilities; no shaving, no sermons. Why he didn't even have to dress. Though he wasn't sure he would want anyone he knew to see him in such a state.

So it was with a mixture of joy and shame that he greeted the unexpected appearance of his own son. Both feelings squared then cubed when his son pointed to him, to him alone, and chose him from among the multitude.

How would his son greet him, the rabbi wondered as he was led along a neon-lit corridor, would he show the respect due to a father, even though that father was now a four-legged swine? The doors to his son's room were pushed apart and the rabbi gained entrance. But where was his son? All he could see was a bunch of masked men.

"Gonifs," he thought, "thieves."

And he was right as usual, for they stole his kidney, and used it to restore life to Father Christmas.

As Joshua stared at the donor pig, still breathing on the operating table, the Angel of Death filled his ear with tempting words. He vouchsafed receipes known only in the Elysian Fields, and Joshua tasted the finished product on his tongue. If mere anticipation sent him into raptures, how could he resist the real thing?

When the operating theatre was empty, he cut the pig's throat with a scalpel, and butchered it expertly. He smuggled the joints into his deep freeze, which hitherto had known only kosher cuts. Although his family did not celebrate Christmas, they were sufficiently assimilated to exchange presents and eat the traditional fowl on December 25.

"My God, Joshua," said his wife, who had never before tasted pork, "that turkey was divine."